Hope Cottage

Catherine McCarthy

Copyright © 2019 by Catherine McCarthy

All rights reserved. This book or any portion thereof may not be reproduced or used in any manner whatsoever without the express written permission of the author except for the use of brief quotations in a book review.

This is a work of fiction. Names, characters, places, and incidents are a product of the author's imagination. Any resemblance to actual persons, events, or locales is entirely coincidental.

Cover Design & Illustrations by Tony Evans

To Tony, my motivator in all things creative

About the author...

Catherine McCarthy is the author of Hope Cottage, a dark and mysterious family saga of triumph over adversity, reconciliation and, well...hope! Penned as a cathartic means of coming to terms with the loss of her own mother it is her second novel, the first being The Gatekeeper's Apprentice, a fantastical adventure for older children. She is currently adding the finishing touches to a book of short stories which also explore the darker side of fantasy.

Originally from the Welsh Valleys, where she taught for almost three decades, she now lives with her artistic and slightly kooky husband in an inspirational old Welsh cottage in West Wales where she writes, reads, sews and bakes...in that order of priority!

Let perseverance be your engine and hope your fuel.
H. Jackson Brown, Jr.

Chapter 1

Marleston, England April 1996

I stood over the unmarked grave and stared at the simple cross which wore a small poppy round its middle. Palm Sunday had passed little more than a week earlier. Artificial poinsettia, now faded pink, lay strewn, as if thrown in a fit of temper across the centre of the grave. How strange, I thought, wondering why they hadn't been removed after Christmas. I concluded that different visitors to the grave had placed their offerings and that the second visitor had not liked to remove the now redundant offering of the first.

But something far stranger had drawn me to this particular plot. The mound of grass and weeds which demarcated the grave was raised considerably above ground level and was roughly human shaped. It rose and widened in the middle before narrowing again at the legs. Because of the shape of the mound and the way in which the poinsettia were strewn one could almost imagine the person buried beneath holding them.

No headstone, no name, nothing but the shaped mound and these floral offerings to speak of the deceased. I thought it rather macabre and shuddered a little at the implication that the body lay just beneath the surface rather than six feet below. Acknowledging that this could not possibly be the case I attempted to dismiss the image from my mind, concluding that recent events in my own life had simply rendered me over sensitive to such sights.

Straightening my back, I gazed around. It was in doing so that I noticed the unusual location of the grave. It stood alone, in the shade of a mature yew tree at the far end of the cemetery, just eight feet or so within the dry-stone boundary wall; a lonely spot in a crowded place.

Turning my attention away from the grave, I gazed towards the dilapidated and unsuitably named Hope Cottage which stood in the lane just beyond the church wall. The angle of the grave meant that it faced almost directly toward the front of the cottage. Any resident would need only to look out of the window to view it plainly.

I shivered and wrapped my unbuttoned cardigan more tightly around my middle. As the early April wind whipped about me like a whirling dervish, I turned on my heels and made my way through the lynch gate and down the lane towards Hope Cottage.

*

I had arrived in the village late the previous evening. Having retrieved the key from the external safe box as instructed by the owner in the information sent to me, I had entered to find a lamp-lit, cosy kitchen and a small, warm lounge. I poured myself a glass of red wine and picked over the remainder of a packed lunch which I had prepared for the journey before dragging myself off to bed exhausted.

Vicarage Cottage had come up in a search for *accommodation, Marleston, England* and I had jumped at the chance of booking somewhere so close to Hope Cottage, thinking it would surely make things easier to be in such close proximity. I had been informed by my solicitor that Hope Cottage was in an uninhabitable state and therefore assumed that I would not be able to stay there for a while, at least until I had spruced it up a bit. I had reserved the holiday let for one week, in the hope that the solicitor had been exaggerating and that I might be able to make Hope Cottage habitable with little more than a bit of elbow grease. After all, I was in no financial position to be frivolously spending my modest nest egg on holiday accommodation. It was all I had put by to begin my life anew. Now, with every step I took, my heart sank for I could see that Hope Cottage was indeed in a far worse state than I had hoped.

It stood on the curve of a narrow lane which wound its way around the back of the churchyard before disappearing around the bend into the distance. Never before had I seen such an overgrown garden, if that was what it could be called, for really it was no more than a small strip of land; an irregular shape which followed the curve of the lane. No hedge, fence or boundary of any kind was present. It was just a space; full of broken, planted pots of various kinds and shapes, most of which now displayed little more than weeds. A few determined spring bulbs had managed to survive long enough to produce bright yellow daffodils which seemed almost ridiculous in their cheer compared to the rest of the house and garden. Glass milk bottles, broken sweeping brushes and other tools along with a few long-dead bushes were scattered at the front of the house.

A large, mature oak stood to the right of the cottage, the branches of which had heedlessly invaded part of the roof, flinging some of its slates to the ground below. A few desperate ones clung on for dear life to the broken guttering.

Five small windows I counted amongst the dead branches and tangle of ivy which clung to the front of the cottage. Two of the window panes were smashed and the wooden frames, once painted white, had peeled and blackened with rot. They looked as though they might disintegrate to the touch.

Key in hand, I cautiously made my way toward the front

door, taking care not to trip over any obstruction. The door yielded with ease as I turned the key in the lock. This wasn't a village that required a great deal of house security I assumed, for I had been informed that the cottage had stood empty for over a year and yet I could see no means of the property having been otherwise secured.

The moment the door opened, a nauseating stench wafted out. Instinctively I covered my nose and mouth with my hand against the acrid smell before stepping inside. Within seconds I retreated. Stepping back into the fresh air, I untied my scarf from around my neck and instead re-tied it firmly around my nose and mouth. Taking a gulp of fresh air, I tried again.

I could scarcely believe my eyes. Judging by the mess, my immediate assumption was that I had indeed been wrong about the security and that the cottage *had* at some time been broken into. I stood in a tiny hallway. A narrow and bare wooden staircase rose directly ahead. No internal doors were present on either door frame to the left or right. I could see that the room to the left had once been a kitchen, though in its current state it was impossible to imagine any person having prepared food in it. The room to my right had once been the sitting room I assumed, though again the only obvious clue was a tattered, musty armchair which waited expectantly in the far corner.

I decided to investigate this room first as it seemed marginally less offensive than the kitchen. I screwed up my nose. The source of the stench which engulfed the house was difficult to identify, as it consisted of a concoction of several foul aromas. I was certain that stale animal urine and faeces, damp earth and mildew were amongst the culprits as well as something else; a human smell, the kind one thankfully rarely encounters, except in the vicinity of the dirtiest kind of person. These odours were unfortunately distinguishable even through my scarf.

Apart from the armchair, the only other piece of furniture in the room was an old sideboard which was littered with bric-a-brac, much of which was cracked or broken. Some pieces had been crudely stuck together with tape or now-yellowing glue. An open fireplace still contained died-down embers as well as a grate full of ash. Only someone with an extremely cluttered and chaotic mind could have dwelt amongst such contents.

I stood gazing into the kitchen doorway for half a minute or so, reluctant to venture inside and instead decided to look upstairs. Thirteen treads led to a tiny landing with bare, creaky floorboards. Two doors, one to the left and one to the right stood closed. The first opened to reveal a room, approximately twelve by nine feet in size. A chimney breast stood in the middle of the wall but the only furniture in the room was a wardrobe of dark wood.

As the room was so bare, it was possible to assess the condition of the walls, floors and windows of the house. It was indeed in a bad way. Part of the ceiling in the far corner had collapsed, displaying an aperture to the roof approximately eighteen inches in diameter. In this corner of the room the walls ran black with mould. Some of the old mortar had crumbled away. The remaining walls were stained an uneven, brownish colour of patchy distemper. The only window faced towards the front of the house and overlooked the cemetery. Its glass panes were cracked and the frame so rotten that it crumbled like ripe stilton to the touch. Fuzzy, black streaks of mildew clung to the surround and where wall and window met, fungi flourished. Several dead bluebottles, legs pointing skyward, lay on what remained of the sill.

I turned to make my way back out on to the landing. Just as I did so, daylight streamed into the room revealing the droppings of vermin. No wonder Mum wanted nothing to do with this place, I thought, though I was more than aware that Mum's aversion had not truly been based on the condition of the house.

The second door from the landing revealed a larger bedroom which seemed to have been the one in which the occupant must have slept. The condition of this room was as bad as the previous yet somehow it *felt* worse, as at least the other room had contained no impression of an inhabitant. Here, I could sense the presence of the old lady. Her metal-framed bed remained unmade along the centre wall. The pillow, still bearing the dip where her head had lain, was stained yellow and a woolen blanket, hand crocheted from a multitude of coloured squares lay crumpled in a heap at the foot of the bed frame.

The scent in this room was more personal and powerful. Again, the room contained a small fireplace which had been left in a similar condition to the one downstairs. I noted the lack of any modern source of heating in the house. An old, threadbare chair, piled high with discarded clothing, a wash-bowl and jug and a tatty wardrobe were also present.

I walked over to the dressing table. Amongst the clutter stood a solitary, faded black and white photograph of a young man in soldier's uniform. The expression on his face was solemn, his eyes seemed to fix on me, full of sadness. I carefully removed it from its brass frame and turned it over in the hope that the soldier's identity would be revealed but was disappointed to find no name. I studied the face again in the hope that it may spark a hint of family resemblance. It did not. Pocketing the photo I left the room.

Having already made up my mind that I would not even attempt a renovation, I headed swiftly back downstairs, deciding that the best thing I could do would be to hire a skip, fill it with the contents of the house then appoint an estate agent to place the cottage on the market as soon as possible. I would be grateful for whatever little revenue the cottage might bring in which I would then spend on a small and likely modern property. Even if I could only afford a one-bedroom flat in a nearby town I now considered it a better option than living in this hovel.

Before returning to the rental property I decided to have a quick peek at the garden to the back of the house. The back door, whose key lay waiting for me in its lock, stood at the rear of the small hallway. I was surprised to see that it opened onto what appeared to be a large area of ground, though as it was so overgrown and had no path I was unable to see exactly how far it reached.

A small, crumbling building was attached to the side of the house. Its broken door revealed a toilet and storage area and was even fouler smelling than the house itself. I should have guessed, I thought, making a mental note of the absence of any kind of bathroom.

Feeling adventurous, I decided to fight my way through the tall grass and concoction of tangled weeds in order to get a better idea of the garden's size. After about a hundred or so paces I reached what I thought must be the end as a simple wire fence now prevented progress. Partly hidden by the weeds I was nevertheless able to follow it around three sides until I eventually arrived back at the left of the cottage. If someone had the time and money this could be a beautiful space, I thought, as from here, it was neither possible to see nor be seen by any other of the village properties. Beyond the wire fence lay a steep drop to the river then the land climbed steeply again on the other side to woodland.

Chapter 2

Back at Vicarage Cottage, I admitted to myself that the morning's discoveries were disappointing to say the least. Hopes that my recent inheritance might provide a means to starting a new life had pretty much been dashed by its appalling condition. I understood that the value of properties in this part of England was a lot higher than back home in the North. Nevertheless I was certain that in its current state, Hope Cottage would not bring in the kind of money needed to get myself out of my financial predicament, nor would it in any way be possible to find the money to have it renovated. I decided that I would telephone a few local estate agents that afternoon, having first contacted a local skip hire company and arranged delivery of a large skip for the following morning.

With the skip ordered, two valuations arranged for the following Thursday and the realization that I would need a hand to shift the larger pieces of furniture, I scribbled out a plea on the back of a blank postcard which I found in a drawer ...

Is there anyone who happens to have any free time tomorrow?(Wednesday 15th) I am clearing out the contents of Hope Cottage, Church Lane and have no-one to help! I would be very grateful to anyone who might be able to lend a hand.

Yours desperately,
Cassie Wilkinson

I understood that this might seem rather presumptuous coming from a stranger and yet I really was desperate. I walked down to the local Post Office cum village store and asked if they would be kind enough to display it in their window.

Bit of a stab in the dark, I thought, but one never knew, someone might be inquisitive and bored enough to offer. After all, I considered it likely that a few villagers had probably been itching to see inside the cottage for some time.

*

Up like a lark the following morning and dressed in the shabbiest clothes I owned, I ambled down to Hope Cottage to take delivery of the skip by 7-30a.m. Back inside its doors for the second time I was hit by a wave of utter despondency. Where on earth should I begin? I had arranged an empty and refill service with the skip company and now that it had arrived I couldn't decide whether to begin inside, outside, upstairs or down. I sat on the bottom stair, head in hands with both the front and back doors wide open in an attempt to encourage the rancid air to leave fresh and air to enter.

I wasn't surprised that no-one had turned up in response to my plea but I still hoped that someone with a bit of muscle and organizational skills might magically appear. How delusional of me, I thought miserably. Still, I decided that sitting there feeling sorry for myself would get me nowhere, so I got to my feet and headed for the living room. I began by opening all the windows and donning a pair of sturdy rubber gloves. After attacking the contents of the room like someone possessed I soon realized that throwing pieces of furniture as they stood onto the skip filled it far too quickly so I returned to Vicarage Cottage to retrieve the tool kit from the boot of my car.

I had just begun to heave the chairs back out of the skip when I was surprised to hear a cautious voice calling from the front door. 'Uh hello ... I've come to help.' An elderly gentleman stood just inside the doorway. I was certain he hadn't been standing there on my return. I squinted towards him in the bright sunlight.

'The door wasn't locked. I just went inside to call. Thought you might not have heard me knock,' he continued, obviously rather embarrassed at having been inside.

I held out my rubber-gloved hand. 'Hello! I'm Cassie. Pleased to meet you. You have no idea how welcome you are!' I beamed.

His face relaxed and he returned the smile. 'Tom,' he said, firmly gripping my gloved hand. 'I live next door to the Post Office. Saw your postcard. Got some time on my hands this morning so I thought I'd come along. No-one else turned up?' he asked glancing around.

'I'm afraid not.'

'Aye, most folk are working these days see. Where do you want to start?'

'Well, I just went to fetch some tools. I think I need to dismantle the furniture before I put it in the skip or it will cost me a fortune,' I laughed.

He nodded. 'Tell you what, why don't I do that while you box up the knick-knacks in the rooms?'

'You sure? We'll have a cup of tea later. It's okay, I brought a flask,' I laughed, knowing that like me he wouldn't wish to drink from any cup belonging to the cottage kitchen.

An hour or so of hard graft and the living room was empty. In some ways, with the clutter gone it looked better but on the other hand the bare walls and floor further highlighted its dilapidated condition. I went back outside to where Tom still worked. 'Come on Tom, let's have a break.' I smiled.

We had hardly spoken so far, largely due to the fact that I had spent much of my time indoors and he outside, trying to organize the skip's contents in the most frugal way possible. Still, I had the impression that he was a friendly and genuine gentleman and his help had certainly sped things up.

We sat together on the wall of the churchyard, facing towards the front of the cottage. It seemed the most obvious place to rest as the cottage garden offered nowhere to sit and inside was too dirty to consume anything.

It was Tom who spoke first. 'You moving in then?' he asked, nodding towards the cottage.

I took a deep breath. 'Well, that was the original plan. I recently inherited it you see. Emily was my grandmother on my mother's side. I assume you knew her?'

'Indeed ... but not well. Nobody knew her *really* well. S'ppose I should say knew *of* her rather than knew her.'

'Oh I see,' I said, sensing his unwillingness to offer more.

'Did you have much to do with her yourself?' he asked tentatively.

'No. In fact I never met her. My Mum was adopted when she was just a baby and any contact with Emily was cut. Mum never spoke about her and to be honest it wasn't until my Mum died recently that I even knew this place existed. Mum had inherited it when Emily died but for whatever reason she'd not mentioned it to me.'

He watched me with a puzzled frown.

'Can you tell me *anything* about Emily?' I urged, aware of the somewhat pleading tone in my voice.

Again I witnessed his hesitancy and he stared at the ground. It was several seconds before he spoke again. 'Thing is see, I don't think she was very well ... in the head I mean. That's why the cottage got in such a state.'

'It's alright,' I assured him. 'You won't offend me whatever you say. It's as I told you. I never even met her so she's a stranger to me. It's just that now I'm here I'm curious, that's all. I'd like to find out more.'

Tom's expression relaxed somewhat. 'Well, I don't know that much myself. I've only lived in the village these past six years see. I moved here after my wife passed on so as to be closer to my daughter and grandchildren. All I can tell you is that Emily was known round here as a bit, well eccentric like.' He glanced at me before continuing. 'She kept lots of cats, strays mostly. They weren't the only four legged creatures in the cottage though,' he chuckled. 'Supposed to be good at keeping out mice and rats but they didn't do a very good job in there did they?' He nodded towards the front of the cottage and smiled. 'Kept herself to herself. Didn't see much of her. No-one did. Truth be told, there were some who weren't sorry to see her go. Thought she was a blight on the village with the state on this place see. Quite a few lining up to buy the old place when she went. Disappointed they were when it didn't come up for sale.'

'What, even in that condition?' I asked surprised. 'It'll cost a fortune to do up!'

'Aye, but property for sale's rare in this village. People don't move from here unless they go off in a box,' he said. 'It's so peaceful here. No crime nor nothing. And there's plenty of folk round here with money to invest in that.'

'I walked around the graveyard when I arrived Tom but couldn't find anything with her name on. Do you know if she's buried here?'

'Well, rumour has it that she left something saying she wanted her ashes scattered down by the river, least that's what folk round here say. There wasn't really a funeral see. We just heard she'd died and that was that. People didn't inquire too deeply. No good pretending to have been a friend is it after the horse has bolted so to speak. Bit hypocritical that'd be.'

I sat in silence for a few minutes, considering what I had heard so far.

'Come on! Let's get back to it. Which room do you want to tackle next?' Tom asked, noticing the troubled look on my face.

Strange, I thought as I began to tackle the kitchen. I was never really curious about Emily but now that I'm here she's like an itch that I want to scratch. As I'd cleared the contents of the living room I'd found myself searching for clues which might help me draw some conclusions. Over recent months, I'd been so immersed in my own problems that I'd merely viewed the cottage as a potential meal ticket, one which would hopefully enable me to begin my life again. But now, with every cupboard I emptied and every box I opened, I found myself seeking amongst its contents some remnant of the person who had lived here. It was still difficult to view Emily as a grandmother but I was indeed becoming more and more curious about her as a person.

The living room had revealed nothing of interest though. Instead, it had merely confirmed the hoarding nature of its former occupant. I was certain I would have no more luck in the kitchen. After all, kitchens were hardly the place for hidden secrets. The only things hidden in this one were insects and worse.

By mid afternoon we had successfully cleared most of the downstairs. The skip was full to overflowing so I telephoned to order a replacement as arranged and invited Tom back to Vicarage Cottage for a sandwich whilst we waited.

'I'm so grateful for your help Tom,' I said as we sipped our tea. 'I don't know what I'd have done without you this morning. I must admit I didn't know where to begin. Just a while ago, when I learned of my inheritance, it seemed the answer to my prayers; a cosy little English cottage I thought. I tell you, I could literally smell the roses! After recent events it seemed like a dream come true. Then to be met with that,' I said, nodding back towards the lane. 'Well, it certainly brought me back down to earth with a bump.'

Tom smiled sympathetically. 'I'll bet it did! Never mind. It *could* be turned into the house of your dreams you know. Take a bit of cash I dare say but it'd be worth it in the end.'

'Oh Tom, I couldn't do it! First thing I need to do is get a job. Without an income my savings won't last long. Then I'd have nothing left to invest in renovating. No, I'll have to put it on the market as soon as it's cleared and get a little flat or something.' My face failed to conceal my obvious disappointment.

He hesitated. 'You mind me asking? You moving here alone?'

I could hear the emotion in my voice as I answered and swallowed hard. 'Yes. To be honest with you I've had a hell of a year Tom. Divorced and lost my Mum both within the space of a year. I came close to breaking point but Mum made me promise to go on, so here I am. It's just not turning out to be quite as straight forward as I'd hoped that's all.' I forced a smile. 'Still, I've got through worse than dealing with some dirt and junk. If I can survive the last year I can surely handle this. After all, it's only bricks and mortar.'

Tom nodded. 'What do you do for work? If you can get a job perhaps you can keep the cottage and do it up slowly like.'

'Well I lectured in English back in the North but I haven't worked for the past six months. I took time off to nurse Mum see. She had no-one else. She had secondary breast cancer and needed the help. It was the least I could do.'

I saw the understanding look on his face and wondered if he'd gone through similar with his wife. 'The nearest university's 'bout forty or fifty miles away but there's a college not far. My Kate works there, in the library. Why don't you see if anything's going there? You never know. By the sound of it you're due a bit of good luck.'

'Thanks Tom. I will. It won't hurt to inquire will it?' I smiled, grateful for his words of encouragement.

Chapter 3

I would have loved to have given the downstairs a good scrub now that it was empty but I knew that the logical thing to do would be to continue clearing out first. Simon had frequently told me to *get my head out of the clouds* and I wanted to prove him wrong, even though he wasn't here to witness it. If truth be told, I also wanted to prove to myself that I *could* be systematic when I needed to. His criticism over the years had worn me down, yet even now we were apart I still felt the effect of his negative comments whenever I didn't behave precisely as he would have wished. Sometimes it seemed as though he were still looking over my shoulder, waiting for me to take a tumble.

I had to admit that in some respects he was right. I could be a bit of a dreamer. I was by nature an optimist; naturally cheerful and always ready to see the best in everyone. He had pointed out many times over the years that I was a mug, gullible and easily taken advantage of. He had affirmed this opinion on many occasions, especially whenever I tried to help someone out. I had wondered for a long time if it was just insecurity on his part; excused it as him simply not wanting to share me. It had not been until fairly recently that a light had switched on in my head and I had been able to see his behaviour for what it really was; simply that he needed to control me. The only person I've been gullible with is you mate, I thought with more than a trace of bitterness.

During our twenty year relationship, he had slowly but surely chipped away at my confidence until I had become a shadow of my former self. People had noticed; indeed I had lost friends because of him but I had still refused to see him for what he really was. A smile hid the tears but laughter was all too infrequent. Still, the shock of his affair had hit me with the force of a hammer, particularly when coupled with the knowledge that *they* were going to become parents.

It had been a joint decision not to have children. To begin with I held no strong feelings either way but he had been adamant. He was unable to think of anything worse he had said. As far as he was concerned that would have been it; his life would have been over, so as no maternal instinct had ever switched to green I had been happy to go along with this decision.

I was thirty seven now, too late to change my mind and in honesty I didn't want to. Even though I felt lonelier than I had ever done, I was still glad that I didn't have the worry of making a new future for myself as well as that of a child. Any children we may have had would have probably been in their early teens by now and so would have been unlikely to want to uproot. I couldn't imagine the horror of having to stay in the North, in close proximity to Simon, her and their offspring, especially without the support of Mum. No, all in all, I was not sorry that I was having to do this alone, however hard it was.

*

It was physically exhausting, dismantling the old bed and wardrobes and carting them section by section down the narrow, wooden stairs to the skip. Poor Tom put his back into it like a man half his age. 'Builder all my working life,' he said uncomplaining. 'I don't mind at all, only too glad to help.'

'You're one in a million Tom!' I answered with heartfelt appreciation.

By the end of the first day we had made a real mark on the place.

'Tell you what,' he said. 'I've nothing on tomorrow. I'll be round by eight and with a bit of luck we'll have this wrapped up by late morning. We can start on a bit of a clean up then, always easier to see what really needs doing when a place is clear.'

'Thanks ever so much Tom. I'm so grateful.' I smiled warmly.

He must have noticed how drawn I looked because he turned and with a look of concern said, 'When you've got things sorted you want to start eating properly ... get a bit of meat on them bones.'

His frankness brought a lump to my throat, 'I know,' I replied. 'I must admit I haven't been eating properly of late. Life's been so stressful. Mind you, I'm pretty hungry now, after all that hard work,' I said brightly, understanding that my being of a similar age to his own daughter meant that he probably viewed me in a protective way, and besides people of his age were always trying to feed you up.

After Tom left though, all thought of dinner and my complaining stomach vanished. I swept out Emily's former bedroom then sat on the floor in the middle of the room surrounded by cardboard boxes full of bits gathered during the day. Rubbish mostly, I assumed, but I still hoped that these more 'personal' belongings might give me a sense of who Emily had been.

A little after eight I suddenly realized that I was squinting badly over what remained of the contents. The outside light was failing and as I hadn't thought to bring any artificial means of light I decided to call it a day. I contemplated carrying a box or two back to Vicarage Cottage in order to continue my quest but as I stood the stiffness in my back from the day's toil warned against it. I didn't even have enough strength left to bend down and lift the boxes. The past few hours since Tom had left had revealed little information. Nevertheless I had been so absorbed in the task that my mind had forgotten its troubles, at least for the present. Stiffly, I made my way down the stairs and straight out the front door, locking it behind me.

Throwing off my shoes and flopping down on the sofa, exhaustion hit like a wave. The stench of Hope Cottage clung to the inside of my nose. It was so pungent that I could taste its acrid bitterness at the back of my throat. Although both hungry and exhausted, I knew I would be unable to eat anything until I had dragged myself into the shower. After scrubbing my face and body and slinging every stitch of clothing into the washing machine I could only muster up enough energy to empty the contents of a can of soup into a bowl and pop it in the microwave. With the steaming soup on a tray on my lap, I reflected on the day's achievements. My first assignment in the morning would be to knock at the Vicarage and see if the cottage was available to rent for a bit longer. I certainly hoped that it was, as I could envisage myself soon otherwise homeless.

'That should have been your first priority today,' I heard the ghost of Simon's voice nagging again. 'It would have taken you what, five minutes to sort? Typical! Now what are you going to do if it's already booked?' The image of his sneering face loomed close.

'What do you care?' I replied silently, determined not to cry.

'Self pity gets you nowhere!' Another frequent quote of his.

'Why were you so bloody often right?' I spoke aloud to the walls, the memory of his look of self-righteousness clear in my mind. Taking out a notepad, I wrote a list of all the positive steps forward that I had made during the day:

- *Made a new and special friend! (That immediately made me feel better!)*
- *Cleared out all furniture and large items from the cottage.*
- *Managed this with only two skips!*
- *Discovered a little about Emily.*
- *Possible contact for job.*

I realized this last entry was pushing it a bit but seeing the list grow made me feel better.

I retreated to bed and as soon as my head hit the pillow I was asleep. However, the ache in my back meant that every time I changed position during the night I had to wake up and do so gradually. Is this what it feels like to get old? I wondered, not without a little guilt. Poor Tom, I bet he's feeling it worse than me.

Chapter 4

True to my word I knocked at the door of the Vicarage at 7-45 the following morning. A rather disgruntled looking man answered with a frown. Not a morning person, I assumed from his disheveled appearance and blank expression. Still, I smiled at him.

'Sorry to bother you so early. It's just that I was wondering if the cottage might be free for another couple of weeks.' No reply and no removal of the frown suggested that I might need to offer further information. 'I'm so sorry, I'm Cassie. I'm renting your cottage this week.' Still he showed no sense of understanding my request. 'Uh ... I was hoping to move into Hope Cottage soon, only it's nowhere near habitable.' Realizing that I was beginning to ramble I stopped speaking and waited.

His expression relaxed a little. 'Hold on, I'll get my wife. She deals with the bookings,' he said before half-closing the front door and retreating back down the tiled hall. I stood and waited. Suddenly becoming aware of my work clothes and the impression my appearance would make, I quickly re-tied my ponytail which had loosened in the April wind in a vain attempt to appear more coherent.

Moments later I found myself being looked over by a rather stern woman whose appearance suggested a retired seventy-something year old school ma'am. As she offered nothing by means of answer to my former request I felt obliged to repeat my plea. I could hear the desperation in my voice. I wondered if the woman was going to give me lines as punishment for disturbing her. The way she continued to stare made me feel as if I were on trial. Perhaps she thinks I'm too untidy to stay in her property. Maybe she thinks I will leave it in a mess; these and other concerns flitted through my mind as I desperately waited for an answer.

After what seemed like an age she finally spoke, her voice equally as curt as her expression. 'You are in luck. I've just had a cancellation. It's free for the next two weeks.'

I felt the butterflies in my stomach relax and breathed a sigh of relief. 'Thank you ever so much,' I beamed. 'I'll write a cheque and drop it in later if that's all right.'

I hopped off the doorstep, eager to retreat from her scrutiny but was forced to return as she spoke again. 'Hope Cottage did you say? You're intending to move into Hope Cottage?'

'Uh yes. I've recently inherited it. I was hoping to move in almost straight away but ... well, as you probably know, it's in a bit of a state.'

'State indeed! Still, I suppose for the right price it could be fixed.' She looked me over again, as if to suggest that I didn't look as if I had the kind of wealth needed to put it right. A few seconds of uncomfortable silence followed before I once again turned to leave.

'Were you related to Emily Willis in some way then?' Her question summoned me back a second time. I noticed the pattern of deep, vertical lines around the woman's mouth and similar horizontal ones around her eyes. Her grey-streaked hair was pulled tightly into a chignon and her skin looked as if it had seen lots of sun and little moisture over the decades. Her expression was steely but I was certain there was a glint of curiosity in her cold, piercing eyes.

'Yes, she was my grandmother, on my mother's side ... but we didn't know her. That is, I mean, my Mum was adopted when she was young.' I wasn't wrong. This woman was indeed interested in what I had to say, though apart from her eyes which gave her away the rest of her face and body tried its best to look disinterested. For all Simon's criticism of me I knew I was good at reading people.

'Oh ... I see,' she drawled. An awkward silence followed as the woman made no effort to move but instead continued to study my face.

'Thanks again ... for the cottage I mean. I'd better be off now. Tom will be waiting for me. He's helping me clear it out you see.' I mentally kicked myself for behaving as though I owed her an explanation. After all, I was paying her the fee which she would have otherwise lost due to the cancellation. As I hurried down the gravel drive leading from the Vicarage I was certain her eyes still bore into me but I dared not turn round.

Tom was already sitting on the church wall. He smiled as he saw my hurried approach. 'You look flustered. No need to rush. I knew you'd be along soon,' he smiled.

'Sorry Tom,' I panted breathlessly. 'I would have been on time but I needed to call at the Vicarage to see if I could keep the rental for another couple of weeks. Ended up taking longer than I thought. I've just received a bit of a grilling from the owner!' I could still feel the flustered heat in my cheeks.

'Oh, I gather you've met Ruth then,' he grinned. 'She *can* be a bit of a dragon. Her father used to be the vicar years ago. Brought up here she was. Went away to Africa apparently when she was about seventeen to do missionary work. Married into the missionary out there. Her husband's a bit of a misery as well. Acts like she owns the village. A real bossy boots she can be. Rents out the cottage and does a bit of B&B from the main house to keep it going like - expensive running a house as big as that.' He nodded back towards the Vicarage. 'Apparently, after both her parents died, she wasted no time in returning though. Knew what a little gem she had on her hands there no doubt,' he laughed.

Chapter 5

Tom's predictions the day before proved to be pretty accurate. Shortly before lunchtime the contents of the cottage were almost cleared and we found ourselves once again sitting on the church wall with a sandwich, planning what to do next. As the skip was now full again and rain forecast for the following day we decided to delay clearing the rubbish from the front of the house until there was better weather forecast and instead turn our attention to cleaning the inside. Tom said that whilst he was out of touch with the labour costs involved in renovation his knowledge and experience in building would enable him to give me a rough idea of the major jobs that would need doing.

'I've got two estate agents coming on Thursday Tom,' I explained. 'Much as I would have loved to live here had it been in a better state I still don't think there's any way I can keep it as it is.' I was annoyed now with myself for not having secured or at least looked for work in the area before having made my move. It had all happened so quickly though. Mum's death coming so soon after Simon's affair had initiated an overwhelming flight response. Even before I knew of the cottage's existence I had made up my mind to flee and start all over again. I had known that as an only child Mum had left everything to me but had thought that meant inheriting the few thousand she had in savings. So when the solicitor had informed me about the cottage it had seemed like a bonus gift from Mum urging me to make the new start I needed. After all, there was nothing or no-one to tie me to the North now.

'Still probably worth knowing what you're up against though, don't you think?' Tom asked, jolting me back to the present.

I had been so lost in thought for a minute that it took a while to register what Tom was on about. 'S'ppose so,' I mumbled unenthusiastically. We decided to tackle the cleaning top down. No central heating meant there wasn't any hot water to clean with so Tom returned home for some wood and coal with which to start a fire in the living room.

'Hope no birds have nested up there!' he laughed.

I couldn't believe that we actually had to boil pots and kettles over an open fire in this day and age but without hot water, tackling the grime would be nigh on impossible. 'She must have lived at least half a century behind everyone else!' I grumbled.

'Thing is, everything comes to us at the flick of a switch these days,' Tom said. 'We don't realize how easy we've got it 'til we have to do without.'

Ceilings, walls and floors were first swept with hard and soft brooms. Buckets of steaming, soapy water were then used to scrub the surface of the walls. The dissolving mildew and distemper ran down our arms, into our hair, and splashed all over our clothes but an hour later the spare bedroom at least felt, looked and indeed smelt cleaner.

'How about we aim to finish upstairs today and tackle downstairs tomorrow?' Tom suggested.

'You *must* let me pay you Tom. Really I insist. I could never have done this without you!'

'I don't want paying! I'm only too glad to have something to do. Anyway, makes me feel young again. Reminds me of my old building days ... I was happy you know. Lot to be said for being happy in one's work.'

'Nevertheless Tom, I would feel much better if I paid.

I feel really guilty.'

'You can do me *one* favour in return.'

'What's that?'

He smiled. 'Just hold off making your decision about selling the place until we've finished clearing it and you know what costs are involved. It could be a little gem this. It's a cracking village, really friendly and welcoming. You could do worse than stay here I promise you.' He saw the lack of hope in my face so continued his plea. 'If nothing comes for you ... in the way of a job I mean, and you decide it's too costly, *then* sell it. Just give it a shot first, that's all I ask.'

I managed a smile. 'Okay Tom. I'll wait 'til I get some quotes and see what the estate agents say it'd be worth, and then I'll make my final decision.'

'Good lass!' He patted me gently on the shoulder.

*

The following two days were back breaking. The kitchen was the worst. All manner of human and animal filth lurked there, including decaying spillages of cat food and bird seed, (at least the bits that hadn't been eaten by rats) hair, fluff, grease and even coughed-up fur balls. We got through several bottles of bleach just sanitizing the kitchen.

By the afternoon of day five though the cottage could, with a little imagination, be considered clean. Tom took out a notepad and pen and we walked, room by room, through the necessary repairs. We made two lists: The first took everything into account from the installation of central heating to fitting a kitchen and even decorating. The second took into account the basics minus jobs we would be able to tackle together. Tom said he would be willing to muck in with me and do the painting, door hanging etc., things that weren't too heavy or didn't necessarily demand professionals. The size of the cottage didn't allow for a bathroom so this would be an additional expense as it would probably entail building an extension on the back.

Once we had itemized the internal works we moved outside and began to list things such as a new roof, windows, down pipes etc. The list was endless and seemed extremely daunting.

'At least you can get a couple of quotes now,' Tom said. 'One for having the lot done and one if you and I do a bit ourselves.'

'Thanks Tom. Would you be willing to come round tomorrow when the estate agents call? I feel a bit out of my depth.'

'Course I will. What time they coming?'

'There's one at eleven, the other at half past.'

'That'll be fine. I'll see you then. It'll be interesting won't it? At least you'll have more of an idea. I paid £125000 for mine six years ago and it's only a two bedroom. I didn't have to do much to it mind, only a lick of paint. Difference is of course, mine's attached to the Post Office. This one's detached and in a lovely little spot. The garden's big with lovely views and lots of privacy out there,' he said, nodding towards the back of the house. 'Tell you what ... it's supposed to be dry tomorrow. See if you can get another skip delivered early and we'll tackle the rubbish out the front before the estate agents arrive. First impressions go a long way you know.'

I breathed a sigh of gratitude. 'Are you sure Tom? You've done so much already.'

'Course! Might as well finish what we've started. I hate doing half a job.' He turned to leave then stopped. 'Oh, almost forgot, if you're not too busy, see if you can call round this evening around seven. My Kate's coming over. I'd love you to meet her. Told her all about you on the phone. She'd been wondering why she hadn't been able to get me all week!' he laughed.

'I'll do that Tom. I'd love to meet her too. I bet she's wondering what type of woman has stolen her dad!'

*

I lay in the bath until my fingertips wrinkled, topping up the hot water every now and then. I was sick of being filthy. Still, the worse was over now. I still had one or two boxes of Emily's possessions to sort through but on the whole Tom and I had wiped the cottage clean.

I dressed casually but neatly in clean jeans and a long-sleeved green top and put on just a hint of make-up; after all I didn't want to give Tom's daughter the wrong impression; goodness only knew what she might be thinking, her elderly father unavailable all week due to helping a strange woman no older then herself. I hoped she wouldn't think that I had taken advantage of his generosity. Typical of me to worry about such things but where I came from people rarely helped others unless there was something in it for themselves. Stop thinking like Simon! I reproached myself. That's just the sort of thing he'd say! There are still people in the world who are willing to do one another favours for no return you know. You'd have done the same in his position, at least your old, unsuspecting self would have.

Chapter 6

Tom's daughter Kate was really friendly. She looked nothing like him but had similar facial expressions when she talked and smiled, which she did often. After a pleasant few hours I truly felt I had gained another friend. She even offered to meet me in the college lobby the following Monday to show me the way to Human Resources where I planned to drop in a copy of my C.V.

'I'm so out of touch!' I said nervously, explaining that I had worked in the same university for a number of years, then given up work to nurse Mum when she became too ill to look after herself. 'I probably should have hung fire and just asked for compassionate leave rather than hand in my notice but at the time I just couldn't see myself going back and I didn't want to mess them around. If I'm honest, I knew Mum didn't have all that long and things were over between me and Simon. I just knew deep down that sooner or later I would need to make big changes which would probably include moving away,' I explained.

'You were probably right. Sometimes something tells us it's time to move on,' Kate replied. 'When we lost Mum I felt as if part of my world had ended too but I had the kids, Mike and Dad to give me a sense of purpose. I think if I had been in your situation I would probably have done the same.'

'He's a treasure your Dad,' I smiled. 'I truly don't know what I'd have done if he hadn't come to my rescue. I only wish I could find some way to repay him.' I hesitated for a moment. 'I hope you don't mind him helping me. I must admit, I've been worried about what you might think.'

'Not at all!' she assured me warmly. 'I worry more about him being lonely. He's pretty fit for his age and he knows his limits.'

I felt a wave of relief. 'Thanks ever so much Kate, for being so understanding I mean. See you around ten on Monday then.'

I ambled back through the village. The evening was warm for the time of year. The air was fresh and still and seemed to promise that spring had finally beaten what had seemed the longest of winters. I suddenly felt at peace. It really had come as a relief to have had Kate's blessing.

Chapter 7

By the time the estate agent arrived at eleven Tom and I had managed to clear the worst of the junk from the front of the cottage. The overgrown grass and multitude of weeds was still evident of course but at least now it appeared less like a scrap yard.

'Clearly someone's been busy!' She spoke in an eloquent English accent, peering over the top of her spectacles at the evidence of our work with a small smirk. 'Pleased to meet you Miss, Mrs.?'

From her words it was obvious that the navy-suited, court-shoed agent was not a total stranger to the property. Bet they've been poking around for months just waiting for this opportunity, I thought.

'Wilkinson, and it's Miss,' I replied, trying to disguise my immediate distrust. Tom had warned me that due to the village's popularity I should be wary of agents who might offer me a deflated valuation with an eye to either obtaining the cottage at a reduced price for themselves or for some eager client already on their books.

'Try not to appear too eager. Tell them you are just considering your options at the moment,' he had warned.

'And you are the owner I take it?' she continued.

'Of course.' I decided to play her at her own game. 'To be honest I am probably less likely to sell than renovate but I would like to have some idea of what both its current and renovated value might be.' On receiving this information her smirk disappeared and was replaced with a frown. Tom nodded in my direction as if to confirm that he liked the way I was handling her.

'Well I couldn't possibly tell you what its renovated value would be,' she said haughtily. 'I mean there are so many factors to consider.'

'But surely you could give me *some* idea,' I continued, determined not to be outwitted. 'If I give you the gist of the alterations I'm planning to make then surely you could give me an estimate. Not anything written in stone I understand but your experience would indisputably allow you a cautious estimate wouldn't it?' I persisted, watching her squirm somewhat in her tight-fitting shoes. Good job I didn't invite her a week ago, I thought, or she'd have likely broken her neck in those. My face retained an innocent smile as I spoke, though inside I was feeling less confident than I sounded.

'Well, let's take a look first and work out what it might be worth in its current state,' she replied, still wearing a severe expression.

I could hear the unspoken phrase *time-waster* desperate to escape from her vibrant, red lips. 'Where would you like to start?' I managed.

'How about inside?' she replied, not without a hint of sarcasm.

Tom gave me a look that said, *She's a feisty one,* and I returned with a small nod to show that I was thinking the same.

As I should have expected, her tour of the property was peppered with, *Oh dear's* and tuts and my new found confidence quickly diminished with each room we visited. When she declined my offer of a tour of the back garden and instead merely stretched her swan-like neck out the door, a wave of concern engulfed me again at the thought of what turning this *slum* into a home would cost in terms of both time and money.

'Hmm ... give me a moment while I make a phone call will you? Then I can let you know what I think,' she said, teetering towards her car.

She sat in the driver's seat and dialed. Tom and I watched from the kitchen window as her head did lots of shaking and her beautifully manicured hands made accompanying gestures towards whomever it was she was speaking on the other end of the line. Tom could see by my face that I was disappointed and giving me a friendly flip on the arm said, 'Come on now. Where's that spirit? Remember, she's probably playing cat and mouse. She likely has this lined up for someone you know.'

'I know,' I sighed and tried to smile but I still felt nowhere near as positive about the possibility of living here as I had done just a day or so ago.

She clip-clopped her way back towards the front door, wearing a forced blank expression and from it called, 'Hello?' As she obviously seemed disinclined to re-enter the cottage, I met her at the door.

'Right,' she began, focussing her attention on the file held in her hands. 'Well it's obviously a difficult one but in its present condition I would advise you to put it on the market at just under £180 000. I've spoken to my colleague and we agree that given the circumstances we would not want to make a projected value in the light of renovation as there are just too many variables. It's a difficult selling market as it is and ...'

'Thank you. At least it gives me some idea,' I interrupted. I was aware of my rudeness but by now was sick of her negative attitude and had had enough.

Her mouth fell open. For the first time she seemed less confident. 'Give us a ring if you decide to put it on with us. Perhaps we could discuss it further then,' she managed.

I merely nodded but was sure that the look on my face

read, *not in a million years would I give you my business!* This kind of behaviour was so out of character for me. I was always such a sucker, as Simon so often called me. I wasn't even sure I liked this new side of my personality. It felt as if I were watching someone else. It was then that I remembered reading about the various *Stages of Grief.* My current attitude suggested that I was at the angry stage. My watch read 11-25 but Tom had poured tea from the flask and handed it to me even though we both knew the next agent was due at any moment.

'I can't take it on Tom. I know she might have had ulterior motives but even so she knows far more about property than I do and she was obviously not impressed by its condition. I really think I'm going to have to let it go for whatever I can get for it.'

'Wait and see now. Don't be hasty. You wouldn't want to regret it later would you?' he warned.

We sat in silence for the next few minutes, sipping our luke-warm tea when we were suddenly both jolted out of our thoughts by the sound of a car door slamming. 'Oh, here we go again! I wish I'd only booked the one now,' I moaned.

'Don't be silly. Where's the enthusiastic Cassie gone?' he said with a smile.

The front door was being knocked. Other than the actual lock, there was no door furniture and the sound of the hollow thudding on the old wood corresponded with the way I was feeling – dull and lifeless. I opened the door to see a tall, middle aged man with a smiling but slightly flustered expression glancing at his watch.

'Sorry I'm a bit late,' he spoke in a friendly voice. 'The previous client didn't seem to want me to leave. Elderly lady, seemed lonely,' he continued, still smiling.

'That's okay. Come in,' I replied, my mood softening a little. 'I'm Cassie.'

He stepped into the hallway and held out a large, warm hand. 'Pleased to meet you. John Burgess,' he said. 'What do we have here then?' He glanced from left to right and back again, the absence of internal doors obvious.

I led him into the kitchen where Tom remained seated on a fishing stool salvaged from his garage, still sipping his tea. He rose to his feet. 'This is my friend Tom. He's been helping me out here,' I smiled. The difference in John's attitude to the former agent had helped me to relax a bit.

'So how can I help?' he asked. 'What are your plans?'

Despite Tom's warning and Simon's voice nagging me about being too trusting I suddenly felt able to follow my instincts and so found myself explaining the bare bones of my situation to him. I told him that I was in two minds whether to sell up or renovate and that I would value his professional opinion. Even Tom seemed to warm to him as he didn't shoot me any warning looks.

'Okay. Well the decision of course will be yours but let's have a little chat about your options first,' he said. 'You've basically got two choices by the sound of it. Now, in the current economic climate, property's not doing so well and no-one, no matter what they try and tell you, has a crystal ball so cannot really say what will happen to prices in the near future. We can only go on past experience of market performance. Taking that into account I personally feel we are in for a long ride before we really see any great rise in prices again. I reckon they'll stay steady for a couple more years. It's a buyers' market at the moment.' He paused to see if I'd taken it all in. 'Having said that, you'd probably need a cash buyer for this as any prospective purchaser would be unlikely to be granted a mortgage given its current condition. On the other hand, this is a very popular location and the plot on which this cottage stands is superb. Therefore, I don't think you'd find it too difficult to find a cash buyer, in fact I believe there'd probably be a few already lined up. Of course, if you *can* find the means to renovate it yourself you'd be looking at a decent profit at the end though. In all honesty, if it were mine and I could afford to do the work I'd likely stay put. It's a beautiful village this.'

I breathed a sigh of relief. I knew he wasn't really telling me anything I didn't already know but at least now I felt he would be more likely to give me a fair valuation.

'Let's have a look around and you can tell me your plans at the same time. I know I probably should be urging you to sell but by the sounds of it you need fair play. Just don't tell my boss,' he laughed.

The three of us toured the cottage and garden and all the while John made notes and took measurements. Half an hour later we returned to the kitchen.

'Right. I think in it current condition you could be looking at putting it on the market at around £179 950. In all honesty though, I think it would sell really quickly at that price. Now giving you an accurate valuation of what it might be worth after your proposed improvements is obviously difficult as it would depend on the spec., any changes in market conditions and how long the renovation took. However, I imagine you'd be looking at a possible value of around £280 000.'

I was shocked at the difference. 'Really?' I said, a look of utter astonishment on my face.

'In this village, a detached cottage of this size on this plot would be worth around that figure. With the size of the garden out the back there is plenty of scope for extending too and that would make it an enticing buy. Someone could end up with a little gem here,' he added confidently.

'See, that's what I told you!' Tom beamed.

I couldn't help but smile. 'Well, thank you ever so much for your time and advice. I'll have to think about it and get back to you as soon as I have reached my decision.'

He hesitated for a moment. 'There is one further option you may not have considered.'

'What's that?'

'Well, it's just a thought, but if this were mine and I was in your position it would be something I'd look into. The land that leads around the corner from the back garden, why don't you think about selling that as a potential building plot? Obviously you'd need planning permission and it wouldn't be a big plot. Plus you'd then have a closer neighbour and that might not be what you'd want but it might bring in the revenue you need to do this place up. I know you'd have to rent in the meantime but...' I could see that he was almost thinking aloud and weighing up the option as he spoke.

'Hey Tom! That's a thought,' I smiled, my cheeks flushed. Tom looked excited too. 'That's something else to consider.'

'I'll leave you to make your decision for now then. If you do decide to sell, the cottage or the plot that is, I'd be only too pleased to do business with you.'

'Thanks, I'll get back to you. Thanks for all your help,' I replied with genuine enthusiasm.

After he left, I turned to Tom in the kitchen. 'Hey, what do you think?'

'Sounds like a really good idea to me. Of course it'd take time and the planners are pretty strict about new building around here but it's worth a shot. Give them a ring and see if someone will call round and take a look.'

'I will Tom. Probably a long shot but it'd be one way of affording the renovation costs wouldn't it?'

Chapter 8

Spotting Kate waiting for me in the entrance lobby I inhaled deeply. Her warm smile put me a little more at ease but I felt like a teenager again; the uncertainty that being on unfamiliar territory brings. I noted for the umpteenth time how much confidence I had lost over the years. This was not down to one single factor but rather for several reasons including the torment of my mother's illness and death, Simon's controlling behaviour towards me, but also because I had stayed put in my previous job for far too long. I had not challenged myself like this in years. It had been been sixteen years since my last interview. I was only too aware of how things had changed in the working environment and how things were now far more competitive than when I had first begun lecturing. Just getting a foot on the ladder, just to be given the opportunity to show what you were capable of was no mean feat in this day and age.

'You look terrified! Come on, Phillip's not an ogre and you've got nothing to lose by simply making him aware that you are available,' Kate said with encouragement.

She had very kindly arranged an informal meeting with the Head of the English Department. As she had worked in the college library for several years she was quite familiar with most of the academics. I quickly wiped the perspiration from my palms onto my navy skirt as a dark-haired thirty-something year old man approached.

'Phil, this is Cassie.'

I managed a smile though I could feel my hand trembling as I shook his. Don't be silly! I reproached myself for being so fearful. 'You're only having a quick chat. It's not even as if there's a job going!'

Kate led the way toward the student cafe in the hope that its informal surroundings amongst the students might make me feel more at ease. Indeed, chatting as we sat amongst the throngs, I did begin to feel more relaxed. I explained my teaching background to him with as much enthusiasm as I could muster under the circumstances and told him that I had prepared my C.V. and accompanying references. I asked if he would be kind enough to consider me should a vacancy arise. He had a friendly enough demeanor and told me a little about the English Department and of the fact that he had only been made Head of Department the previous year. He assured me that if any vacancy were to arise he would let me know. 'In honesty though, it's not likely until after the summer term and even then it'll probably be part-time if anything; you know some evening classes etc. Would you be interested in that sort of thing?' he asked.

'I'd be grateful for any opportunity to be honest,' I replied, whilst at the same time trying not to sound too desperate. I didn't want to tell him anything of my personal circumstances as I didn't think it appropriate.

Coffee break was over and he excused himself. Kate and I headed over to Human Resources. I thanked her again and left, not wanting to impinge on her working hours. Besides, I had managed to arrange a meeting with the Planning Officer in the council offices across town at twelve to discuss the possibility of selling part of the cottage land. 'Grab the bull by the horns!' was what Mum always said and I hoped I might get a more positive result if I actually met with someone rather than simply telephoned. I had taken some photos of the cottage and gardens over the weekend and whilst I knew this would not be enough to get any kind of decision, I felt that at least I could explain more clearly what I wanted to do if I had a visual image to focus on.

As expected the planning officer was rather stern, being probably used to giving little away through facial expression, but he did at least appear to listen. 'I know the village well of course; in fact, I even know the very cottage you are talking about. Do you mind me asking how you have come to own it? I know a few people who'd been hoping it'd come onto the market,' he said.

My heart sank, hoping this would not mean he would be biased against my idea. I put on my best pleading expression and explained the outline of my story. I wanted him to at least be aware of my situation and perhaps even manage a little sympathy.

'I see,' he said, still wearing the same stern expression. 'Well of course this discussion can only preempt what would be a long process if it were to be passed. I can call round later in the week to take a look, and then at least I can give you more of an idea as to whether or not you would be wasting your time going for planning approval. All I can say at the moment, and this is strictly off the record you understand, is that you'd probably have a bit of a battle on your hands with some of the villagers if they thought the place might turn into a building site. Also, looking at the photos here and from my memory of the place you would be highly unlikely to be granted permission for anything other than a small, single-storey.'

He must have read the despondency on my face as he added with the tiniest hint of a smile, 'That doesn't mean it's a complete no-goer of course. People have been granted permission in all sorts of places and after all sorts of battles with neighbours. Wait until I've had a look then we'll discuss your options further.' Quickly tapping into his computer, presumably accessing his diary which was not visible to me he said, 'How does Thursday around eleven sound?'

I managed to thank him for his time but returned to my car with a sinking feeling.

Back at Vicarage Cottage I telephoned Tom and invited him over for a quick lunch. The morning's events had made me feel lonely and I really needed someone to talk things over with. It was at times like this that I missed Mum the most and even Simon in a perverse kind of way.

*

'What you must focus on is that neither of them said no did they?' Tom tried to reassure me about both my morning's meetings. 'You need to be a bit patient. These things don't happen right away you know.' He patted my hand in a fatherly gesture.

'I know Tom. It's not like me to be impatient. Really it isn't. It's just that I worry because time is not on my side right now. I mean I can only stay here for one more week and I haven't even sorted anywhere else to live yet and as you know, my finances are not exactly in the best of health!'

'Something'll turn up girl. You mark my words if it doesn't. Anyway, I'd not see you out on the streets. I'd put you up in my spare room first.'

'I couldn't possibly Tom! What on earth would the villagers make of that? I'd never want to damage your reputation,' I laughed.

'I'm too old to worry about reputation! *We* know we're good friends and nothing more. Kate knows the same so that's all I care about.'

His innocence cheered me. 'Tom, you're a treasure! I don't know how I'd have got through the last few weeks without you you know. I feel as if we've known each other for years.'

'Come on,' he said, getting to his feet stiffly. 'Let's go and tackle the rubbish in the back garden. Make a better impression when the planning officer calls on Thursday.'

'You sure Tom?'

'Absolutely! I'm a bit bored myself today. Can't think of anything better to do!'

Chapter 9

After a sleepless night, tossing and turning, I realized that my main focus now needed to be on finding somewhere to live and then finding some sort of paid employment, however menial, as long as it contributed towards the rent. My thoughts had been so wrapped up in the cottage that I had rather stupidly neglected both of these. Regardless of Tom's generous offer of a room, there was no way on earth I would take him up on it. Of course we both knew it was a completely innocent proposal but I had no intention of sallying either of our reputations in *this* kind of village.

At 9-00 a.m. sharp I telephoned John the estate agent to ask whether there were any properties available to rent in the area.

'What sort of thing you after?' he asked.

'Small and cheap as possible!' I replied, my jovial tone belying the fact that I actually meant what I said. 'And I would need to move in next week if possible, otherwise I'll have to resort to a hotel.'

'I'm afraid you wouldn't find anything that quickly. I'd say you'd be lucky to be able to move into anything without at least two weeks or so notice. Landlords expect references, bonds and usually a minimum contract of six months these days. That's assuming we've got anything that fits your requirements. Give me a few minutes and I'll have a look and ring you back. Is that okay?'

I put down the phone and inhaled deeply in an attempt

to calm myself. The thought of homelessness was looming ever nearer. I'd fleetingly wondered about knocking at the Vicarage to see if there was any room in the B&B for a few weeks but Ruth's attitude on the morning I'd approached her about extending the let had been really off-putting. Still, it may come down to that, I thought. After all, beggars can't be choosers.

Within a few minutes John called to say that the cheapest available rental was £250 a month on a studio apartment back in town. I arranged to view it the following day.

No sooner had I replaced the receiver than it rang again. It was Tom and he sounded excited. 'I may have some good news for you!' he said breathlessly. 'I'm friendly with a chap called Mr. Ghent, lives at the end of the village, got some animals - chickens and a few rare-breed goats and a small garden allotment. I bumped into him when I went out for the paper this morning and he told me that his daughter in Australia has been admitted to hospital for an emergency hysterectomy. She wants him to fly out to help look after the kids for a month or two. He was in a bit of a state worrying about the animals and garden so I hope you don't mind but I grabbed the chance and filled him in on your position. Said you'd likely be only too glad to house-sit for him whilst he was away and that I'd help you take care of things. He said we could call round at teatime today for a chat. Did I do the right thing?'

I laughed with joy. 'Right thing? Tom you may have saved me from a breakdown!'

*

Mr. Ghent was an old dear. I could tell he was a little wary of me at first and, like most people, didn't relish the thought of a stranger moving into his home but I managed to reassure him that I would most certainly take good care of things. 'I was going to look at a studio flat in town tomorrow and they were asking £250 per month in rent. How would it be if I paid you the same?" I suggested.

'I don't want rent girl! Just promise me that you'll look after my little un's out there.' He nodded towards the smallholding out the back. 'I'll likely be gone two months. That's how long they've told my daughter she will take to recover properly and if I don't go my son-in-law will have to take a lot of time off work. He's self-employed so that would cause them even more stress.'

'Mr. Ghent, I really can't thank you enough but I insist on paying rent.'

'Shan't hear of it! Tell you what you can do for me though... Would you give me a hand booking my flight? I can't handle that internet business. Don't know where to start!'

I laughed. 'No problem. There's internet access back at the rental cottage. Come round with me now if you like and we'll get it sorted.'

The flights were booked for the following Tuesday, leaving me with just one night of potential homelessness. Tom insisted that I should stay the night in his spare room and I really felt too drained to argue. Besides, it was a blessing in disguise. Perhaps at last my luck is beginning to change, I thought hopefully. I telephoned John to cancel the viewing on the studio apartment. Now all I needed to do was to find a job.

Chapter 10

An on-line search produced nothing that looked even vaguely hopeful within the immediate search area so I decided to register my C.V. with a few recruitment agencies and hope for the best.

I took a trip back into town to visit the local jobcentre and left my details with them. It was the usual scenario, overqualified and over-experienced for most, under qualified and totally lacking in experience for what remained. Still, it was all I could do for the present. Up until now, I'd been too exhausted and too busy to visit the local pub but I'd promised to treat Tom to a bar meal there that evening in return for his help in finding me somewhere to stay.

At seven o'clock sharp we stepped through the sturdy black door of the Moon and Sixpence in a jovial mood. I felt more relaxed than I had done in weeks. A weight had lifted in knowing that at least for now I had a roof over my head. Give yourself a chance to look into the building plot and then at least you'll be able to come to a decision about what to do with the cottage, I'd told myself in the mirror as I was getting ready for the evening.

The pub was gently bustling and had real old-fashioned warmth with a roaring fire in the far corner. Several heads turned and greeted Tom as we entered. It was obviously the kind of village where everybody knew everyone else and even though they glanced inquisitively towards me, once

Tom introduced me, they seemed genuinely welcoming. I sensed that a few were bursting to ask questions when my ownership of the cottage was mentioned but for now I didn't want to offer any further information.

As I ordered our meals at the bar, broccoli bake for myself (being vegetarian I was pleased that they had something to offer) and home-cooked ham for Tom, a handwritten notice pinned to the side of the bar caught my eye...

Kitchen and bar help required four days a week, lunchtimes and evenings, Thursdays to Sundays

Drinks in hand, I returned to our table smiling. 'What do you think Tom? Should I make inquiries? I've got no experience in catering of course but it'd do for a while. Better than nothing don't you think?'

'Won't hurt to ask.' He smiled encouragingly. 'Bessie the landlady's alright. Tells it as it is. Won't put up with no messing but she's nice enough. You never know. They don't always find it easy to find people for jobs like that. Too out of the way for some folk to travel twice a day and if you don't live in the village you might not want to be travelling home on your own late at night. Besides, I'm sure you'd soon pick it up. It's not exactly rocket science is it,' he laughed. 'Go on, Bessie's at the bar now. Go and have a word.' He nudged my arm and pointed toward a stout, grey pony-tailed lady who stood chatting to one of the locals.

I suddenly felt nervous. 'Oh I don't know Tom. I'll have a think about it while we eat.' My broccoli bake went down in lumps as I *ummed* and *ahhed* over what to do. I tried my best to glean what I could about Bessie's character through her interaction with the customers and also tried to take in more of the atmosphere in order to establish what I would be up against. By what I could see she seemed friendly enough and the place was not too busy. After downing another half a cider for dutch courage

Tom persuaded me to go and speak to her.

She called to the barman who stood in the middle of a conversation with a customer on the other side of the bar. 'Jim, hold the fort for a few minutes! Come into the back and we'll have a quick chat,' she said smiling at me.

I couldn't believe how nervous I felt but ten minutes or so later, having filled her in on my background and coming clean about my total lack of experience I was surprised when she said, 'Pop round at eleven tomorrow before we start for lunch and I'll show you the ropes. The pay's not great I'm afraid, £5 an hour but I like the look of you and I know old Tom wouldn't pal up with anyone who was no good! You know what? I'm fed up with those bloody youngsters from the town. They get their parents to fetch and carry them and then they phone in sick half the time. Can't rely on them. Now I'm not saying you're long in the tooth yet but you're no spring chicken either. Age counts for experience in my books.' She gave me no signal that she was joking.

I was a bit taken aback by her abruptness but was beginning to understand that this was often the way people in such small communities spoke so was not offended. 'I'll certainly do that and thanks for the opportunity,' I replied gratefully.

Tom was watching my face anxiously as I returned to our table. 'I think I just had an interview of sorts,' I told him with a grin. 'I'm coming round for a trial tomorrow lunchtime.'

He laughed. 'There you are. Worth asking wasn't it?'

'I can't believe it Tom. If it works out then I'll have found somewhere to stay and a job all in the space of two days!'

Chapter 11

The trial went well, all things considered and Bessie and I seemed to hit it off. I stayed and helped through the lunch hours and found it to be less stressful than I had imagined. I left at two thirty, having arranged to begin the job properly the following day.

The day dawned bright and warm. The sky was cloudless as I returned to Vicarage Cottage via the cemetery, once again passing the unmarked grave which had caught my attention the morning following my arrival. I couldn't help but stop and stand for a few moments. It was exactly as I had first encountered it, apart from the fact that the strong April sunshine had seemed to fade the poinsettia a little further.

The cemetery was empty as I made my way toward the church, intending to take the short cut through the back to the lane which lead to Vicarage Cottage.

Suddenly, I had an overwhelming feeling of being watched. Looking up, I found that indeed I was right for there, in the lychgate, stood Ruth. Her thin mouth twitched slightly as I approached. I wondered if it were her attempt at a smile. I returned the gesture with a friendlier version. It was she who spoke first as I drew adjacent. 'You *are* leaving on Sunday aren't you? Only it's as I told you, I have other guests arriving in the afternoon.'

Why does she have to be so rude? I thought but replied politely, 'Yes of course. I haven't forgotten. Don't worry.'

She appeared to breathe a sigh of relief and I saw the tension in her stance ease a little. 'I suppose you'll be returning home to wherever you came from. I mean it'd take so much work to make it habitable. You'd never do it on your own,' she said, gesturing in the direction of Hope Cottage.

What on earth does this women have against me? I wondered, for it certainly seemed that she not only wanted me out of Vicarage Cottage but also out of the village. I decided that as I had done her no harm I wouldn't give her the satisfaction of thinking I was leaving.

'Actually I'm staying here; at least for a while that is. I'll be working in the Moon and Sixpence and remaining here in the village.'

The disappointment on her face confirmed my suspicions. 'Oh I see ... And what about Hope Cottage? Are you selling it?'

How nosy, I thought, hesitating a little before deciding to keep her guessing a while longer. 'Oh no. I'm intending to renovate it then we'll just have to wait and see. No definite plans yet,' I replied, still with an innocent smile on my face.

She looked peeved to say the least. 'Oh. Well be sure to hand in the keys by ten o'clock Sunday morning,' she said, abruptly turning her back on me and walking toward the church. I watched as she entered. Without so much as a backward glance she closed the door loudly behind her.

How rude that woman is, I thought. I wonder if it's something personal or if she's like it with everybody? It's certainly no way to attract business!

*

Tom and I had decided to pull out all the stops in lieu of the planning officer's visit and spent Wednesday afternoon cutting the overgrown grass and weeds at the back and side of the cottage with the hire of an industrial petrol strimmer. I told him of my rather strange encounter earlier that day but he seemed unperturbed. 'I wouldn't go reading anything into that,' he said. 'She's like it with everyone.'

Perhaps I am being over-sensitive, I thought and got back to raking. The tidy up was almost complete now and certainly did the job of making the garden appear larger which was exactly the effect I'd hoped for. I knew the planning officer would go on position and measurements rather than the visuals but at least now I felt the area could be viewed more clearly.

He arrived at eleven precisely the following morning. Fortunately it was another clear, bright day. Having carried out the usual formal greetings, I led him straight round to the back of the cottage where he stood and gazed silently for what seemed like ages. 'So what exactly would you like to do with this?' he asked finally.

I sighed nervously. 'Well, as I explained, I hope to be able to perhaps sell off the land at the side as a potential building plot. You can't see any of the other village houses from there and it wouldn't interfere with anyone towards the back either as that land goes down to the river. The only potential nuisance during building would be to the resident of Hope Cottage and as that would be me, well ...'

I was silenced as he interjected, 'But it's not as simple as that you see. This being a conservation area, the Council and residents frown upon any kind of new build which potentially detracts from the character of the village.'

My heart sank. He must have noticed the look of despondency on my face as he quickly added, 'Let me measure up and have a better look round the corner then I can give you more of an idea.'

Not knowing whether to follow him around or to let him get on with it alone I decided to go with the latter and sat dejectedly on the crumbling, stone step at the back door. All my current plans rested on his decision as there was no way on earth I would be able to afford the renovation on a bar-maid's salary.

He returned a few minutes later and stood looking down at where I remained seated. I had always been told that being eye-level with a potential adversary was more advantageous but at that moment I couldn't care less. The advantage was all his.

'Basically, you've got three choices. Firstly, you could apply for what we call Outline Planning Consent which means the council would consider the erection of a dwelling on the plot. If that were to be passed the advantage would be that the plot could go up for sale more quickly. The disadvantage is that there would be no guarantee of eventual full planning approval and this would need to be reflected in what you could potentially ask for it.

Your second choice would be to apply for full planning permission which means that you would need plans drawn up and approved by council before putting the plot up for sale. The advantage of this is that any potential buyer would know exactly what they could and couldn't do with the land. However, this sort of permission would take a lot longer and to be truthful, in my opinion, would unlikely be granted.'

Shielding my eyes with my hand, I squinted up at him through the sunshine. He watched me closely, awaiting my response. 'Oh I see. And what might be the reasons for rejection?' I asked.

'Well, as I said earlier, new builds are unwelcome in conservation areas and also, something you might not have considered, is that a new plot would require separate road access from the lane. If I'm honest this does not look particularly feasible given how narrow it is.'

I paused in thought. 'How long might full planning

permission take?' I asked tentatively.

'Probably around six months, even longer if someone disputes it. There is also no guarantee at this stage that you would obtain either outline or full permission, it depends on so many factors so if I'm in honest both are risky. You could spend a fair amount of money getting plans drawn up only to be refused permission altogether.'

'But are you in a position to tell me what my chances are?' I asked, all hopes of my solution quickly disappearing.

'If it was in any old village I'd say you'd have a good chance. However, the conservation status of Marleston realistically reduces your chances to lower than fifty per cent I'd say. Worth a shot if you can afford to be patient but if you're desperate I'd advise you to sell instead. Even if planning were approved it would likely be on condition that specific reclaimed, local materials etc. are used.'

I paused again, trying to assimilate what I'd just been told before remembering what he had said earlier. 'And my third option? You said I had one of three options,' I reminded him.

'Yes. Your third, and in my opinion the option with most chance of success would be to apply to erect a small holiday let on the land. The council would be more likely to favour that option as Marleston is rather short of such accommodation. Plus a holiday let wouldn't require separate road access.'

'Okay. Well thank you for your honesty. I'll have to think about it.' I wanted desperately to be alone so got to my feet and began to walk back indoors.

'In the meantime, if you simply decide to forget the plot and go about renovating the cottage for yourself I can provide you with a list of council-approved builders,' he offered.

'Okay thanks, I'd appreciate that,' I replied, my face unable to hide my disappointment.

My mind was a whirr as he drove off. Back to square one! I thought. Still, no time for self pity. I've got to be at work in fifteen minutes for the lunch shift. The last thing I want to do now is let Bessie down.

My shift at the Moon and Sixpence lifted my mood somewhat and strengthened my resolve to find a way of staying. I was beginning to really appreciate the kind of life on offer here and felt determined to try and make it work.

Having filled Tom in on the details of my chat with the planning officer, I decided to write down my options so that I could at least consider them in black and white. It felt good to have the freedom to do this without it being met by a sarcastic comment from Simon. He always made fun of the frequent notes and lists I made. I telephoned the planning officer and asked him to read off a few builders' names and numbers then arranged for two to visit early the following Saturday.

My list of course didn't tell me anything I didn't already know but I was now able to visualize my options to a degree, though as soon as I could fill in some renovation figures those options would be made all the more clear.

Chapter 12

The first builder had said he would be able to come around eight thirty as he worked Saturdays when the weather permitted. He was amiable enough, though rather quietly spoken for a builder. He listened carefully as I explained my ideas, measured up and made a thorough examination of the place, both inside and out, then promised to send me a quote in the post within the week.

The second, apologetically arriving a little late at 10-00a.m., was more chatty and inquisitive. As he was more forthcoming, I found myself opening up to him and mentioning my idea for the plot. Tom had also arrived by now and with his builder's knowledge I felt more self-assured in asking questions. 'I'd definitely give it a shot if I were you!' he said confidently. 'You could be sitting on a little gold mine there. Don't bother with outline planning though. You won't make half the profit from that. A lot of people won't go for it, especially in an area like this ... too risky. They'd want to see it in black and white first. Shame you've got to consider it at all mind. If this were mine I'd want it all. Nice bit of land out there!' he laughed.

'To be honest with you, it's the only way I'll be able to afford the renovation,' I admitted.

'Ah, well that's different. I mean I don't know your financial situation, but another option, if you're patient, would be to get the basics done, you know roof, windows, and such, make it water-tight then add the non-essentials bit by bit. Trouble with you women is it's usually only the non-essentials you're interested in!' he said with a cheeky wink.

Just like the builders back home, I thought but as he seemed genuine I was surprised to find that it didn't really put me off.

'Tell you what I'll do. How about I send you two quotes? One for the basics and the other with all the works, and then you'll have more of an idea.'

'That'd be great thanks,' I said.

'And don't let those planning officers put you off. You never know, you might get permission for the right type of build there.' He nodded back towards the corner of the cottage. 'Take your time then couldn't you. Get the basics done here so it doesn't decay any further then sit on it 'til you can sell the land. Then you can use the money for the fancy jobs. Opportunities like this don't come up very often you know.' He paused, examining my expression as I took it all in. 'Anyway, I'll leave it with you; none of my business what you decide. That's the trouble with me, can't resist saying my piece. I'll get those quotes out to you within the week all right love.'

Tom and I considered the options over a cup of tea before I left for work. 'Can't do anymore now until I get the quotes,' I said.

'Aye, try and put it out of your mind for a few days. You can end up going round in circles some times. Tell you what, how about I come round after your lunch shift and we move the majority of your stuff in with me. Saturday's usually pretty busy in the pub you know and after a late night I don't suppose you'll feel like a really early start in the morning. As you said, she wants you out by ten - mean devil!'

'Thanks Tom,' I laughed. 'That'll be great. See you around three.'

'Where's the rest?' Tom asked, looking down at the two suitcases and four small boxes packed ready by the kitchen door. 'Got it in storage have you?'

It was then that it hit me exactly how few possessions my life consisted of. Before leaving the North I had indeed trimmed them down to the bare minimum. I had taken very little from both the house I had shared with Simon and Mum's home, preferring to hold on to only a few, precious keepsakes.

I supposed, on reflection, it was to do with wanting a complete, fresh start; not wanting to carry any past baggage with me in more ways than one. Now though, as I tried to justify my lack of possessions to Tom I felt slightly embarrassed. The look on his face was somewhat puzzled but still, people of his generation tended to hold on to things more than mine. After all, they were the post war generation, not the 'throw away' generation I still felt I was just about young enough to belong to.

One trip in the car was all it took and I thanked Tom again, promising to go straight round the following morning after handing in my keys.

Chapter 13

Not wishing to give the fearsome Ruth any opportunity to have a go at me, I found myself knocking rather timidly on the Vicarage door at nine thirty. I had considered posting the keys through the letterbox but thought better of it; after all, I was still a customer and as such should have no rational fear of her.

To my relief, her husband answered almost immediately, as though waiting. He took the keys from me without so much as a word. I hesitated for a moment, expecting at least an attempt at courtesy but when nothing seemed forthcoming, even in the way of feigned conversation, I simply muttered, 'Thank you,' and left. The door was closed behind me even before I had reached the bottom step. Once again I found myself annoyed by their rudeness. The only unfriendliness I have felt from anyone since my arrival here, I noted.

Still, I was cheered greatly by the warm welcome which awaited me at Tom's. His spare room was immaculately prepared and he had even put out a spare kettle, cup and some biscuits for me. 'Bless you!' I said warmly, giving him a quick hug. For the first time in a few weeks, I felt tears threaten. Don't be soft now! I scolded myself.

*

As we prepared the Sunday lunches, I warily told Bessie of the cold reception I had received from Ruth and her husband. I was guarded about criticizing any of the villagers as it was quite possible here that one might find themselves criticizing someone's relative. Besides, I didn't want to give the impression of being a gossip-monger. Over the past few weeks, I had begun to feel a greater sense of belonging here than I had done in all my thirty seven years in the North. Back there, with the exception of my childhood years, something had always felt slightly amiss.

'You don't want to worry about that old bag!' Bessie said emphatically. 'She's not got a good word to say to anyone! Nosy old thing mind you. Likes to think she's back in the olden days when the clergy more or less controlled what went on in the village!'

I couldn't help but smile at her frankness.

'Truth is, nobody likes her!' she snorted. 'Oh yes they tolerate her. Some of them got to, 'specially the church-goers, but she's not got any real friends.' Her face was screwed with distaste as she spoke of Ruth. 'Shame really,' she sniffed. 'Her mother was a lovely woman.' She shook the water from her hands before wiping them swiftly down the front of her apron and heading to the pantry to collect another sack of potatoes. Quickly she returned and took up the conversation where she had left off. 'Typical old-fashioned vicar's wife she was; nicely spoken and always friendly. Genuine she was. Always welcomed villagers with their problems. Bit of an olden day's therapist I suppose!' she laughed. 'After her husband died she lived there alone like a recluse and that bloody daughter of hers never came to see her! Yes, she was off in Africa doing her charity work but what about charity beginning at home? There was her mother, a lonely soul and years went by without her even stepping foot in the place. A real good mother she had been to her too. Deserved better than that!' Her plump, reddened hands worked deftly at the potatoes. 'Ruth wasn't long in coming back mind once she realized her mother didn't have long. Oh no! She wasn't going to let anyone else get their hands on that place. One of the best houses for miles that is and there's some crackers around here mind. Probably why she was so cold with you. Doesn't like the thought of newcomers in the village. Especially with you owning the very property she can see from her front window. Like I said, she still likes to think she can control things round here.'

'I suppose you're right,' I muttered. 'Still, I won't have anything more to do with her now will I?'

'Too bloody right! Your own cottage being practically next door or not I wouldn't bother with that one if I were you.' As she opened the oven door, the sizzling fat hissed like her temper. 'Right then! Let's get these bloody roasties in!'

Chapter 14

The move into Mr. Ghent's house went smoothly. Before he left for the airport, he spent most of the day familiarizing me with the animals and giving me instructions about how best to care for them.

'Call me by my first name - John,' he told me with a friendly smile as I had followed him round the land like a sheep. Though I assured him I would be fine, truth be told I was feeling a little apprehensive. For years I had daydreamed of the *Country Life* and now I was getting first hand experience, even if it was only for a lend. Being with the animals extinguished any feelings of loneliness and the sense of duty and care that came with them was remarkably rewarding. What, with the animals and the pub I was busier and more fulfilled than I had been for a long time.

On the Friday, a written quote from the first builder arrived at Tom's. It was very detailed and professional, just as I had expected but also conveyed to me that the cost of full renovation would be around £29 000. That would include all the basics; roof, windows, guttering, turning the old out-house into a single story bathroom extension etc. as well as installation of a kitchen, bathroom and central heating. It seemed a fair price and around what Tom and I had imagined. Nevertheless, it was also £6000 more than I had in savings. My current job would not be sufficient to mortgage a sum anywhere near the deficit so really it just confirmed what I already knew; that I would either need to sell the land or, by some miracle, find a better paid job.

My lunchtime stroll back to John's after my pub shift took me past Tom's house. I was rather surprised to see him chatting on the doorstep to the second builder.

'Hello again!' he called cheerfully as I approached, feeling rather bedraggled after what had been a busy shift. 'I thought I'd deliver your quotes by hand so I could just brief you on the options. I hope you don't mind?'

Quickly, I attempted to re-pin the escaped sections of grown-out fringe blowing in front of my eyes.

Without waiting for an answer, he launched into his explanation. 'Basically, the quote for making it water-tight - roof, guttering, external rendering, doors and windows and new internal floors and walls as well as re-wiring and updating plumbing would cost around £20 000. I'd say you'd be wise to spend an extra £3000 at the same time and get a central heating system put in so that the majority of the pulling about's done in one go. Of course, bathrooms, kitchens etc. cost as little or as much as you want them to. That estimate also includes turning the old outhouse into a small bathroom but doesn't include any fittings. The rest'd have to wait but at least if you spent around £23 000 you'd be guaranteed the house would be watertight and wouldn't depreciate further. I've not included additional things like internal doors etc. so if you're really up against it with the budget you can more or less tailor it to what you've got to spend and what you're prepared to wait for.'

I hadn't spoken so far but had simply nodded as he had talked, partly because he hadn't really let me get a word in edgeways and partly because I was genuinely trying to take it all in.

He paused for a breath. 'Anyway, I don't want to put any pressure on you to make a decision. I think you've got plenty to consider there,' he said, passing me the paperwork. 'Anything you'd like to ask or shall I leave you to mull it over?'

'Just one thing really; if I decided to get the basics done and wait for the rest, how long would it take to make it fit for habitation?'

'Let's see. Where are we now? Mid-May.' He scratched his chin. 'I'm in the middle of a couple of jobs but nothing too big at the moment so I could probably make a start in around three weeks time. You'd be looking at about the end of August for the basics to be completed.' He looked at me and grinned. 'Now I could tell you a lie and promise it'd be done sooner but the truth is that's how long it'd take ... Oh, by the way, I've also had a re-think about the plot. I know what I'd do if I were you. Rather than try to sell off the land and lose your privacy, I'd apply for permission to have a single-story timber frame holiday let built on it, as and when you can afford it of course. I think it'd be the cheapest option as well as the most likely option to be agreed by the planners. It'd more than pay for itself in the long run.'

I smiled. 'That's exactly what the planning officer suggested when he came round. Well, thanks ever so much Steve. I'll have a good look at the options and get back to you,' I told him feeling somewhat cheered.

As he drove off in his van Tom asked, 'Fancy a cuppa? I was just about to put the kettle on.'

We sat in his small, neat kitchen. 'You know Tom, it's really strange,' I said.

'What is?'

'Well £23 000. That's exactly what I've got put away.'

He laughed, somewhat embarrassed. 'You don't have to tell me that girl. That's your business.'

I smiled. People of his generation were always embarrassed when it came to discussing personal wealth whereas my generation didn't seem to mind. 'I don't mind telling you

Tom,' I assured him. 'To be honest, I really don't feel able to make the decision alone and you're the only one I've got to discuss such things with.'

'Then I don't mind either,' he said. 'I just don't want to lead you up the wrong path that's all. It's like spending someone else's money see. I promise to give you my honest opinion as long as you understand it to be what *I'd* do if I were in your shoes. Just advice that's all; The final decision has to be yours.'

'Of course, I understand.'

Sat at his kitchen table we poured over the detail of the quotes.

'Let's see ... you know you're ensconced in John's till at least the middle of July so you're not going to end up homeless. If the build took a couple of weeks longer you could either move back in here or I'm sure Bessie'd spare you a bedroom in the pub for a couple of weeks. She's done that before. Used to run a B&B there 'til last year but found it too much with the pub. D'you think your wages can cover your basics like food?'

'I think so, just about. I know I don't earn that much but it's enough to live off, especially as it's just me and in the meantime I'm still going to keep looking for a better paid job.'

'You could move in say end of August, buy a microwave, kettle and so on and manage until you got something better paid. I know you wouldn't have real home comforts but still, what d'you think? If you don't mind roughing it for a bit I know it's what I'd do.' Bless him, he was trying so hard to motivate me to stay.

I sighed with the weight of the decision. 'I'm still unsure Tom. It's the fear of being left with absolutely nothing that worries me. I mean every penny I have would be gone. What if it all went wrong? What if I can't find a better job?' It was at times such as this that a lack of confidence still threatened to control me.

'Ah but you wouldn't *really* be left with nothing would you? You'd still have the house and if worse came to worse, you'd have to sell it. Property's always a good investment you know. You'd make more on it than what it's worth now.'

'That's true,' I nodded. We sat in silence for a few minutes mulling it over. Simon's smug expression reared large in my mind. Suddenly I shot up. 'You know Tom, I've decided! I've only got myself to worry about so I'm going for it! No more indecision. I'll phone Steve back this afternoon and tell him to start as soon as possible.'

'Good girl!' He breathed a sigh of relief. The chiming of the grandfather clock in the hallway interrupted. Tom laughed. 'Now get back and feed those animals or John'll have your guts for garters.'

'Goodness me; I didn't realize the time. I'd better shift! Thanks again Tom.'

Walking swiftly down the lane to John's place, I felt a lot lighter for having made my decision. There would be no more wavering. My mind was made up. For too many years I had been unwilling to take a risk, even when my instinct told me to, but I'd promised myself change and I was going to keep my promise.

I rang Steve, my heart beating fast. I took his bank details and promised to transfer a ten per cent deposit the following day. Animals fed, I poured over the options he had given me and decided to play safe. I would forget the luxury of things like internal doors and a kitchen for the present and instead opt for a central system. At least this way I knew I had a better chance of staying on budget. How on earth I was going to furnish the place though was anyone's guess but that was something I could consider at a later date; after all, people had managed for centuries without fitted kitchens.

Chapter 15

The next three weeks passed by almost uneventfully except for an unexpected, and I must say unwelcome visit from Ruth. Reflecting upon it later I realized that she must have been watching out for me as I had only returned to Hope Cottage a few minutes earlier. I had been wistfully sitting at the top of the stairs trying to picture how the house would look when a hammering at the door jolted me from my reverie.

There she stood, face as stern as a Victorian headmistress and eyes of steel. She offered no pleasantries as a means of explaining her presence.

'You may think it none of my business but I've noticed a few builders snooping round here. Do you mind telling me what it is you intend to do with the place?' she huffed emphatically. 'I hope I'm not about to be subjected to months of noise!'

My mouth fell open and I began to stammer. I had never been good at fighting battles and had often been caught unprepared by more aggressive sorts. Indeed, my first instinct was to allay her worries and explain my plans in a friendly manner but I paused then to my surprise found myself saying, 'Actually, you are correct. It *is* none of your business!' before calmly closing the door in her face. My legs trembled as I re-climbed the stairs yet I grinned triumphantly. I heard her footsteps retreat up the path and seconds later the church gate slammed loudly as she made her way back to the Vicarage.

*

True to his word, Steve began the building work during the third week of June. The weather was glorious which aided progress and I could not remember a time when I had felt more optimistic. I visited the site to check on progress almost daily. I didn't want to get under the builders' feet but I was so excited I couldn't resist. I would only stay for a few minutes but found it incredible to watch! As the cottage slowly but surely transformed from an ugly duckling into a beautiful swan, my sense of hope also grew. It was the first time in as long as I could remember that I felt truly independent.

One afternoon, during the third week of the build and just as I was about to start my lunch-time shift at the Moon and Sixpence I received a call from Steve. 'Hi Cass,' he said cheerfully. 'Do you think you could pop round?'

'Oh Steve, is it urgent?' I asked with a groan. 'I've just started my shift at the pub. I'll be finished by three though.'

'No worries,' he replied, 'it's just that I've found something.'

'What is it?' I asked in trepidation, hoping that it didn't mean he'd uncovered some problem which would incur more expense.

'It might be nothing,' he went on, 'but we're working upstairs this morning, pulling up the rotten floorboards. One of them was particularly loose and when we pulled it up lo and behold, hidden beneath it was an old box. It's locked though and there's no key. Obviously it may contain nothing of value but I wouldn't want you to think that we'd been snooping.'

I felt a shiver of excitement. All the work Tom and I'd done to empty the cottage had revealed nothing. I'd been desperate to find some clues as to Emily's past. Maybe the box would contain photos or even paperwork. 'Thanks Steve! I'll be round as soon as my shift's over if that's okay,' I replied excitedly.

'Course. I'll lock it in the van to keep it safe.'

I decided not to tell Bessie just then, wanting to keep the box and its contents secret until I'd had chance to explore inside but how I got through that shift without giving myself away I do not know. Luckily we were so busy I didn't really have to spend time with Bessie for I felt sure that I would not have been able to conceal my excitement. At three o'clock on the dot I raced up the lane towards Hope Cottage. Steve and two of his men were busy hauling the old wood onto the back of the lorry. He smiled and jumped up into the cab, retrieving the box from where he'd placed it under the dashboard.

'Here 'tis,' he said, thrusting it into my hands with a grin. From the way he held it, I could tell that the contents were not heavy.

'Great! I've been on pins all afternoon,' I said jiggling the brass lock.

'You never know, perhaps there's a couple of grand in there,' he winked. 'That'd boost the coffers a bit no doubt! Might even be able to buy yourself some furniture.'

I returned his smile. Strange as it may seem, the thought of the box yielding extra cash had not entered my mind. Maybe I was too much of a romantic but I had instead been focused on the possibility of it revealing more about my family's past; that for me seemed more valuable than cash. 'Do you think you could break the lock for me?' I asked, fingers trembling. 'The box itself is obviously not valuable and I can't wait to see what's inside.'

'Course!' Steve delved into his toolbox and retrieved a hammer. Placing the box on the ground he gave it a whack. The lock was not sturdy and it yielded on the second thud. The lid remained closed as he once again handed it over. I was bursting with anticipation, yet I also wanted to decipher the contents in private. Steve seemed to understand this and changed the focus away from the box. 'Everything's gone straight forward today. We'll be putting in the new floor joists tomorrow so I suppose I'll see you then,' he said, giving me permission to take my leave.

'Sure, thanks again Steve,' I replied before scurrying off back to the little farm house. All the way, I had to refrain from stopping in my tracks and simply delving inside the box. I guessed that the whole thing weighed only about a pound but I could feel its contents sliding about gently as I walked so I knew it must contain some kind of paperwork.

*

Once inside the kitchen, I placed it on the table and lifted the lid. A cloth of now discoloured but once-white satin revealed itself, wrapped around something firmer. Gently, I unwrapped the cloth and held it in front of me. I saw that it was a gown made for a baby. My heart beat fast as my immediate guess was that it may have been made for Mum. Along its folds the satin was brighter. Around the neck of the garment a delicate circle of lace had been sewn which was repeated around the tiny cuffs. It revealed no label and upon further examination I could see that it had been meticulously hand stitched. No other embellishment was present, but the bodice was carefully gathered below the chest and the full-length skirt delicately pleated into the seam. I held it to my face and breathed it in, half expecting it to bring Mum's scent to me. Ridiculous! Instead I inhaled only dust which felt poignant all the same.

Through misted eyes I now saw what the gown had protected. It was an old book made of brown leather with a worn gold spine. I opened the front cover and saw that its pages were hand-written in a cursive font. Gently flicking through to the back I could immediately see that although the hand that had written in the book was one and the same, the precision and deftness of the script had weakened towards the latter end and had become shaky. This book may yet reveal to me many secrets, I thought. Armed with a strong, hot cuppa I retreated to the sofa.

Chapter 16

The inscription just inside the front cover read,

Christmas Day, 1938.

To Emily, with fond memories of childhood and a genuine offer of friendship.

Yours,
Richard

The next hand, and the one which continued throughout was different. It began...

What a wonderful day! I do not believe that I have been this happy for such a long time. Today even begun well with Mum seeming relatively lucid when I took her breakfast on a tray as I always do on Christmas morning. The sadness in her eyes seemed temporarily extinguished and she even smiled at me and patted the bed for me to sit awhile.

Mind you, Grandpa soon spoiled it by yelling at both of us to get up and stop being so bloody lazy! He's so cruel to Mum. I can bear it myself but the way he treats her when she is obviously so very ill breaks my heart. Then again, I truly believe that it is he who has caused her illness down the years for she was never sick in this way whilst Father was alive.

Anyway, I began by saying that it has been a wonderful day and so I will not spoil it by dwelling on the negative.

At church, I sensed Richard watching me from his pew. I was sure I could feel his eyes on me all the way through the carol service and I was not wrong. I wondered if he would speak to me again, as he had done last week in the village, and I hoped that he would. After the service, I saw him hurry outside but by the time the three of us had made our way out there was no sign of him. I was holding on to Mum's arm in the usual way, steadying her along the path towards home when I heard his voice. "Merry Christmas to you all," he called, rather nervously I thought.

"And the same to you Richard," I replied, glancing down at my worn shoes and hoping he wouldn't notice the hole in the toe. Mum stared ahead, oblivious and Grandpa merely grunted.

"May I speak with you Emily?" he began hesitantly. He fell into step beside us as we continued our way home. I didn't reply straight away as I was taken aback and a little nervous in Grandpa's presence. "It's just that Mum is thinking of setting up a fund-raising group in the New Year and ... well ... she wondered if you'd like to join. She appreciates your wonderful sewing skills and thought that perhaps they could be put to good use in mending and making clothes for the poor. Would you be interested?"

The gate to our cottage was within touching distance. I knew that Mum would not be able to give me her blessing to speak with him but hoped that as it was Christmas Day, Grandpa might be in a better mood and allow me a few moments. I decided to try my luck. "Grandpa, may I speak with Richard for a little while? You know how much I love sewing. I really would like to help out in the group."

The look on his face was thunderous and I fully expected him to deny me but before he could reply I continued, "I'll only be a minute; just to find out what day the group will be held then I'll be in to prepare lunch."

He turned towards Richard and scowled before grunting, "One minute then or I'll be out looking for you."

I placed Mum's elbow in his rough hand before he could change his mind and raced back through the church gate to where Richard had stopped.

As Mum and Grandpa continued down the path towards our cottage, Richard took something from behind his back, held out both hands towards me and said, "For you Emily … Merry Christmas!"

He beamed so warmly that I felt as if my heart might burst. He placed in my hands a gift, wrapped in brown paper and I trembled both with embarrassment and joy. "Thank you Richard! Whatever did you do that for?" I asked, my face reddening.

"I like you Emily … You know, you can always talk to me if you need to," he said nervously and I understood then that he guessed a little of the misery of what my life entails.

"Do you think we might meet … perhaps when you're out on an errand? I would like to be your friend again Emily, you know like we were as children, before …"

His voice trailed off and I knew then that he was also embarrassed and found it hard to speak of what had come to pass.

"I have very little free time Richard," I replied, turning my head towards the cottage. "And you know, Grandpa is very strict."

"I do understand Emily but I feel that you could do with a friend." I realize he is only trying to help yet I am so afraid of letting anyone in, afraid of what Grandpa might do if he finds out, yet at the same time I long for some company my own age.

"I visit the market in Winchton every Tuesday," I told him. "Maybe if I hurry, I could meet you briefly afterward.

I wouldn't have long though, he would know if I was delayed and then ..." I knew I should say no more.

A look of joy came over his face. "Then I'll see you Tuesday. I'll wait for you in Brewer's Lane. No-one will see us, and please Emily, please don't change your mind. I'll take great care to hide. No-one will be able to tell your Grandpa if we are not seen together."

He smiled at me but I could see pity in his eyes. I cannot be sure if he only suggested the meeting because of this but still I know it will be worth the risk. I cannot bear this incessant loneliness much longer!

Just then, I heard Grandpa growl, "Get back here girl!" so I quickly turned and ran through the gate and down the path, hiding the gift beneath my cloak, prepared to confront his temper. However, when I entered our cottage I was surprised to see him simply sitting at the table smoking his pipe. He didn't even glance up. I rushed straight to my room to put on my work dress and apron before returning to the kitchen to prepare lunch.

It wasn't until this evening that I could safely find either the time or opportunity to unwrap the present and find ... you! Yes, you Dear Diary; though you are simply a book of blank pages which I can fill as I please, I know instantly that I will pour out my heart to you and that I will keep you secret. You are the first Christmas gift that I have received since Father died. You have no idea how precious you are! I do not think I have ever been as grateful as I am now for the schooling I received during my younger years. Without it, you would be of little use.

I paused the reading to catch my breath. Yes, I had always wanted to discover more of my heritage but what I was now reading hinted at a very troubled past. I was desperate to read on. I didn't want to put the diary down until I had absorbed every last word but the sound of impatient clucking from the garden reminded me that I had not yet fed the animals. I hurried outside, determined that once fed I would return to the diary and devour its contents.

Chapter 17

Marleston, England December 29th 1938

Emily had been unable to sleep the previous night for today was Tuesday. She had fretted at the thought of someone seeing them together but had managed to convince herself that should it happen, there would be no harm done; after all, they were only going to talk for a few minutes. Then she fretted that perhaps somehow Grandpa already knew of her plans. Maybe he had found her diary? Surely that was not possible! She knew that if he had, she would most certainly have received a beating by now. However, she really *must* loosen a floorboard under her bed at the first opportunity. She would do it when he next went to the pub which was likely to be New Year's Eve. She knew Mum wouldn't notice; however much noise she made in doing so, Mum would remain oblivious.

She would have loved to have worn her best dress to meet Richard but she knew this would certainly raise Grandpa's suspicions and then he would stop her going. So she donned her old grey slip and tatty boots and set off as usual, hoping that her face wouldn't give her away for she sometimes felt that the old man could read her mind.

As it was mid-way between Christmas and New Year, she'd hoped that the market would be quieter than usual. However, she was dismayed to find that this was not the case; in fact it was busier, probably due to the fact that Christmas Day had fallen on a Friday she thought. She could hardly concentrate on what it was that she needed to buy before hurrying back out of the crowded market hall. She raced along the High Street, her basket heavy in the crook of her arm.

It took her five minutes or so to reach the turn into Brewer's Lane. As she approached she was suddenly overcome with anxiety. What if Richard wasn't there? Maybe he hadn't meant it after all. What if he *was* there? What would she say? She almost changed her mind and was about to carry straight on down the road instead. However, she plucked up courage and turned right. She could not see him at first but after passing the brewery she spotted him, leaning up against the metal railings watching her, a broad grin on his face.

'Emily, I'm so glad you came!' he announced with genuine warmth. 'I was afraid that you might change your mind. Here, let me take your basket. It looks very heavy.'

'Thank you Richard,' she said, gladly handing it over. She felt suddenly shy, lost for words.

'How about a little walk along the tow path?' he suggested. 'We could follow it almost back to Marleston. It'll only take a couple of minutes longer than the road.'

Emily had timed her journey to the minute. She knew that she would be expected home by noon. That meant there were thirty five minutes remaining. She knew the tow path route from childhood but was forbidden to walk it alone and therefore had not done so for several years. How hypocritical of Grandpa, that he would forbid me from doing something like that in the name of protection yet at the same time treat me so cruelly, she thought bitterly.

'That should be fine,' she answered. 'It'll be nice to see the countryside for a change. I'm sure it'll bring back fond memories. Dad and I used to walk along here most Sunday mornings. We should still get back to Marleston by twelve o'clock. If we are a few minutes late, I can blame the post-Christmas frenzy of the market, though if he's in a bad mood he will not need an excuse to ...' She paused, knowing that thanks to her nervous jabbering she had already revealed more than she should.

Richard looked at her and sighed. He felt almost helpless. Everyone in Marleston knew the way both she and her mother were treated but little was said in public of their dire situation. People understood that Emily had no choice other than to stay and look after her sick mother and that she was not legally old enough to leave home without parental consent even if she cared to.

One or two of the villagers had plucked up the courage to tackle the old man in the past but had simply received the sharp end of his visceral tongue and been told in no uncertain terms to mind their own business.

Richard knew that Emily would soon turn eighteen and that were it not for her sick mother she might have been able to seek employment somewhere with lodgings. But her mother's illness made this impossible. All who knew her mother spoke of her fondly. They remembered a young woman who had seemed much like any other, if not a little shyer than most. They remembered that her husband, Emily's father, had died quite suddenly around his late thirties and that soon after Emily's grandfather had come to live with them. Within no time at all, Emily's mum had become a shell of her former self. She was hardly ever seen outdoors and Emily too had suddenly stopped playing outside. At first, the villagers wondered if the changes were down to the shock of the bereavement but before long gossip and rumours suggested that the old man who had come to live with them might be the cause.

'Do you remember how we would spend long days playing in the woods behind the Vicarage?' Richard asked warmly, daring to grasp her by the elbow for a moment.

Emily blushed. 'Of course! I remember those days with

such fondness. I was so happy and carefree.' She paused. 'When does your mother intend to begin the fund-raising group? What sort of things would would she like me to make?'

'Oh silly-billy!' Richard replied with a grin. 'There *is* no such group. That was just a ruse to get to speak with you. I've wanted to for such a long time but have never managed to pluck up the courage, especially as I rarely see you without your grandfather in tow, and he always looks so ... well, I don't mean to be rude but he looks so cross.' He frowned, afraid that she might now be angry with him or think him deceitful.

Instead she giggled. 'Yes you're right. It's not easy you know. But I'd really rather not talk about it right now if that's okay.'

'I thought that if we were able to pretend that Mum was running a fund-raising group then it might give us opportunities to meet. What do you think?'

She hesitated and looked despondent. 'Oh Richard, I don't know. I must be so careful. You have no idea of the trouble I'd find myself in if Grandpa got wind of it. What if he asked about in the village and no-one else had heard of the group? He visits the Moon and Sixpence once or twice a week you know, though I know for a fact that he merely sits in the corner and rarely engages in conversation with anyone ... I don't know why he goes there really.' Her glazed eyes stared into the distance.

'Well I hope you don't mind but I've been a bit presumptuous ...' He stood still and looked at her. She saw that his green eyes were still flecked with gold, just as they had been when they were children. 'Mum and I happened to be talking about you the other night and saying how we never see you around. It was sort of *her* suggestion in a way I suppose ... I know it's very unusual for a minister's wife to tell a fib but she said that if anyone ever asked, she would cover for you and say that you both often sewed together.'

Emily was shocked. Her instinct was to behave defensively. 'I'm okay you know ... I mean I know Mum is ill but I cope, and anyway I wouldn't want to be away from her for long just in case ...'

'Oh Emily, I hope I haven't offended you. It's just that Mum and I thought that a girl your age should have some company at times that's all. We just felt that maybe you deserved a break, what with caring for your mother as you do.'

She saw that he looked disappointed and felt sorry for him. After all, he had only been trying to help. 'I tell you what. I'll give it a go. I'll need to catch Grandpa in a rare good mood and ask his permission of course ... and I wouldn't be able to meet for long. I can't promise he'll even agree to it but I'll try.'

Richard's face brightened and with his free hand he reached over and held hers. She felt her face redden again. By now they had almost reached the place where the tow path adjoined Marleston High Street. 'If you don't mind, I'll say goodbye here Richard.'

He understood and handed back the basket. 'Shall we say Saturday at six? Meet me in front of the church if you can.' He flashed a genuine smile. 'It's been lovely seeing you again and *please* do your best to come.'

'I will,' she replied.

As she passed the Post Office she saw that the clock in the window read ten past twelve so she hurried down the street as quickly as she could.

Chapter 18

Over the next few months, Richard and Emily met in secret most Saturdays for an hour. Late at night, while the rest of the house was asleep, Emily would sit up sewing and knitting with wools and fabrics provided by Richard's mother Elizabeth so that she might produce the odd piece of work and announce that she had made it at the fundraising group. She was still surprised that her Grandfather had agreed to her going and wondered if somewhere buried deep inside him there might be a God-fearing, charitable side. Maybe he saw it as a form of penance for his sins. Anyway, thus far she had managed to keep her meetings with Richard a secret and was the happiest she had been in years. She felt as if she existed only for these meetings for they allowed her to feel a sense of normality, even if it was for a short time.

Often they would meet in the woods and sit and talk about the old days, when they were children and the games they used to play. If the weather was bad, Elizabeth was kind enough to allow them to sit in the study at the Vicarage and talk. Emily and Richard re-kindled their friendship and she developed a deepening closeness to Elizabeth too. Not once did either of them ask her difficult questions but their friendship provided her with a feeling of warmth and comfort, a feeling that she *was* worth something.

There was only one worry she had during this time, and that was that Richard's younger sister Ruth seemed to have taken a dislike to her. She remembered little of Ruth from childhood, only that Richard would talk of his younger sister as being a bit of a nuisance, a bit spoiled and demanding but then probably so did all boys with younger sisters and she hadn't found it unusual at the time.

Now however, when Emily saw her in the churchyard or during her visits to the Vicarage, Ruth would scowl at her and storm off. Emily had tried on numerous occasions to engage her in conversation but Ruth gave her little opportunity to do so. It worried her. She was afraid that she might have done something to offend Ruth in some way and so after a few months she plucked up the courage to ask Richard what he thought.

'Oh don't worry about her, she's always been a toffee-nosed madam,' he replied but the look on his face told Emily that Ruth's behaviour *did* bother him.

'Maybe she is upset by my humble background,' she said sadly. 'After all, you and your family are much better off than mine and are treated with great respect within the village.'

Richard's warm eyes clouded with anger for a moment and Emily feared that her suggestion might have offended him but instead he said, 'The trouble is Emily that no-one or nothing is ever good enough for Ruth. I don't know where she gets it from. I mean it's not as if Mum or Dad have ever behaved that way. Despite their standing in the community they treat everyone as their equal and do not judge others by how much or how little wealth they have nor where their family comes from. *Please* don't let her bother you. She's not worth it. She needs to be put in her place!'

'Don't be so harsh on her Richard. Maybe she's just a bit envious that I'm stealing her elder brother's time. After all, I'm sure she admires you so.'

'Maybe you're right in part. She has always seemed

desperate for my attention but lately I can hardly bear to be in the same room as her. She's so precocious!'

But Emily *did* worry about Ruth. Not only did she worry that her presence offended her in some way but she also worried that if Ruth got to hear that she spent time with Richard under false pretenses she might try to stop them meeting. Maybe she would even be mean enough to inform Emily's grandfather of the real reason for their meetings for by now, they both knew that they were falling in love.

Chapter 19

As the year progressed, Emily, along with everyone else in the country, grew more and more afraid that war might be imminent. As well as all her worries at home, she grew increasingly concerned that should war break out then her beloved Richard might be called up to fight. He was just nineteen years old and fit and healthy. Richard on the other hand didn't seem to worry unduly about the prospect but Emily believed that underneath every young man's bravado there lay a deep fear.

He worked by day as a trainee accountant in Winchton and at weekends often helped his parents out with church business. He, like them, held a deep-rooted Christian belief and always managed to look on the bright side when things went wrong. Emily on the other hand, though having been brought up to believe in God, had found her belief waning after the early death of her father and events which had ensued. It wasn't that she felt bitter about what had happened; she truly believed that her family had simply been unfortunate. It was just that she found it difficult to keep faith in a benevolent God who looked down on everyone from above. Sometimes she discussed her Christian misgivings with Richard and although he felt differently it never led to arguments between them. In fact, she strongly believed in the moral message of Christianity but no longer held any belief in an omnipotent being.

Despite the ongoing difficulties at home, her personal

happiness during the year of 1939 grew and grew, due solely to the time she spent with Richard and Elizabeth. Even so, the threat of war loomed ever large until it was a constant presence at the back of her mind. She couldn't bear the thought of Richard going off to war and with it the possibility of losing him.

By the time war was actually declared she had resigned herself to the fact, though this still did not prepare her for the great sense of loss which she felt on the day his call-up papers arrived shortly after New Year 1940. She felt as if her heart had been torn in two and knew that Elizabeth, along with all other mothers in the same position, felt the same. 'You have no choice son,' Richard's dad Hubert told him. 'We will pray for your safety every day and you must do the same.' The glisten in his eye as he spoke belied his brave words.

Elizabeth could not show such bravery and took to her room. 'I'll look after myself Mum,' Richard tried to console her. 'I have too much to live for to allow anything to happen to me.'

He was to leave on the Sunday morning. Even though they had been meeting each other regularly for a year now, both Emily's grandfather and her mother still remained ignorant of the fact.

Emily often longed to be able to talk about Richard to her mother but she knew that it would have been pointless. Her mother may have understood in part what was being said but she would not have been able to share in Emily's joy. It was as if her mother's emotions were in complete shutdown. An occasional smile played around her lips but even then her eyes were a dark, empty chasm. Emily could not be certain as to whether this was in part due to the medication she took or not. All she had been assured by the doctor was that without it her mother would not be safe to live at home and would likely have to be placed in an institution. Emily could not bear the thought of this. She still dreamed that one day, maybe after Grandfather had passed away, she might be able to help restore her mother to some semblance of health.

Although she had been very young, she could recall snippets of conversation which had taken place between her mother and father which had suggested that they had made their escape to this village upon marrying in order to free her mother from her own father. What she could not understand was how on earth her mother had allowed him back into her life after Emily's father had died. Could it have been that she had simply been too weakened by grief to have found the strength to deny him? Emily could not be sure.

The meeting between Emily and Richard that particular Saturday was filled with sadness. She was still restricted to just one hour in his company and *so* wanted to make it a happy one. However, she found this an impossibility. 'How long will it be until I see you again?' she asked tearfully.

'I have to go into training for six weeks then I will be allowed home for a short time before I am informed of where I will actually get posted,' he replied, gazing deeply into her sad eyes.

'Six whole weeks!' she sighed. 'How am I going to bear it without you? I'm sorry Richard, it's appalling that I'm feeling sorry for myself at a time like this but you are the only joy in my life.'

He held her close in his warm arms and kissed the top of her head. 'Emily,' he began. 'When the war is over, will you marry me?'

She could not believe what she was hearing and stared up into his smiling eyes. 'Do you mean it Richard?'

'I have never been so serious about anything in my whole life,' he assured her.

She felt as if her heart would burst. 'I would dearly

love to,' she said and then paused, 'But I can't Richard. I cannot leave mother. She would not cope without me.'

'But I mean for her to live with us too,' he replied. 'I earn a fair income, we could buy a little house somewhere nearby and your mother could come with us.'

'Oh Richard. Are you sure?'

'I am indeed ... but I have to tell you truthfully Emily. Although I have tried not to pry into the way your grandfather treats you both, I would not be prepared for him to also share our home. I hope this will not mean that you will say no?'

She shook her head vehemently. 'You have no idea Richard,' she gasped. 'One day I will tell you everything but for now, whilst I am still living under the same roof I cannot bear to talk about it. No, he can stay at Hope Cottage alone and Mother and I will be free at last!' She searched his face for any sign of uncertainty and found none. 'Oh it is a dream come true! Are you really sure you mean it?' she cried.

'I have never been so certain of anything in my life. I love you Emily, I believe I have loved you since we were children. It broke my heart when you became estranged from me during those years after your father ... I thought I had lost you forever. Now we just need to be patient until this war is over, which we are assured won't be long, and then we can be together for ever.'

Emily's face suddenly fell. 'Have you spoken to your parents about this Richard?'

'I have and they are both delighted. Mother said that she could not have chosen a kinder and more gentle daughter-in-law if she had searched the world over.'

'I feel as though I am dreaming ... But what about Ruth? Does she know?'

A fleeting shadow passed over his face and his warm, green eyes darkened. 'No, not yet ... I didn't want to tell anybody else until I had asked you ... But don't worry about her. It's none of her business whom I choose to marry.'

'I know but I *do* worry. I would love to be her friend Richard but she won't even let me try.'

'She *has* no real friends Emily. She never allows people to get close. The trouble is that she is so selfish. She always wants things all to herself and that includes people. I suppose in a way she is to be pitied but it can be so annoying. Anyway, let's not spoil what little time we have left together worrying about Ruth. I shall tell her in the morning before I leave. I'm sure not even *she* would be able to cause a row about it on the very day I go off to train for war!'

Emily kissed him gently as she said goodbye at the church gates at two minutes to seven o'clock. Even though at that moment she considered herself to be one of the luckiest girls alive, he was still leaving and so she was also one of the most miserable. 'Take good care and be sure to come back safe to us,' she pleaded, her eyes glistening with emotion.

He held her chin gently before once again planting a small kiss on her lips. 'It's only training Emily. You are allowed to say that to me when I actually leave for war. Now sleep well and look after yourself for me. You have no idea how much I will miss you. I will write to you via mother and let you know exactly when I am due home. Will you tell your own mother of our plans yet?'

Emily's face saddened, 'It would be of no purpose Richard. She is too sick to understand. No, I will tell her when the war is over and things are final. Do you think we can marry at your church? Wouldn't that be wonderful?'

'Of course my love, I wouldn't want it any other way.'

It was hard to part but she knew she had no choice. All she could do was to wish away the months to come and hope that war would soon be over and their lives together could begin.

Chapter 20

The following weeks ticked by in a cloud of gloomy foreboding. Emily hardly dared give too much thought to her engagement. The hand that life had dealt her thus far did little to turn her thoughts to optimism. She still went to the Vicarage every Saturday for an hour, partly because she did not want to rouse the suspicion of Grandpa, who seemed so used to her going now that he didn't even protest, and also partly because she had grown very fond of Elizabeth and Hubert too. Each week, there would be a letter from Richard waiting for her over which she poured once alone in bed at night. She cherished every word but had the good sense to keep the letters hidden.

Elizabeth seemed to guess that Emily would have no money with which to buy postage stamps and kindly offered to post her letters to Richard at the same time as she posted her own. During these visits, not once did Ruth make an appearance. Instead, she remained squirreled away in her bedroom. Emily did not like to broach the subject with Elizabeth for fear that she might think she was criticizing her daughter.

The last few days before Richard was due home for the last time passed by so slowly that Emily felt as if the day would never arrive. He had written that he would only be allowed home for two days and so Emily had thought and thought of a way that she might be able to convince her Grandfather that she needed to be away from home for longer than an hour. She knew only too well that if she angered him in any way she would pay the price and that might mean her forbidden to see him at all. Once again it was Elizabeth who came to her rescue. The Saturday before he was due home, she suggested to Emily that they should arrange a farewell gathering not only for Richard but also for the two other village boys who would be leaving for war at the same time. 'How would you feel if I had Hubert announce it at church tomorrow with an open invitation to the entire village?' she asked.

Emily's stomach flipped. 'Grandfather would decline, I'm sure of it,' she replied anxiously.

'Then I will ask him personally as we are leaving church. I will reinforce my appreciation of the exceptional fund-raising work you have undertaken for the war effort with your sewing and ask that both he and your mother attend. He'll be less likely to refuse then don't you think?' She smiled encouragingly.

Emily knew that she had so much to be grateful to her for. 'Oh Elizabeth it's worth a try, but what if he still says no?'

'Well that's a chance we'll have to take. This is a wicked thought for a vicar's wife, but once we have him in attendance we will ply him with drink and hopefully dull his senses. I'll keep a careful eye on your mother then you and Richard will be able to slip away and spend a bit of time together. Goodness only knows you deserve it! Your fiancé, even if it is a secret at the moment, will soon be off to war! You have to be able to say your farewells properly.'

Emily reached across the little table at which they sat and took Elizabeth's hand. 'Thank you Elizabeth. You have been so kind to me. One day, when Richard and I are set up in our own home, I hope I will be able to repay you. You will always be welcome at our house and I will do my utmost to be the best daughter-in-law you could wish for.'

'Don't be silly now! Leave it with me. I've already discussed it with Hubert. We'll glean your grandfather's response after church tomorrow and take it from there. If he says no, then I'll try another tack.'

Chapter 21

Although her grandfather was disinclined to attend any social gatherings, he wasn't one to resist a free meal and drink. Elizabeth had not only personally invited him but had also respectfully asked at the same time whether it would be possible for Emily to be spared for an hour or so in the morning to help prepare the food and tables for the party.

Her grandpa had grudgingly agreed to this request with strict instructions that she return to see to her own mother within the hour. So on the following Saturday morning Emily set off for the Vicarage.

As she flew up the path, she could see Richard waiting for her in the doorway. He looked so smart and handsome in his uniform but seeing him dressed in this way only made the realization of what he was about to endure more real. Although he beamed a genuine smile at her, Emily could also see that the six weeks of training had taken its toll for he was already paler and thinner.

Once safely inside the house, he held her closely, breathing her in. She lay her head on his shoulder, determined not to cry. 'I've missed you so much,' she managed, her voice choked with emotion.

'As I have you,' he replied, stroking her hair.

Elizabeth appeared, smiling. 'Now you two, off you go for a walk. It's a beautiful day and I've got everything underhand. The preparation is all done so you would only be in my way if you stayed.'

Emily knew that what she was really doing was granting them some deeply-needed privacy and for this she was truly grateful. After all, not only was Emily soon to be giving up her fiancé, but Elizabeth was giving up her only son. The selflessness of Elizabeth's actions touched Emily deeply.

It was indeed a beautiful day. Although it was only the first week of March, there was not a cloud in the sky as they scrambled to the top of Scar Rock. Richard held her by the hand all the way, helping her climb the steep ridge to the summit. They held on to each other as they gazed back in the direction of the village and town beyond, the wind blowing Emily's long, chestnut hair free of its ribbon.

'How is it possible to be both the happiest and most miserable person in the world all at the same time?' she asked, her innocent, dark eyes moistening in the wind.

'Because love can be so beautiful and also so painful,' he replied, sweeping strands of hair away from her eyes before gently planting the lightest of kisses on her lids. 'I will be fine Emily. I promise you. This war will not separate us for long, I just know it. Soon it will all be over and we can be married and settle down to a new life; a life in which you can be free and happy.'

'Do you really believe it Richard?' she asked, clinging on to his words of hope.

'I honestly do. I can't explain it Emily, I just know it will all work out fine. Now come on, we've got to head back soon or I'll be late for my own party and that would ever do!'

He took her hand in his and began to run back down the hill.

'Not so fast!' Emily screeched with both fear and joy though she knew she was safe in his grasp. In fact, she could never remember a time when she had felt safer.

Having dutifully washed and dressed her mother in her best pale-blue dress before seeing to her own clothing, Emily was ready. She tried her very best to appear cheerful but calm so as not to arouse the suspicions of her grandfather who, she knew only too well, was capable of ruining the best laid plans at any given moment.

She hooked her own arm through her mother's and stroked her hand. 'You look beautiful,' she beamed as her mother stared beyond her with her usual, unseeing gaze. 'Come on, it'll be fun. It'll do you good to have some fresh air.'

Leading her down the path and across the lane towards the church she half expected to hear her Grandpa say that he had changed his mind and they wouldn't be going after all but, casting a quick glance over her shoulder, she saw instead that he was in tow, just a few paces behind them.

The Vicarage garden looked beautiful. A white marquee stood close to the house and long trestle tables were piled high with food and jugs of cold beverages. Bunting had been draped above the tables on string and ribbons of red, white and blue danced in the trees. Emily knew that Grandpa would not wish to sit at the long tables alongside everyone else from the village and she also understood that such a situation might prove too overwhelming for her mother. The last thing she wanted was for the occasion to bring on one of mum's 'episodes,' so she passed on by and led them to a small garden table which stood at a little distance from the crowd.

Elizabeth appeared almost immediately and greeted them warmly. 'What I would have done today without your Emily's help I don't know,' she said, directing this comment towards Emily's Grandpa whilst daring to look him straight in the eye. Oh how Emily wished she had half of Elizabeth's courage! He simply grunted by means of reply before turning his gaze towards Emily and saying gruffly,

'Well girl, get me and your mother some refreshments. We didn't go without lunch for nothing you know.'

Emily watched nervously from the marquee entrance. She had not yet spotted Richard and knew that she could not risk seeming over keen on his company once the party got into full swing. Even now, she saw that her Grandpa kept glancing from where he sat in the direction of the marquee, anticipating her return. He was her jailor. He baited her with her mother's illness, knowing that she could not leave to make a life of her own and he relished his power. If it wasn't for this damn war, thought Emily angrily.

A sudden squeeze of hands around her waist jolted her out of her thoughts. She let out a small squeal and turned to see Richard, still holding her and smiling down at her face. 'Penny for them,' he teased.

'It'd cost you more than that ... and anyway, you wouldn't like what you heard.' She tried to smile back whilst anxiously removing his hands from around her waist in case anyone should see.

He stared deeply into her eyes. 'I don't need to pay, I can read your mind,' he said earnestly. 'It'll all be over before you know it Emily. We'll make our own life, you'll see. It'll be full of everything we ever wished for, I promise.'

Emily sighed. She did not want to spoil these last few precious hours with him but the joy of the morning's walk in his company was already in jeopardy of being overthrown by her usual feelings of gloom and pessimism. She gazed deeply into his warm, gold-flecked eyes and managed a smile. 'I know. I believe in you with all my heart and I know that you will do your utmost to return safely to me. Now I'd better get back with his plate. He'll likely storm off in a temper otherwise.'

She turned to go but he caught her by the elbow, almost causing her to drop the plates. 'Emily, meet me by the church gates at midnight. Please! We have to say goodbye properly.'

She hesitated. 'I'll try Richard. If I manage to ply him with enough beer this afternoon he'll likely fall deeper asleep. But if I don't come, know that I love you and will hope every hour of every day that you are safe.' She turned then, before the tears had opportunity to escape.

She was in luck. Not only did Grandpa guzzle down several pints of beer during the afternoon but Hubert made several appearances with a whiskey bottle and plied him with a few large glasses. Emily was surprised at this as her Grandpa, for all his faults, was not a heavy drinker. She knew that during his visits to the Moon and Sixpence he rarely drank more than two pints. She couldn't help but wonder what spurred him on this afternoon. Maybe it was the heat of the day that had made him thirsty or the fact that he wasn't paying for it; she could not be sure but was grateful all the same. She was also surprised by how long he remained at the party, for it was past five thirty when he suddenly stood up and declared it time for them all to go home. He had not passed more than a word with any of the villagers during the afternoon; in fact, most had given him a wide berth. He had simply sat with a grizzled look upon his brow and observed the comings and goings.

If Emily stopped to consider her mother's interpretation of events she was filled with sadness, for she too sat in one spot for the duration of the afternoon, neither speaking nor even showing awareness of anyone or anything around her. Indeed, the only sign of life she had shown was when she began to shiver at around five o'clock as the afternoon had chilled. Emily had dutifully wrapped a cardigan around her shoulders. She wondered if it had been worth her mother coming at all for she had merely nibbled at a few items on the plate but had seemed otherwise completely and utterly disengaged from the whole situation.

Even when Richard and his fellow 'brothers in arms' had given a rousing and moving farewell speech to the crowd her mother had neither turned in his direction nor shown any expression of understanding. Still, though physically able, she so rarely left the house at all that Emily had hoped that perhaps by bringing her, deep within her consciousness, some remnant of comprehension might take place. She feared deeply that should anything happen to herself, her mother would be committed to an asylum as there was no-one else in the world that would be willing or able to give her the same round the clock attention. She hoped and prayed that Richard would be proven correct in his optimism and that she would soon be in a stable home of her own, away from her Grandpa.

All three were ensconced in their own beds by ten. Emily listened anxiously for her Grandpa's snores, still dressed in her day clothes until she heard the clock downstairs guiltily chime midnight ...

Chapter 22

Marleston, England, July 1996

I could barely believe what I had read! I was glad to finally have so many questions answered. At the same time however I felt deep sadness at being unable to share this knowledge with Mum. I could not wait to devour the whole of Emily's diary as well as the letters which lay bound by a red ribbon at the bottom of the box. Having read thus far, I guessed that they might in fact be love letters written between her and Richard during the war.

It was then that I remembered my recent conversation with Bessie regarding Ruth. So Ruth had a brother ... strange that Bessie had not mentioned him when she had spoken about her.

Although I felt as if I were intruding on what were obviously very private feelings I hoped at this point in the reading that what lay ahead for Emily and Richard was true happiness though even now I had a nagging suspicion that all had not gone well. After all, if indeed Emily and Richard had married then why had Mum been given up for adoption? It crossed my mind that perhaps Mum's father had indeed been someone else, someone whom Emily had met after the war had ended. After all, such happenings were quite common during that time. After reading what I had about Emily and Richard thus far I simply could not imagine that if their relationship *had* resulted in marriage and Mum had been born to them then the outcome of Mum's upbringing would have turned out as it had.

I felt desperate to share this new-found information with a loved one but there really was no such person in my life. I knew I could talk to Tom and that he would be a listening ear, but as close friends as we had become it would still not mean the same to him as it did to me.

I could second guess the outcome all I liked but I would simply need to read on if I wanted to discover what had actually happened between them.

Pausing for a few moments, I put down the diary and picking up the bundle of letters instead, untied the ribbon that held fast their secrets. I scanned the postmarks at the corner of each. The first ten or so were contained in plain brown envelopes and had been written in the same hand as the greeting from Richard at the front of Emily's diary. I therefore concluded that they had to have been written by him.

They were postmarked *Kent* and dated between 25th of March 1940 and the 18th of May the same year. Subsequent letters had been sent from various places in France, including Dunkirk and were dated between the end of May and the 16th of August 1940. However caught up in war Richard had become he had still found the time to write to Emily as often as twice a week by the look of things. But why had the letters stopped so abruptly and so soon? Had he been killed in action? My stomach lurched at the prospect and yet I already had a strong feeling of foreboding. I worried now that maybe I had more of Emily's genes than I realized, as from what I had already gathered she too tended to look on the black side. Don't be silly, I scolded myself. You know that you are naturally optimistic. It is just the events this past year that are making you think this way.

Of course there was another possibility - perhaps Emily

and Richard had simply fallen out of love. After all, war seemed to confuse even the strongest of emotions. Tempted though I was to immediately skip to the last letter I refrained from doing so. I really wanted Emily's story, for good or bad, to be revealed to me as a journey, from start to finish.

The last few envelopes within the bundle were held within fine, pale blue envelopes and postmarked Ilfracombe, Devon. The hand which had addressed these was unfamiliar to me. My fingers trembled with anticipation for I knew that Mum had been raised there. I recalled that as a very young child she and I had taken several seemingly endless train journeys from the North to Devon to visit Grandma and Granddad. They had seemed so old and indeed they were, for I later learned that they were already in their mid-forties when they had adopted Mum. These journeys had not continued past the age of about six though as by then Mum had lost them both. I was hungry to devour the contents but had promised myself that I would be systematic and so turned my attention back to the diary.

Chapter 23

Marleston, England August 1940

'Oh my darling boy! Just look at you! Are you alright?' Elizabeth hugged Richard cautiously, as though he might break to her touch. Hubert had just returned, having collected him from the train station. 'Now Elizabeth, don't fuss. Of course he's alright. He wouldn't be standing here in front of you if he wasn't would he?' Hubert managed to put on a brave face but Elizabeth was only too aware of the anguish they had both suffered over the past few weeks after having been informed of Richard's injury.

'Come inside and make yourself comfortable son then you can tell us how you really are,' she managed. She followed just a step behind as Hubert led Richard to the sitting room. He was exhausted. That was plain to see. His face was drawn and pale and spattered with small, fading scars here and there. His cheek bones were chiseled and his uniform hung from his shoulders as if from a slender, shop mannequin. The usual glint in his eyes was extinguished, as if a candle had been snuffed out and both Elizabeth and Hubert could see that he was struggling to put on a brave face.

Hubert took his crutches from him and supported his right arm as he lowered himself into the armchair. He breathed in sharply, as if in pain, or perhaps it was simply out of relief of finally being in the comfort of home. Elizabeth decided to believe it was the latter.

The past month had been an agony, both physically and mentally. He was lucky to be alive, he knew that only too well and yet knowing it was still not enough to bring him joy. Yes, he was grateful to be home for now but he could not bare to think about what recovery would mean for him. His right leg had been pretty broken up by the blast but the doctors had done a good job and had managed to re-pin the bones. He knew that three months of rest and recuperation lay ahead before he would be expected to return to duty, albeit at a more sedate pace for a time to 'ease him in' as they had said. His injuries, although fairly serious, would not protect him from eventual return to the front.

The only joy he felt was knowing that tomorrow morning he would once again see Emily. Oh how he ached for her day and night! He had forbidden Elizabeth from letting her know that he was coming home. As far as she was aware he was to remain in the hospital in London. He had wanted to keep it as a surprise. But now that he was so close it was all he could do not to insist that she be brought to him this very evening. He could sense her presence; indeed, as he sat peering out of the sitting room window he could just make out the glint of light from her own cottage.

Elizabeth followed his gaze and must have read his thoughts for she swiftly walked over to the window and drew the curtains from the dusk; perhaps selfishly she thought, for as much as she had grown to love Emily she had longed to have him to herself, even if it was only for a short time.

It was only as the curtains stole his view that he turned and noticed that Ruth was also in the room. She had not spoken yet, nor had she been there to welcome him in the hallway. He saw that she stared at him from the furthest corner of the room, her cold, green eyes narrow and cat-like. 'How are you feeling Richard?' she managed, her gaze moving away from his face to his splinted leg. She approached him now but before she got close enough to offer an embrace seemed to think better of it and instead sat down stiffly in an adjacent armchair. It was close enough that, should she have felt so inclined, she could have still held out her hand and held his. Instead, she stared ahead, towards the fireplace watching the coals burn brightly. Richard did not even bother to answer as he could see that her question had been merely one of formality.

As usual, his mother tried desperately to make amends. 'Ruth's been so worried about you, haven't you Ruth?' she fumbled in embarrassment before turning her full attention back to him. She feigned a nervous smile. 'Now what can I get you to eat? I'm sure the months of army rations must have made you long for some home-cooking. I've made all your favourites.' He did not reply so she pressed harder. 'You must let me spoil you Richard, you need to re-build your strength. Look how thin you've become!'

'I'm not really hungry mother, just exhausted.' He turned and saw the look of concern on her face and felt guilty about rejecting her offer. 'I tell you what, some cheese on toast would go down a treat. I've missed real cheddar.' Elizabeth beamed and scurried off to the kitchen quickly followed by Hubert. The silence that ensued was a chasm; though Richard felt too weak to even care.

Within seconds Ruth also stood. 'I'll bring the newspaper,' she drawled in a pompous tone and left the room. Alone again, Richard gazed about him. There was so much warmth in this room and yet he felt cold, not physically but emotionally. It was almost as if he were non-human. He tried to conjure an image of Emily's face but found that he failed to do even that.

Minutes later, Elizabeth returned with a tray laden with tea and his childhood favourite which he did his utmost to finish for her sake. 'I'm so sorry but I desperately need my bed. I've imagined my own pillows every night.' He tried to smile. He *was* tired, utterly exhausted, but more than that he suddenly felt desperate to be alone. Even the cold emptiness inside him was preferable to this nervous cheer.

Hubert helped him climb the stairs and waited while he used the bathroom before supporting him along the landing and seeing that he had all he needed in his room. 'Call if you need anything in the night Richard,' he said sadly before turning and leaving him alone.

*

Whilst he had been at the front, he had imagined the comfort of his own bed over and over again; so why was it that now he lay in it it brought him no comfort? He lay still on his back, his injured limb supported by a feather pillow and tried desperately to feel a sense of belonging. He was numb. He could only hope that emotion would return in the morning when reunited with Emily.

Eventually, he managed to drift into a dream-filled sleep but awoke in the early hours, once again aware of the strange void. This was worse than the fear, the adrenalin, the anxiety ... at least then he had felt alive! A strange thought entered his mind. Perhaps he had actually died on the battlefield. Perhaps this last month of pain and hospitalization had not been real. Maybe this was the reason for his current lack of feelings. Deep down, he knew there was no real logic to this.

Pushing down hard with the heels of his hands in order to raise himself into a sitting position, he grasped his left knee and carefully turning his injured leg until he sat at the edge of the bed. His head swam and he was afraid for a moment that he would pass out so he sat a while longer, inhaling deep, slow breaths until the feeling subsided.

He listened for sounds beyond his bedroom door.

Nothing. A glance at the bedside clock told him that it was just past three a.m. He felt in urgent need of the bathroom and so, reaching carefully for his crutches which leaned against the sturdy chest of drawers like two soldiers having a cigarette, he pulled them to him and cautiously stood up.

The landing was silent. He made his way as stealthily as he could towards the bathroom. He did not wish to wake anyone, not out of a sense of caring he realized but merely because he did not yet feel able to face any ensuing conversation or attempts at joviality.

He was on his way back and had just passed the door to Ruth's room when he heard the slightest of clicks. Her door opened. He pretended not to have heard and was about to take another hobble towards his own door when her voice stopped him in his tracks. 'You intend to marry her don't you?' Her tone was cold and as emotionless as he too felt. He half-turned to face her. Even at this hour, she stood fully dressed, about three feet in front of him, a look of pure spite on her face.

He sighed. 'I take it you're referring to Emily?' he replied, meeting her icy stare.

'Well who else?' she retorted indignantly, glancing down at her neat, black-laced shoes and swiping away an imaginary speck of dirt.

It was that one small action that seemed to jolt him back to the real world; for it was as if in that one swift and perhaps seemingly insignificant motion she spoke volumes.

'Do you consider her beneath you?' Up until now, he had avoided having it out with her. He held her steely gaze, feeling a ball of hatred within his very core. So much death and loss and cruelty and here she was, his own sister whom he had loved dearly as a child and she had the audacity to belittle his love over something as insignificant as material wealth, for he felt certain that it was this which made her despise Emily. He could think of no other reason, for Emily was pure and good and liked by all who knew her.

She snorted at him and he felt repulsed by her. He knew that many considered her attractive, what with her fashion sense and immaculate appearance but at this moment he found her truly ugly. 'You could do far better than *that* Richard!' she retorted.

He felt himself tremble with anger. What had become of him? He had always been so gentle; a model son and he knew that he would make a model husband and father one day too, and yet here he stood loathing, despising his own sister. He failed to reply, knowing that if he did so his words would likely be so bitter they may permanently damage any relationship he had with her forever. But she was not prepared to give up the fight so easily.

'Marry that peasant and you will bring shame on all of us!' she hissed. 'Her grandfather is a stinking brute and her mother the living dead! Who knows what sort of retarded children she might bear?' She paused, still smirking, awaiting a reply. When he offered none she continued to berate him. 'The condition is probably hereditary you know! Consider *that* before you go any further.' The horror of her words rendered him mute and frozen. She sensed his weakness so went in for the kill. 'And have you thought about this? There's rumour in the village that she sleeps with him.'

He turned on her angrily now, spitting his words, his face ashen. 'What ... what are you talking about?'

'Why, her grandfather of course! She might even be carrying his child as we speak!' She smirked like a cat and lazily stroked her hand along the length of her glossy hair.

He had never before felt such anger, not whilst face to face with the enemy nor when his body racked with pain from the bullet. 'I *will* marry her ...' he spluttered, 'and you will know that you are wrong. You will never be half the woman she is. You are nothing but evil!'

He turned away from her now and gripping his crutches tightly, hopped one more step, away from the top of the stairs towards his room.

The force took him by surprise. His body, rigid with anger, gave to the blow like a skittle in an alley. In the split second it took to hit the bottom, he knew he would never again see the face of the one he loved most.

Chapter 24

The emptiness she felt was indescribable. She was an old oak, struck by lightning, her core burned hollow. Though the church thronged with sympathetic well-wishers and the melancholic sound of their singing filled the space to the rafters she felt completely alone. She stood transfixed by the wooden coffin draped with flag, unable to convince a single word of the hymn to pass her lips. She had known loss; it was not a new experience for her, yet this was different. This loss meant that all hopes and dreams, not only for herself but also for her mother had blown away like embers on the wind.

There was no-one to hold her hand or offer her words of comfort and tell her that all would be well in the end. Both Elizabeth and Hubert had been more than kind to her over the past week but their own grief was so immense that they were barely holding up themselves.

He had been so near to her on that fatal night and she had not even known. She could have held him and comforted him if only she'd known he was home. But Elizabeth had explained that Richard had wished his homecoming to have been a surprise and had requested that she be brought to him the following morning, after he had had chance to rest from the journey. But it had not happened as he had wished. Instead, she had been summoned to the Vicarage to be told the worst possible news; that he had arrived home the previous night for a spell of recuperation only to have met with an accident even before he could see her. She should have known the life he had promised her would not come to pass; yes, somewhere deep inside she *had* known it all along.

The coffin was being lifted now. She was vaguely aware of six men holding it aloft and carrying it back down the aisle. He could not be in that box! It was not possible! He was more full of life than anyone she had ever known – it could not be over. No tears - too numb. Too immersed in disbelief by the horror of the situation. She had been half prepared to lose him to battle; indeed, when she had first heard of his injury she had expected the worst, but to have lost him like this was beyond belief.

When it was her turn, she vacated the pew like a lamb and trooped behind the others into the churchyard. The procession followed the path all the way to the bottom, away from the other graves and stopped just in front of the old yew which stood opposite her cottage. Words were softly spoken as his body was lowered to its resting place in the earth. Still she did not cry.

Glancing towards her own home, she realized that Elizabeth and Hubert must have chosen this plot with her in mind for she would need only to look across from her bedroom window to see where he lay. This gesture of selflessness on their behalf was what opened the floodgate. Her shoulders shook uncontrollably and for the first time, someone offered her comfort. Hubert, his left hand holding Elizabeth's, slid his right arm across and held her in his grasp. She was grateful and faced him with as much warmth as she could muster.

It was only then that she noticed Ruth. It was not so much that she *saw* her but rather that she *felt* her presence; for her steely eyes bore into Emily's back like a cold blade. Glancing momentarily over her shoulder she saw that she was right. Ruth stood just behind her, not at the side of her parents as one would have expected but a step or so back. Her eyes met Emily's but Ruth's eyes reflected no pain, no loss, only hatred.

Too consumed by her own grief, it had not been until later that night that the oddity of this really registered with her. After the service she had not joined the family and other mourners back at their home, though of course Elizabeth had invited her to do so. Instead she had returned to the cottage where she had vomited until she felt purged. No words of sympathy had been forthcoming from her Grandpa nor had she expected any and her mother remained ignorant of the situation. She had no-one; just a memory of what might have been almost within touching distance of her own bedroom window.

Chapter 25

Marleston, England July 1996

Having devoured the letters that had been sent by Richard during his short time at war, my appetite was still not satisfied. I turned my attention to the others, those which were written in a different hand. The glue of the faded envelopes had re-sealed over time and wanting to handle them carefully, I resisted tearing them open. Instead, I retreated to the kitchen for a sharp knife. Carefully, I opened the first, dated 18th March 1941.

Dearest Emily,

Our darling Rebekah is doing well, in fact, she is thriving! She has put on several pounds in weight this past month and last night turned herself over on the mat for the first time. She smiles all the time and hardly ever cries, except when she is hungry. She has taken to her formula really well and by the look of her it is doing her nothing but good.
I'm sure that you think about her often but I would once again like to reassure you that what you did was for the best. She is a very bonny and contented child. Fred and I will continue to raise her as our own and do nothing but our very best for her. Your selflessness has made our dream come true and we love her as though she were our very own flesh and blood. She will want for nothing.
I will write again soon and let you know how she is

getting along. As I promised you when you gave her up to us, should you wish to write to her, I will keep your letters safe and let her have them when she is of a suitable age and ready to understand.

Take care of yourself,
Marjory and Fred Wilkinson

Finally I was beginning to piece together the puzzle of not only Mum's life but in doing so also my own. I felt sad but also a sense of warmth. It brought me comfort to know that Mum had been raised in what by all accounts appeared to have been a loving home. I knew that in those days to have given birth a child out of wedlock would have been very much frowned upon. Surely given the temper of her Grandfather, Emily couldn't have taken such a risk. But then again, she would not have been the first to have found herself in such a predicament nor would she be the last.

Poor Emily. Mum had only ever spoken of her adoptive parents so it must have been either that Emily had not brought herself to write to Mum or that Mum's adoptive parents had not fulfilled their promise and handed over the letters. After all, I was certain that if Mum *had* been in possession of such letters she would have at some point shared them with me or at the very least I would have come across them when I cleared her things after she had died. She had never been the secretive sort, at least not with me, and I also knew almost beyond doubt that had she ever received such letters she would not have destroyed them.

However, I was beginning to understand what Mum had possibly never come to realize; that Emily had been very much a victim of unimaginable bad fortune whichever way it went. I wondered how her Grandpa had taken the news when he had discovered her pregnancy and felt sick at the thought of how he must have treated her.

Chapter 26

Marleston England, August 1940

She had thought the vomiting due to the sickness of her grief, but when it continued day after day she began to worry. Could it be possible that she was pregnant? It had only been the once, that night before he had gone to war, when she had met him at the witching hour and they had climbed the hill to the woods. Both had wanted to feel alive, for different reasons but with the same result.

Undressed and alone she stood in front of her bedroom mirror and studied her image. She had lost weight, not gained it. Her collar bones protruded and she could count her ribs without even breathing in, and yet there was a distinct roundness to her abdomen, all the more noticeable perhaps because of the slenderness of the rest of her body. She reached down and stroked her stomach with circular movements. Something told her she was right. A warmth spread throughout her hand as if it detected life though she felt no reciprocal movement.

The constant sickness along with her grief had rendered her so empty that at this moment she did not even care if it were true. In a way she thought she might be glad. Perhaps then she would feel that she had not lost him entirely, that a part of him lived on inside her. She dared not consider what the reality might mean for her at home nor in the community. For the present, she was just glad that it made her feel less empty.

Another four weeks passed by, four weeks of endless drudgery. She somehow carried out her daily tasks as if she were a clockwork toy. She felt no emotion, not for her mother's plight nor her own.

She had not visited Elizabeth since the day of the funeral though she had observed both she and Hubert making their regular homage to Richard's grave. They sat and talked, often glancing towards her cottage where she stood and watched from behind a chink in the curtains. She could not really understand her present feelings towards them both, for whilst she shared their broken heart she wished for no communication. It just seemed too painful. She did not want to talk about Richard to anyone except herself, in her own head, where she spoke to him almost constantly. In doing this she felt he was still with her.

She noticed that Ruth had not on any occasion, at least to her knowledge, visited her brother's grave and she considered this strange. Then again, each to his own she supposed. Not everyone gained comfort from a six by three foot plot of ground.

Several weeks had passed now since that unbearable day, the worst day of her entire life but it was almost six months since the best, the day of the farewell party when they had sealed their love. By now she knew that she was not mistaken. She felt his life move within her, giving her reassurance that he lived on inside her. He was *not* in the ground in front of her window after all; his life endured. She felt his warmth and cared for him as well as she could by feeding him through her own need for sustenance. She sang to him when they were alone and caressed him through her flesh, feeling him respond with little kicks and flutters.

There was just one act that she had to perform though which worried her; one thing that she thought could possibly cause him harm, yet she had no choice. During her weekly trip to market, she had purchased several strips of bandage. Each morning, before she made her presence known downstairs, she stood in front of her mirror and carefully bound the growing roundness of her body until it appeared a little flatter, all the while apologizing and promising to release him from his bounds come evening.

The previous Wednesday her heart had skipped a beat. Whilst she had been serving dinner her Grandpa had grizzled that she seemed to be putting on weight and he had suggested that perhaps he should cut the food allowance. She had in-taken a sharp breath before mumbling that she had merely been feeling poorly and so had been trying to pick herself up a bit. She assured him that she was not being wasteful with the money he gave her. He had retorted with a grunt before tucking heartily into the steaming shepherd's pie she had placed in front of him For now at least, her answer had seemed to quell any suspicion he might harbor.

She had calculated that she only had around twelve weeks to go and was wise enough to know that it would be during this time that she would most likely pile on even more weight. She would need to keep her eating to a minimum and once again let out her two pinafores. She refused to consider what would happen when her time eventually came nor would she think about how she could possibly raise a child given her personal circumstances. She only knew that the child she carried, the life of Richard, was worth more to her than anything she had ever known and that she would somehow bring this life into the world, for she could not bear to live in a world devoid of him.

Another seven weeks passed by and she continued to struggle to hide her secret from the world. Her mother, too lost within her own void, was the only one who posed no threat to Emily but each day she grew more fearful of her Grandpa's looks and words and avoided being seen in public as much as she could. She was thankful that winter was fast approaching for she could throw her cloak about her, rendering her form shapeless whenever she visited town for provisions. Feigning eternal cold she wore a shawl that she had knitted to try to hide her ever-increasing waistline but was still as twitchy as a hare in the presence of her Grandpa.

Perhaps due to old age, he seemed to have mellowed slightly of late. Verbally he remained as curt and malicious as ever but at least now he rarely took a swipe at her and practically ignored her mother entirely. He had even given up his weekly visit to the pub in the last few months and, in the main, sat in front of the fire issuing commands, snoozing or else eating at table. He also retired to bed early most nights and so it was with great relief that she would rush to her room and release the life that continued to grow inside her from its bounds.

It was on one such night, at the beginning of November that she first felt it. She had noticed that he had become more still of late and had been concerned. Having no one to ask and no access to medical help she counted and calculated every little movement and response alone, still refusing to consider what she would actually do when the time came. But it would not be yet; she knew that much. She had almost another month to go before she would need to face the reality of giving birth. She did not want that time to come. For now she relished in the selfishness of not having to share him. He was hers and hers alone.

She had freed him of his bonds for the day and had just climbed into bed exhausted. She had begun to struggle with every little task over the past few weeks and by the time evening came she could not wait to crawl into bed and rest her swollen and aching legs.

No sooner had she lay down than she felt the first twinge. Her abdomen contracted in a spasm – as she peered under the sheets she could see it happening. Her heart beat fast, fear and reality momentarily washing over her but within seconds he had settled down again. Eventually she calmed and drifted off to sleep.

She had no clue as to what the time was. She only knew that something was very wrong. She had never before experienced such pain. It was all she could do not to cry out. It could not be time! She was not ready for this!

Breathing rhythmically and loudly she managed to calm herself and the pain abated. She was soaked in perspiration though the night was cold. Slowly she turned in her bed and swiveled her legs out from beneath the covers until she sat on the edge waiting.

Minutes later and the sweat had dried. She shivered with the cold which caused her bladder to weaken. Not wishing to awaken anyone she tiptoed silently around the bed and lowered herself onto the chamber pot. Another sickening wave of pain hit like a blow from a prize fighter, rendering her double. She shoved her fist into her mouth to stop herself from screaming. Panic hit her for the first time in eight months. Gripping the bed frame she tumbled back in to bed and lay with her knees as close to her chest as the bump would allow. The pain lessened once more.

Eventually, she drifted back into a dream-filled sleep though she could not be certain whether or not it was sleep or delirium for she was with Richard. She felt his arms about her as surely as she felt the coolness of the sheets; but she could not breathe – his embrace was suffocating her. She struggled to release herself from his grip.

She awoke again to the pain. She began to sit up but before she could complete the movement she felt herself soaked. She thought she must be bleeding. It would be over then! She would die and with her so would he. She was certain now that he had visited her just minutes earlier to take her with him. She managed to light a candle and examined her legs. No blood, just fluid.

When the pain returned again she knew she could bear no more alone. She would have to seek help. With the next pause of agony, she left her room as quietly as she could and, grabbing her cloak from where it hung waiting on a hook in the kitchen, stumbled out of the cottage. Once outside, the cold night air hit her full in the face but was a relief from the searing heat of the pain. Slowly, she stumbled across the lane and entered the churchyard, knowing that at most she had only minutes before the Monster would return. She did not pause at his grave for there was no need; he was with her, holding her hand in his as she staggered towards the Vicarage.

She hammered on the door.

Chapter 27

'Oh my goodness Emily, what on earth ..?' Hubert saved her from falling over the threshold when she failed to raise her leg high enough to clear the step at the front porch. The door was swiftly closed behind her to shut out the cold night air. She said nothing, nor did she look him in the eye. She merely gripped his arm as he led her through the hall towards the sofa in the living room.

As he set about lighting the lamps, Elizabeth leaned over her and attempted to untie Emily's cloak from her shoulders, her own face white as a sheet. 'Whatever is the matter? Is it your mother?'

Emily shook her head vehemently and let out a moan. Still she could not look either of them in the eye. The pain overcame her once more and this time she cried out.

'Has he hit you? Oh my Lord, what has he done to you?' Elizabeth was trembling now. She released the cloak from Emily's shoulders. It slid to the floor like a corpse, where it lay curled in a heap, as though the life it had held had been suddenly extinguished.

Now Elizabeth saw what was wrong. She gasped loudly, raising her hand to her mouth to quell her shock as the mound of Emily's stomach was revealed to her beneath the nightgown.

The pain was so severe now that Emily was beyond shame. She only knew that she had to get through this. She had promised him that he would continue to live and therefore she would see it through. At this moment she felt that she would not have cared if the whole village had been present.

She had not spoken a word thus far, only groaned with the pain. As it once again released its grip she looked at Elizabeth for the first time. 'It's his,' she managed and Elizabeth saw the fire of determination in her eyes.

'Do ... do you mean Richard's?'

Emily only nodded. She glanced towards Hubert who up until this point had been busying himself trying to get a fire going and saw him pale. He said nothing; he simply froze on the spot before muttering something incomprehensible and hastily retreating from the room.

Emily could see the shock on Elizabeth's face and yet she managed to smile at her warmly. Her eyes sparkled and Emily saw their green warmth flickering. Richard had inherited his mother's eyes. She knew that what Elizabeth was feeling at this moment was similar to what she herself was feeling – that knowing your child lived on was more important than any morality in this world.

Seconds passed in silence before Elizabeth managed to once again take charge. She called out to Hubert, 'Help me get her to his room! We must help her Hubert.'

Somehow, between the surges of the storm, they managed between them to climb the stairs. She lay on the bed, realizing that this was where he too had lain. She could sense his presence strongly now. Though the sheets were newly laundered she inhaled his scent and for the first time felt tears sting her eyes. Then the monster roared once more and she was overcome.

From somewhere in the room she heard a cry. 'Send for the doctor!' She floated now, above the bed. She watched from above as the writhing shape that was her own body eventually calmed. Looking down she felt no fear. She knew that this time he would be saved ...

Chapter 28

Marleston, England, July 1996

Looking at the dates, I could see that Emily had failed to complete her diary for several months, though of course I could not understand without reading on the reasons why. And then it continued again, only briefly; just one more entry in the form of a letter.

My Darling Rebekah,

You will never know the enormity of what I felt for you when Elizabeth placed you in my arms that very first time but I want to write it down, to record it so that it is not lost, so that you do not become a mere memory.

It was a shock that you had not been born a boy, for I had been convinced that your Father lived within me all those months. Still, I suppose it does not mean that he did not; just because you are a girl, a precious, tiny slip of a thing. You are still him and he is still you. You looked at me with his eyes and I knew he was not lost. But I had to lose you, for your sake I had to lose you and I wish you could know that my heart was broken all over again in doing so.

The doctor had been a family friend of Elizabeth and Hubert, a trustworthy friend who, after delivering you safely, made his way to Hope Cottage. He awoke Grandpa to tell him that I had been found in the churchyard delirious with infection and must be left to rest at the Vicarage for a few days. He had assured Grandpa that there would be no financial cost to himself and that he would even send a nurse for Mum to compensate for the loss of my presence.

He returned to assure me that though the news had not been met with gratitude, having reinforced that I would likely die if I did not receive rest, Grandpa had grudgingly conceded.

Needless to say, he made no attempt to visit me and I was able to spend three incredible days in your presence; nursing you, loving you and telling you everything you would ever need to know of my life and my love for your father. Oh how I tried to make you understand! If only babies were born with memories then I know that you would have, for as I talked you would stare at me and frown with a wise expression and it was as if you heard.

But all too soon my heart was broken once again and I know that this time I will never recover! You are gone from me. I have to let you go so that you can live without bounds, without anguish and fear and you can be free.

But I will never stop loving you.
Your Mother,
Emily

I read each word and my own stomach contracted with the pain that she must have felt.

But it is too late. I can never tell you Mum that you were loved and you were wanted more than you could ever have imagined! It seems that from beginning to end you were destined not to know the truth. If only Emily had been brave enough to have sent it to you Mum, this letter, then you would have known. Why ever did she not? I could only guess her reasons.

Chapter 29

Just after sunrise the following morning, I made my way up the lane towards the churchyard. I had spent the previous night restlessly, putting two and two together and tying up pieces of the puzzle that even Emily's diary did not solve.

I reflected back upon my first day in Marleston, when I had stood at the unmarked grave. I could hardly believe now that it was indeed my own grandfather's grave. The small poppy cross was now gone; the poinsettia too. Perhaps they had blown away in the late-spring wind. Other than a mound and an empty glass jam jar which lay on its side there was no marker to show that this plot of ground belonged to anyone.

I stood and pondered. There was still something I could not understand. If this was Richard's grave and he had been so well-loved by his parents, then why on earth was it unmarked and uncared for when his own sister lived only a hundred paces away.

Yes, the diary had revealed how Ruth had felt about Richard and Emily but surely she could not have hated him so much that she would stoop to this. Surely whilst his parents had been alive they would have provided him with a head-stone. I wondered if there might be anyone in the village whom I would be able to talk to who might be able tell me more.

I decided to wander around to see if I could find Elizabeth

and Hubert's grave. After all, being the parish rector, I was almost certain that they would have been buried here. I headed towards the church, thinking that this would surely be the most likely place to find them. After all it seemed traditional to bury a member of the clergy in a prominent spot. It was strange now, knowing that they were in fact my great grandparents. Stranger still was the knowledge that Ruth was my great aunt! Was she aware of this I wondered? Perhaps she was. That would explain her iciness towards me. But then Emily's diary also stated the secretive nature of mum's birth and subsequent adoption. I could not be certain as to how much or how little of the story Ruth actually knew.

It did not take me long to discover their grave. I stood and read;

Hubert Harrison
1890-1963
Rector of this parish and loving husband to Elizabeth
and devoted father to Richard and Ruth.
Also Elizabeth Harrison
1893-1974
Reunited

Strange that there should be no loving words attributed to Elizabeth but then knowing what I now knew of Ruth I should not have been be so surprised. No floral tribute was present on their grave. Indeed, just like Richard's, it too appeared rather unkempt. She really is a cold fish, I thought to myself.

Hearing the sound of footsteps I looked up and saw that a gravedigger was busy placing a green ground sheet over a newly re-opened grave a little way off to the right, in preparation for a funeral, I assumed. I slowly made my way over to where he worked, not wishing my intentions to appear too obvious.

'Morning!' he greeted me with a cheery smile as I drew close.

Thank goodness! I thought. 'Busy day?' was the first thing I could think to say. I smiled at him genuinely, but stood at a little distance.

'Aye, funeral later,' he replied. 'Not often we get them here now what with it being full. Only re-openers these days.'

He had a friendly face. His ruddy complexion evidenced his outdoor occupation. Probably in his early fifties, I thought, considering if this might mean he would be likely to know a little of the history of the place.

'So you usually work elsewhere then I assume?' I continued, not wishing the conversation to end.

'Aye. Four days out of five I'm up at the big cemetery in Plowdon but I know this place like the back of me hand. Been here since I was a kid *and* my father before me and his father too. Three generations of gravediggers we are,' he chuckled. 'Seen so many laid to rest it's like cleaning me teeth now.'

I couldn't believe my luck, he should indeed be able to give me some insight into Richard's grave. Before I could think of how I was going to broach the question he asked, 'You new around here then or just passing through?'

I smiled and nodded towards Hope Cottage, 'I'm moving into the cottage when it's ready.'

He frowned and looked confused for a moment, 'I thought *she'd* never let it go to anyone!' he continued.

'He cannot know that Emily is dead,' I surmised. 'Oh but she died quite a while back. I ... I'm her granddaughter.' The word still sounded strange on my tongue.

'I think there's some mix-up here love,' he said, looking at me as if I were the one who was mistaken. 'Cos if *she's* dead, then I must have spoken to her ghost 'bout an hour ago and secondly, if you're her granddaughter, then she must have had a secret love-child 'cos she's never had any children.'

I laughed. 'You're right in part. She did have a love-child ... my mother,' My stomach flipped with a sense of betrayal, though I supposed if I was to make this village my home I wanted no secrets. He watched me intently, waiting for me to say more so I continued, 'But Emily's definitely dead. In fact she's been dead well over a year.'

He smiled then, 'Oh *Emily* was your grandmother. I thought you meant her up there,' he said, nodding back towards the Vicarage. 'Could never imagine her ever having had a secret love affair with anyone but herself!' He grinned at his own joke then his smile turned into a frown. 'Sad affair what happened to poor old Emily though ... I never knew *she* had a child either. Always lived with her poor old Ma. Sick she was, in the head like ... without wanting to speak out of turn. And the old man ... pig he was, though I don't remember him meself. His reputation goes before him so to speak.'

'Emily's grandfather you mean?'

But his thoughts were elsewhere so he did not answer.

'I could have sworn *she* owned it though, not Emily.' Once again he gestured towards the Vicarage. 'Her Da was the vicar see. Owned half the village and rented the houses out to locals. Never ripped them off. Kind they were ...' He paused, lost in thought before continuing. 'But not 'er. Soon as Elizabeth died, folk said she doubled the rents within weeks ... said her own mother had been a soft touch and that they had taken advantage of her good nature for far too long ... I was *sure* she owned it.' He paused again, shaking his head. 'Still, already made one mistake today haven't I?' he laughed again. 'Thinking you were *her* granddaughter. What a scandal that would have been hey! Me Da would have known for certain but don't suppose

I can ask him now.' He nodded back in the direction of an old yew tree under which stood a grave.

I smiled back at him. 'I wonder if you could tell me anything about the unmarked grave down at the bottom there?' I nodded towards Richard's grave, not yet wishing to disclose that he was also my grandfather. Ruth obviously felt that she had enough ammunition to fire in my direction without me giving her more by divulging to the whole community that her brother had had a child out of wedlock, even if it had been a very long time ago. 'Only it looks as if it's been there a long while and yet there's no stone.'

'That's 'er brother's grave.' Once again he gestured towards the Vicarage. 'Only they didn't get on apparently. Funny you should say,' he scratched his head. 'It did have a headstone up until about a year or so ago though she never tended to it. She had the stone removed, said she wanted the lettering re-done ... though she's not had it put back on since.' Again he paused, seemingly perplexed. 'No love lost between them. S'pose at least she's not hypocritical 'bout it. Never cared for him in life so doesn't pretend to care after he's gone.'

I decided to push my luck further, 'Do you know why they didn't get on?'

'Not really. *She* never got on with anyone very well. Thinks herself high and mighty she does. Went to Africa for years. Good riddance too. I don't know of anyone who was pleased to see her return. No ... I think it was just her way.' He nodded again now, in the direction of the unmarked grave. '*He* went to war so my Da told me, and was badly injured. Never really recovered. Died soon after he came home.' He paused deep in thought before continuing. 'Now come to think of it, I'm sure me Da told me he was sweet on your grandmother. Friends when they were just kids but they became more than friends before the war apparently.' He winked. 'I wasn't born then so never knew him myself but *she* wouldn't have liked that,' he said, gesturing in the direction of the Vicarage. 'Him taking up with the likes of Emily would have been well beneath her station as far as she would have been concerned!'

He smiled then embarrassed, his ruddy face turning even redder. 'No offence mind. I'm not saying Emily wasn't worthy of him, just how *she* is, that's all.'

I wanted to help him out of an embarrassing situation. 'Please don't worry. I know what you mean.' I laughed. 'I've been on the sharp end of her tongue already myself in the short time I've been here. Did you know Emily? Everyone I've spoken to simply says that she was an old eccentric who kept herself to herself. Nobody seems to be able to tell me more.'

'Aye ... but she wouldn't always have been old would she? Sad life is all that I know. As I've said, her own Ma was ill and she had no Da growing up. Her Grandpa, her mother's father lived with them and was a bit of a swine apparently. Treated Emily like a slave they say. By the time I was old enough to remember anything Emily was already living there alone.'

I nodded, thirsty for more. He continued, 'Quiet she was, blank like, never smiled at us kids when we passed by. The house she just left to rack and ruin. Would put food out for the birds. Had a few stray cats which came and went. Neighbours weren't keen truth be told. Said the place attracted rats what with it backing on to the river and being so dirty. But *you're* seeing to that now aren't you? Doing it up a treat I notice.' He gazed towards the cottage, his hand shielding his pale blue eyes from the early morning sun.

'Yes, I am ... I think Emily became ill, perhaps like her own mother or maybe she was just lonely.' I pondered aloud.

He smiled warmly. 'Same here, can be a lonely job this you know. You can talk to the clients all you like but not one of them has ever answered me back as yet!'

I glanced at my watch. 'Anyway, thank you so much for the chat. I'd better go or your funeral will arrive and we'll still be talking!' I smiled.

I realized that I would need to get a move on if I were to do the rounds of animal feeding and mucking out before my lunch shift at the pub. I had stood chatting for longer than I had intended. In fact I could not believe my luck in having found someone with whom I could feel so openly able to talk to. After all, I had only visited the churchyard that morning because I had felt compelled to after the revelation of the previous night's reading.

I headed for the side gate which would take me past Hope Cottage even though this would mean a longer walk back via the lane. I did not wish to walk past the Vicarage at present after having gossiped about Ruth. Even now, I imagined her watching me from one of the high, gothic windows of the house. I felt sure she was aware of my time spent with the gravedigger. She would likely put two and two together and know that her own name would have come up in conversation.

As I passed Hope Cottage I could hear the builders hammering away in one of the upstairs rooms but knowing that I was already up against the clock, I swallowed my curiosity to take a peek. Seeing to the animals would take at least an hour. I had to be in the pub by eleven and would need to shower and change beforehand. Still, I could see that it was coming along nicely. Every day made a difference now and Steve had assured me that it would be ready to move into within the next few weeks.

*

The morning post had arrived by the time I returned.

I quickly flicked through the contents in case anything addressed to Mr Ghent looked important. His mail was stacking up to quite a pile now. Still, he was due home in two weeks time. It was looking likely that I would either need to move back in with Tom or else take a room at the pub for a week or two before I could move in to Hope Cottage.

Not expecting to see my own name on any of the envelopes, I was surprised to find a brown, official looking envelope addressed to me. I had obviously missed Tom. He must have posted it through the letter box whilst I was at the cemetery for it bore his address. I had paid to have my mail re-directed to his for the time being even though I was not really expecting anything of importance. Hoping it might be from the college with news of a possible vacancy I tore it open and skimmed the contents. I was surprised to discover that it was in fact addressed from a local solicitor, Messr's Jenkins and John asking that I telephone regarding a legal matter to do with Hope Cottage. The old witch I thought! Just the previous week I had sent a letter to the council planning officer confirming that I would like to consider erecting a timber lodge holiday cottage on the land and asking whether it would be possible for someone to call again to discuss the matter in more detail. She must have got wind of my plans and is trying to put a spoke in the wheel before they even get off the ground. Anyway, it would have to wait until later this afternoon. The last thing I felt like doing right now after what I had discovered last night was dealing with any form of confrontation regarding Ruth, even if it were via a third party.

My shift at the Moon and Sixpence was unusually busy for a Thursday lunchtime but I was glad of the distraction for my mind kept returning to the letters and diary. I realized by two-thirty that I was in fact quite exhausted, having been awake for most of the previous night. By the time I got back to Mr Ghent's at three o'clock I was feeling rather irritable and so decided to put off ringing the solicitor until the following morning.

Chapter 30

'Good morning, Jenkins and John Solicitors.'

I could hear the tremble in my voice as I spoke and hoped that the person on the other end of the line wouldn't notice. 'Uh ... I've received a letter asking me to contact you regarding Hope Cottage.'

'Ah yes. Can I take your name please?'

My reply was followed by three minutes or so of elevator music whilst I held the line, my nerves growing increasingly fraught. Finally, I was told that the matter could not be dealt with over the phone and was instead advised that I should make an appointment to visit the office whereupon it could be discussed. I pressed the clerk for further information but she was not in the least bit forthcoming. My appointment was made for a week the following Friday and so I was resigned to the fact that I had nine days to wait before I would be enlightened, nine whole days and nights during which I knew I would fret and imagine all sorts of uncomfortable scenarios ahead.

I simply could not keep it to myself for that length of time. I rang Tom to ask him if I could pop round for a cuppa, telling him that I had a worry that I needed to share.

'But it was only last week that you sent the letter to the council,' he said, as confused as I was. 'Surely she can't have got wind of it yet? I mean I wouldn't be surprised if she isn't in with a few of the councilors but they'd have to watch what they were doing before gossiping to her about individual plans. I mean they could get into a whole heap of trouble if they spoke out of turn and anything came of it! Alright, if it goes as far as public consultation then she'd have the right to object but if she's got wind of it this soon then someone's in the wrong.'

'But it's got to be about her objecting to the holiday let Tom. After all, if I go ahead with it her own holiday let will face competition.'

'Ah come on girl, I've told you before, she's like it with everyone. She was probably hoping to have snapped up Hope Cottage for herself; build up her own little holiday let empire then couldn't she?'

I hesitated for a moment, but being me I felt I needed to share what I had recently found out about my family with him. Even though we'd only known each other for a relatively short time, I knew that I could trust Tom. He had become a father figure to me. I knew nothing of my real father as my mother had fallen pregnant with me during her student years and their relationship had soon fizzled out.

He listened without interruption as I filled him in on all that I had learned over the past twenty four hours.

'Ah now Cass ... I see what you're up against. Makes more sense now why she wants you gone from here. Afraid you might learn too much about her past I reckon.' He hesitated for a few moments, staring out the window and beyond into his well-tended back garden. 'Poor old Emily! Heartbreaking that must have been. All she'd put up with living with him and her poor mum ... then to have lost the love of her life *and* her only child ... must have been the straw that broke the camel's back. Probably what made her turn out as she did if you know what I mean ... enough to make anyone give up on life.'

'You know what makes me most sad Tom? It's too late to tell Mum that she *was* loved, that she *had* been wanted.

If she'd known Emily's circumstances she would have understood the reasons behind her adoption. She wouldn't have borne a grudge ... she wasn't like that. I mean, the circumstances of *my* birth were far from ideal. Perhaps that was why she was so determined to keep me though, having been adopted herself, she wouldn't have wanted her own child to go through the same. After all, it was a struggle for her having me when she was just a student. I know her adoptive parents were very disappointed in her at the time. They were getting on a bit when they adopted her you see and she'd had a very moral upbringing. They'd funded her to go to art college, just as she'd always wanted, and then she got pregnant before she could even finish her degree. Anyway, like I said, she'll never know about Emily's life now. It's too late.'

He looked me straight in the eye. 'What are your thoughts on the afterlife Cass? You think when we die it's all over? The end of everything?'

'Yes Tom. I do. I mean you have your memories, and your loved one lives on in you in some ways. I mean I often look in the mirror or at a photo and I see Mum looking back at me. Same eyes, same expression, especially as I'm getting older but I don't believe she's in another place Tom. I think it's over.'

He breathed a heavy sigh. 'Well girl, each to their own I s'ppose. For me it's different. I talk to my Harriet every day. Perhaps I'm daft but I feel she's still with me. I thought I might feel different when I moved down here but I don't. It's like she came with me in some ways. Sometimes I have to turn round and look 'cos I sense her presence so strong.'

He must have read the look of doubt in my face as he appeared slightly embarrassed.

'Anyway ... it's just *my* way that's all. If I were you see, I'd still tell her ... your Mum I mean. You haven't even got to say it out loud ... she'll hear you.'

I felt a lump in my throat at his words. Even though Tom's beliefs were far different from my own it was still touching to hear him speak in that way. I *wished* he was right. Like so many others who have lost a loved one I wished he was right; that death was not the end. But for me it was... and there was no going back. For me, the notion of a protective God, one who took you to his home after death but allowed you to still communicate in some unseeing way with those you loved was akin to Santa Claus delivering your presents on Christmas Eve. Not wishing to upset him I turned my thoughts back to the present. 'So Tom, *now* what do you think Ruth's up to?'

He shook his head, 'Have to admit Cass, I'm as puzzled as you are. Don't think I want to interfere like but if you want me to come with you next Friday, to the solicitor I mean, I will do. Don't want you to think I'm poking my old nose in your business mind. You just say if you'd rather go alone. I could come and sit in the waiting room if you like ... you wouldn't even have to tell me what was said. I'd just be there for a bit of moral support.

'Oh Tom ... would you really? I know it's silly but she frightens me. Even though my fear of her makes me annoyed with myself I just can't help but feel intimidated by her. I'd love you to come ... and no I wouldn't want you to stay in the waiting room. I'd only come out and tell you everything anyway. That's me Tom, an open book!'

He smiled. 'Righto then. We'll go together and if those solicitors make her out to be holier than thou, I'll be putting them straight ... tell them a few home truths about her I will!'

We both laughed at the time but over the following days my stomach still did a flip whenever I thought about the likely protest she was about to make. If I couldn't get permission to erect a holiday let and in doing so make some income from Hope Cottage then unless I found a better paid job pretty quickly my plans for a new life here in Marleston might soon be over.

Quite how I would afford to pay for a timber lodge though I had no idea. I'd done a little research and they were nowhere near as expensive as other kinds of builds. Nevertheless, they were still way out of my price range. I only hoped that the council would approve it as a possibility and that should I get a better paid job I could then take out a loan and pay it back over time from the income it would bring in.

Looking on the bright side though, by the end of the week Hope Cottage was not only water-tight but it actually resembled a home. The bathroom extension was complete to roof level and each of the rooms upstairs had new floorboards whilst those downstairs were damp-proofed and newly concreted. Thank goodness it did not turn out to be listed I thought, realizing that if it had, the repair costs would most definitely have been beyond my meager budget.

Chapter 31

Marleston, England, November 1940

Emily sat up in bed, exhausted but calm now. By her side stood Elizabeth. She looked down at the delicate creature lying peacefully asleep in Emily's arms. Emily smiled and handed her the baby.

The serenity of the moment was soon interrupted however as Richard's bedroom door suddenly flew open with such a bang that it hit the wall. On the threshold stood Ruth, her face full of rage and her body as frozen as a tailor's dummy. 'What on earth?' Her voice trailed off as she saw her mother gently rocking a sleeping baby in her arms.

'Hello Darling ... come and see ...' Elizabeth was cut off mid-sentence. During the previous night, in the midst of all the pain, Emily had been vaguely aware of someone mentioning that Ruth was spending the night at a friend's. She recalled now that she had felt a sense of relief at this news, even though in the state she had been in she'd had little care for the feelings of others. Now it was eight thirty in the morning and Ruth had just returned. Emily's heart quickened in her chest and the baby, who had been fast asleep in Elizabeth's arms, began to cry.

A nervous smile played around Elizabeth's mouth. She passed the infant back to Emily before taking a step towards Ruth who remained frozen to the spot. 'Darling, I know this will come as a shock but come and meet your little niece.' She had taken hold of Ruth's elbow, as if to lead her towards the bed.

Ruth violently shrugged her off and remained rooted. 'My *niece*!' she spat. 'What on *earth* do you mean?'

Emily could no longer bear to look in her direction and so concerned herself with attempting to hush the baby who was now wailing in protest in her arms.

Elizabeth stammered nervously. 'She's R-Richard's child Ruth. Emily has borne Richard's child.' She smiled weakly and her face burned red. 'A part of him lives on in her,' she continued, still trying to persuade. 'It has come as a shock of course but your father and I are delighted!' She returned to Emily's side in the hope that Ruth might follow.

Emily dared to glance again at Ruth. In contrast to her mother her own pallor was white, her lips thin and curled ready in retort, '*Richard's* child?' The words seemed to stick in her throat. Then she laughed, a sneering, malicious laugh. 'Oh *Mother*, are you *so* naïve as to believe *that*?' She paused for a moment, raising her eyes to the ceiling as if calculating. 'Where are we now..? November. Let's see ... Ah yes, that would mean that *it* would have been conceived in February. How strange that Richard was in the middle of training at the time!' She paused to allow Elizabeth to digest her words. Elizabeth appeared dumbstruck. 'Are you really so gullible Mother as to be tricked by a *whore*?'

Emily watched Elizabeth's face turn from red to ashen. She herself remained numb. She did not even care that Ruth called her such names. Nor did she care that Ruth believed the baby not to be Richard's. *She* knew the truth and that was all that mattered.

Elizabeth was flustered and embarrassed. Her voice sounded weak and unpersuasive. The room was filled with her fear. 'Oh Ruth, how can you say such things? The darling's just arrived a few weeks earlier than expected that's all. Come and see her and you will see for yourself ... she has his eyes you know.' Emily could see that Elizabeth was trying to make the best of things but was all too aware of the tremble in Elizabeth's voice as well as the tremor in her hands. Richard had often said that it was for all the world as if his parents, Elizabeth in particular, were afraid of his sister and that they would often give in to her in order to keep the peace. Now she could see how right he had been.

Ruth stood firm by the door, her face contorted. It was the first time that Emily had ever considered her ugly, for as smartly dressed and polished as she was her expression wore such a look of distaste that it made her appear grotesque.

'I want nothing to do with that whore nor her bastard offspring Mother and I strongly suggest, for the sake of your standing in the community that *you* have nothing to do with them either!' She turned abruptly on her heels and stormed from the room.

Upon her leave, the baby soon relaxed and cuddled back into Emily's breast. Neither Emily nor Elizabeth spoke for some moments. The sound of doors slamming carried from downstairs and sharp voices told them that another short altercation was taking place between Ruth and Hubert, though this soon ended with the slamming of the front door.

Emily's voice sounded frail even to herself. She was suddenly exhausted by what had happened. 'I'm so sorry Elizabeth. Perhaps we should leave today. I could always find a hotel for a day or so until ...' Only now did the tears fall, but it was not because of what had just ensued. It was at the thought of what was to come, for she already knew in her heart that she would not be able to keep her child.

'You will do no such thing!' Elizabeth snapped, her face still ashen.

Emily, for the first time since knowing her, could sense anger in Elizabeth's tone. 'It is *I* who should be sorry.

Sorry for the way my own daughter has behaved ... sorry that Hubert and I have spoiled her down the years and sorry that she *dares* to make such an accusation in light of what has happened.' She appeared to Emily as though she might faint for she shook from head to foot and her face was completely drained of colour. She slumped down on the bedroom chair, her breathing laboured.

A few moments of silence ensued whilst Elizabeth attempted to recover her breath. 'I hope that *you* believe me Elizabeth,' Emily said, a little guardedly. 'She really *is* Richard's you know. We didn't plan for it to happen ... it was just the once ... before he left for war ... It was just that we both felt so, well *empty* is the only way I can describe it ... dead almost. We did not stop to think that this might happen.' She looked down, her eyes full of love at the sight of the child in her arms. She pulled the baby closer, breathing her in.

'You have no need to convince me Emily.' Elizabeth had managed to calm herself and spoke without tremor now. 'I know you well enough to believe that there was no-one but Richard for you. And besides, I only need to look at her eyes for proof that she is his.' She paused, watching intently as Emily gently stroked the damp, dark hair of the now-sleeping infant. 'But what are you going to do love? I mean, what with your Mother and Grandfather ...' She failed to complete the sentence. She did not wish to appear as if she were taking control of what would after all be the biggest decision of Emily's life.

There was a silent pause, each with their own thoughts before Emily spoke again. 'I have never known love like this Elizabeth. At least not since Richard. But even that love was different. With him *I* felt like the child. He took care of me. I knew that when the war was over he would have rescued me and loved me forever. *This* love is different. *I* am not the child ... this innocent little bundle in my arms is and I know that for her sake, so that she may have a chance in life, I cannot keep her.

I was awake most of the night considering it Elizabeth but no matter what mad schemes I concoct there can be only one conclusion.' She paused, shuddering as she inhaled. 'We both know what it is that I have to do don't we?'

Elizabeth gently took her hand. 'I will help you Emily. Hubert and I both wish things could be different too. We sat up talking most of the night and I believe we came to the same conclusion as you; though we would not have suggested it had you not done so yourself.' She paused, half afraid to venture any further but when she saw that Emily did not protest she continued. 'We know of a couple, through the church, who dearly wanted children but have been unable to have any of their own. *You* could be the answer to their prayers love. Your self sacrifice would mean that three lives could be enriched; both theirs and this darling little one's.'

She looked at Emily, all too aware of the pain her words must cause but she also read the determination in Emily's face. 'You could write to her you know ... I would see that the letters were sent. I could even visit her myself from time to time; you know to see how she's getting along and let you know. What do you think love? They really are a wonderful couple, very loving and kind and money would not be an issue either. She would have all she could wish for.'

Emily couldn't answer for some seconds. 'Thank you Elizabeth. It will break my heart to let her go but I know it will be for the best. I couldn't bear to think that she would otherwise be destined to lead the life that I have led.' She paused then, deep in thought. 'You know Elizabeth, it has taken only what ... eight hours or so of motherhood to understand what being a parent really means ... and that is that you must put your child's life before your own, whatever the cost.'

'You're right love.' Emily saw that Elizabeth looked so utterly sad, as if the bottom had dropped out of her world too. 'You know, I often wonder where Hubert and I went wrong with Ruth. I wonder if we indulged her too much. She was always very demanding; not at all like Richard. He was always so good, so kind, always putting others before himself whereas she seemed incapable of thinking of anyone but herself. In Ruth's world she always came first. She's still the same, as you've seen ... where did we go wrong?' Emily saw that she looked so deeply hurt. At that moment she pitied her.

'Perhaps you did no wrong Elizabeth. Maybe that's just her way and no matter what you'd have done she would have ended up the same. I *have* tried to please her you know. I never wanted to make an enemy of her but no matter how I would try to draw her in she would never engage with me. I'm still sorry though Elizabeth; sorry that it's come to this. I never intended to upset her you know.'

'I know love. She'll come around. Just takes her longer than most people, that's all.' She sighed deeply then and Emily could see that she too was exhausted by what had happened. 'Anyway, I'll let you both get some rest. I could do with a nap myself.' She turned to leave the room but before she reached the door she hesitated and turned back to face Emily. 'Are you sure about what we discussed love? Only I could arrange it should you wish, through the church I mean. I don't want to push you at a time like this but the longer you wait the harder it'll be.' Her face was solemn.

Emily bravely met her worried gaze. 'Go ahead Elizabeth. Set the wheels in motion today if you can. If I hold on to her for much longer I fear I will never be able to give her up ... and where would that lead us both then?'

Elizabeth merely nodded and left the room, closing the

door as softly as she could behind her.

Alone with the child now, Emily gazed down at her sleeping face. 'I want to name you before I have to give you up,' she whispered. 'Do you know what your father would have wanted to name you little one? He would have called you Rebekah ... from the bible. It was his favourite name. It means 'captivating' and that's just what you are.

*

Over the next two days of her confinement, Ruth never again visited Emily's room. She was vaguely aware of her presence in the house from time to time and yet, even when she needed to visit the bathroom, she never once set eyes on her. 'Do you think she might tell someone?' she asked Elizabeth on the final evening.

'You are not to fret over that love. I can assure you that Ruth will not tell a soul though not out of the goodness of her heart I'm afraid. She has hardly spoken a word to either of us these past two days. When she did it was just to ask how soon you would be leaving and to say that neither her Father nor I should tell a soul as she didn't want our 'good name' sullied. I tried again to make her see sense but she simply stormed off. Knowing her, once you're gone she will never again raise the subject.' She glanced in embarrassment towards Emily knowing that her words, although true, were harsh. 'I'm sorry Emily ... Truly I am.'

'Don't be sorry Elizabeth. I don't know what I would have done without you and Hubert these past days. It doesn't even bear thinking about.'

Silence ensued, both afraid to broach the subject of what would take place the following morning.

Chapter 32

Still exhausted by the events of the past few days, Emily did not need to feign illness when she returned home. Her Grandpa moaned and groaned for a few minutes about her absence. Not once did he ask how she was feeling for which she was glad, for she felt that if he had provoked her she may even have been tempted to tell him the truth. The emptiness inside her was a physical void but her mind was not empty. For the first time since Richard's death she was consumed by anger. It was a boiling pot of molten lava, oozing just beneath the surface and it took all her strength to stop it from erupting. She only did so by avoiding him as much as possible, merely placing his meals in front of him and leaving the room. Not once did she sit at table; in fact over the following weeks she barely ate enough to stay alive.

She had decided one thing though; and that was that as painful as it was she had to cut the tie with Rebekah. Although the Wilkinsons had offered to pass on any letters she might send she knew that she would not write. Her reasons for this, though they might seem strange to some, were clear in her own mind. She knew that she would never forget Rebekah but that she could never be a part of her life. She would therefore remember the insurmountable love which she had felt during the months of carrying her and the precious three days she had spent with her following her birth. To think of her in another place, with other people was unbearable and so she would put the memory of the precious time they had shared in a box and close the lid on it.

She asked only one thing of them and that was that they would keep the name that she had chosen and have her christened Rebekah, just as Richard would have wanted. They in turn had promised to do so and she trusted that they would.

She had not cried when she had handed the baby over; she had merely turned around and walked the path back to Hope Cottage. As she had passed by Richard's grave she had paused. Silently she had spoken to him, 'She is safe now. She will not suffer the life that I have been destined to. You may rest peacefully my love.'

She had not been surprised to find that her mother seemed totally unaware of her absence these past days. However it did, for a few moments, fuel her anger and cause her to consider why she had made such a sacrifice when she had not even been missed. She buried her anger deeply though, knowing that it was not her mother's fault and that had she not returned then once the nurse left her mother would have been subject to institutionalization.

On the first night, once she had retired to her room and locked the door, she had written just one letter to Rebekah; one letter that she had no intention of posting. That letter she put in a box, along with her diary. She turned the key in the lock and replaced it under the floorboard.

Chapter 33

Marleston England July 1996

My appointment with the solicitor wasn't until two thirty but as it was my day off I had arranged to meet Tom at the Moon and Sixpence at one for a quick bite. I ordered a simple sandwich, as I couldn't stomach anything more and had a small glass of red wine in an attempt to quell the butterflies.

We parked in town and traipsed the short distance to the solicitor's office which was located in a rather grand Victorian building close to the car-park. In typical Cassie fashion, I was twenty minutes early but as on other occasions found this not to my favour as it simply meant I had longer to wait. At precisely two thirty five, Tom and I were summoned to the solicitor's office. The clerk led the way up a set of steep, narrow stairs to a room on the top floor. My hands were clammy and my face flushed from the wine and nerves.

'Good afternoon ... Robert Gibbings,' the man behind the desk said, holding out his hand. I shook it rather weakly, embarrassed by the clammy state of my own hand. He looked friendly enough though I thought; not as austere as I was expecting and rather younger, probably around the age of forty. 'Well ... thank you for responding,' he continued before gesturing for us both to sit.

I remained silent, waiting for the 'attack' which I was sure was imminent.

'Of course you must be wondering why we contacted you.'

Over the past nine days since receiving the letter I had been determined to appear strong. However, now that I was here and finally facing reality my resolve seemed to fly out the window. I merely found myself mumbling, 'Uh yes, I have been rather worried about what it might mean.' Tom remained silent beside me but I was still grateful for his presence.

The solicitor gave a small throat clear before continuing. 'Well ... it's rather a complicated situation ... it may be a lot for you to take in. Did you bring along the identification we requested?'

I wished he'd simply get to the point. 'Umm yes, I have it here,' I said, fumbling in my handbag and producing the brown envelope containing my passport and driving license.

He took the envelope from me, slid out the paperwork and studied both items for a moment before standing up. 'Excuse me for a moment, I just need to make a copy,' he said, walking over to the machine which stood towards the back of his office. I glanced at Tom nervously and he smiled and gave my hand a quick squeeze of encouragement.

He returned to the desk. 'That's fine thanks,' he said, handing me back the envelope. Hands folded in front of him he leaned forward. I felt my lip tremble as he began to speak. 'Okay, well this might come as quite a shock to you. Firstly let me ask ... did you recently inherit a property known as Hope Cottage in the village of Marleston?'

'Here we go,' I thought. 'Uh yes,' I mumbled. 'Why? Is there some kind of problem?'

'No not really,' he continued. He smiled now and the heavy feeling in my stomach lifted a little. 'Can you confirm whom you inherited the cottage from?'

'My mother. Her name was Rebekah Wilkinson. I was

her only child but she ...' I felt my throat constrict and was appalled at the thought that I might actually cry. It had all been too much. I inhaled deeply in an attempt to gather myself before continuing, 'She passed away a few months ago and it wasn't until afterward that I discovered that she had herself inherited Hope Cottage from her own mother, Emily Willis, my grandmother.' He continued to watch me intently and without interruption.

'Do continue,' he said.

I didn't understand exactly what he wanted me to tell him but as he seemed to be waiting for more of my story I continued. 'She had not been brought up by her you see ... her mother I mean. She was adopted as a baby and had not known her. Emily I mean ... so I think she must have been upset and shocked by her inheritance.' Still he said nothing. 'At the time, she knew that she herself did not have long to live and although there had never been any secrets between us she must have ...' I paused. 'Well for whatever reason she obviously felt unable to discuss it with me. I suppose she knew that she would never get to see the cottage and didn't want to actually put into words that we didn't have much time left together ... if she'd spoken about it she would have had to broach the subject of it passing down to me and at the time we were just grateful for every day we had.'

I was rather pleased that I had actually managed to get to the end of the explanation dry-eyed and felt a little stronger for having done so.

'I see. So you didn't learn of your inheritance until I assume your own Mother's will was read,' he said in a rather kind voice, aware of the delicacy of the situation. I nodded.

'Yes, that's right,' I answered, still wondering where on earth this conversation might be leading.

'Okay,' he continued, 'Well then I think you are probably

unaware of the link between Hope Cottage and Marleston Vicarage. Is that correct?'

I glanced at Tom. 'How much should I give away?' I wondered. 'Uh ... well I have very recently learned of some connections through some paperwork I found at the cottage,' I offered.

'Ah! Then I'll not beat about the bush. I doubt that you are aware of the fact that upon the death of the current residents it is *yourself* who will inherit the property?'

My heart sank. I couldn't think straight. 'Oh! So I *don't* actually own it yet?' I frowned. Of course, I thought, remembering back to my recent conversation in the cemetery with the gravedigger. 'He had been right after all! But if this were true and Ruth was still the legal owner of Hope Cottage then why had she not yet forced me to leave.' My heart beat fast and words failed me. Glancing at Tom I could see that he too was confused. I felt my face burn with embarrassment and shock.

The solicitor interrupted, 'Oh no, not at all. I'm sorry, perhaps I didn't explain it clearly enough ... I mean Marleston Vicarage. Upon the death of Mrs Ruth Fitzworthy you are to inherit Marleston Vicarage.'

'Wh ... What?' The blood pounded in my head and my heart raced. 'B ... but there has to be some kind of mistake,' was all that I could manage.

The solicitor remained leaning in my direction, smiling. I met his gaze, searching his eyes for some enlightenment.

He lifted the phone on his desk. 'Hi Anne, It's Robert. Could you bring us some ...' he addressed both Tom and I, 'tea ... coffee? What would you like?'

I continued to stare at him, mouth agape. 'You look as if you could use it. It's come as a shock, I know.'

'Uh tea please ... Cass?' Tom nudged me, jolting me from my stupor.

I still did not understand. Just a moment ago I believed

that I was to lose Hope Cottage and now this man was informing me that not only was I the rightful owner but that I was indeed likely to inherit the whole bloody lot! My mind raced, 'Uh same please,' I managed, though I had no idea what Tom had asked for.

'Three teas please Anne,' he said before replacing the receiver again. 'Now let me explain more thoroughly. As I said at the beginning of our meeting, the situation is complex.'

Chapter 34

Over the course of the next thirty minutes the conundrum became clearer. To some degree the gravedigger had been right. Hope Cottage had previously been owned by Elizabeth and Hubert along with several other village properties. Long back they had tenanted it to Emily's mother and father. Emily's grandfather had died in 1943, just two years after Mum's birth and it seemed that Emily had then continued to care for her own Mum at the cottage. However, not long afterward her mother had also passed away. Elizabeth and Hubert then gifted the cottage to Emily and so she had become the legal owner.

I imagined that all this would likely have taken place whilst Ruth had been living in Africa and couldn't help but wonder whether or not Hubert and Elizabeth had discussed it with her. Perhaps they had merely felt that Emily deserved it. After all, she *had* been betrothed to their only son and had borne their only grandchild. They must also have realized that upon Emily's death the cottage would pass down to Mum and so they would ultimately be gifting it to their own grandchild.

I did not know whether or not they had ever visited Mum as she had grown up; perhaps circumstances had not allowed them to do so after all. All I knew was that Mum had never mentioned any grandparents. Moreover, and what was even more shocking to me, was what the solicitor had told me next. Some years after Hubert's death,

Elizabeth had changed her will. I was sure though that she and Ruth had been reunited for I remembered Bessie's words a few months back saying that Ruth had returned to the Vicarage when Elizabeth had become ill. I could not for the life of me therefore work out what must have occurred to cause Elizabeth to dis-inherit her own daughter in favour of an estranged grandchild. I could only assume that Ruth must have treated her cruelly upon her return or else surely she would never have done such a thing.

The solicitor had instructed me that Elizabeth's will read that upon her death, Ruth should be allowed to *reside* at the Vicarage for the remainder of her days. However, when Ruth herself died, should my mother be traced then *she* should in fact inherit. I had not felt any sense of pleasure at having this explained to me, only numbness. It was just too big to comprehend for the present. However, I was now beginning to understand why it was that Ruth had behaved so rudely towards me.

Upon leaving the solicitor's office, Tom and I had sat in my little car for over an hour discussing what we had just learned. He was as flabbergasted as I. The news was still not really cause for celebration however as the solicitor had also left me with a seed of doubt. It seemed that upon Elizabeth's death Ruth had contested the will but had lost. Now, after so many years of estrangement, she must have presumed it unlikely that Mum would be traced. However, now that I had appeared on the scene as the eventual inheritor she was prepared to do battle again. This ultimately was the reason for me having been called to the office today.

Although he seemed pretty confident that it was unlikely that Elizabeth's wishes would be overruled, I was neither presumptuous enough nor optimistic enough to consider the fight over. I understood that if Elizabeth's wishes were to be granted then I would probably have a long and complicated battle on my hands. I also understood that it was likely to cost me in legal representation as although he had ensured me that Ruth would need to bear the brunt of the costs I would still have to pay some myself, though such costs could be taken out of any eventual gains. That's all very well, I thought, but what if I should lose. How would I find the money to pay then?

What I had come away with most of all was a strong urge to try and fathom the reasons behind Elizabeth's thinking. Surely something gravely serious must have happened in order for her to have spurned her own daughter in this way.

Chapter 35

Marleston England, March 1941

It was a Sunday morning and the three of them were seated at the breakfast table when Ruth made the announcement. 'I'm going away,' she said without even raising her head from the newspaper she was pretending to read. 'To Africa ... I'm joining the missionary. I leave next week.'

A sharp intake of breath from Elizabeth was followed by an icy silence which sat in the room like an unwanted visitor. The past few months had been hell for both she and Hubert. Ruth had always been difficult, that much was certain, but recently she had seemed to baulk at their every suggestion and had done her utmost to avoid them as much as she could. Elizabeth, being the kind of person she was, had tried on several occasions to lighten the mood and strike up a conversation but each time Ruth would simply cast her a look of indifference and find an excuse to leave the room.

'Why ever didn't you talk to us about it dear?' Elizabeth spoke now, once again pussy-footing around her own daughter. 'Are you unhappy? Is it anything your father and I have done?'

Ruth merely snorted, 'I do not wish to discuss the matter further. I have arranged for my luggage to be sent on. The company will be collecting it on the 23rd of the month. I would appreciate it if you could ensure you are at home on that day.' She had stood then, about to leave the table but was unprepared for what was to follow.

'How dare you!' Hubert also stood, looming over the table. His large, kindly hands pressed into the wood so that his knuckles shone white. He appeared angrier than Elizabeth had ever seen him in all her life. His stance seemed to knock Ruth's confidence for a moment for she hesitated, frozen to the spot.

'After all we have done for you! Given you!' He almost spat the words at her, his face turning redder and redder. 'You know Ruth, as far as I'm concerned you can go! I've had enough of your appalling behaviour these past few months ... no not months ... years, it's been years! You've *never* shown any appreciation or care for anyone and now you have the audacity to speak as if we mean nothing to you. We're little more than pawns to be used at your convenience aren't we?'

Ruth was momentarily bowled off her feet. Never before had she seen her father so angry. For a few moments she sat back down, her face ashen, features pinched with shock. However, she did not give up the fight for long. She stood again, both hands on the table, emulating his stance. She leaned toward him, making herself appear as threatening as she could. It was as if they faced each other in the ring. Elizabeth sat between them, head in her hands. 'Stop! Let her go! If that's what she wants then it's for the best,' she pleaded.

'Huh! Let me go?' Ruth mocked. 'You could not stop me even if you wished!'

'Oh yes we could my girl!' Hubert replied, his anger still fierce. 'You are only eighteen years old and still therefore legally within our care. Should we wish we could *indeed* stop you!'

She grinned mockingly at him now, her old self-assurance having returned. 'But you wouldn't dare would you?' She paused. 'Cross me and I could drag *her* name through the mud ... hers and that precious son of yours and you know it!' she gloated.

Elizabeth was crying now, 'You wouldn't dare!' she sobbed. 'How can you be so unkind? Your brother cold in the ground and that poor girl having to give up his child...You wouldn't dare!'

'Well that's where you're wrong Mother!' she spat, seething with anger.

Hubert was stunned. His hands trembled. He spoke again, more calmly now. His eyes fixed on Ruth and this time he spoke with greater control.

'What happened that morning?' he asked, breathing heavily, his face now devoid of colour. She did not reply but he pursued. 'You know ... I've wanted to ask you for such a long time. What *really* happened that morning on the landing?'

Now it was Ruth's turn to be flustered. 'What morning?' she stumbled. 'What are you talking about?'

'Oh but I believe you *know* the morning to which I refer Ruth ... the morning Richard died.'

Her mouth fell open. 'He fell! You know that he fell! What are you trying to say?' Her voice was shrill as a whistle. She did not meet his gaze. She remained standing but appeared smaller now, more fragile, as if deflated.

There was silence in the room for a few moments then Hubert spoke again. 'Ah but I *heard* you Ruth.' He still stared directly at her. 'I heard every word you said to him on the landing. I *heard* your visceral attack and it took all my strength to stop myself from coming to his rescue.' She stared at the table. 'After all he had been through at war and then to be injured, and there you were, belittling the love of his life. The things you said to him Ruth, they were unforgivable.'

She still did not look at either of them. Both could see that for a moment the fight had gone out of her.

It was Elizabeth who spoke next, her voice trembling and her chest heaving with emotion. 'Leave it now ... please ... both of you. Before things are said that might be regretted. Leave it for God's sake! For Richard's sake!'

Ruth glanced towards her mother, who had once again seemingly come to her rescue. But Hubert was unwilling to leave the matter. 'I want you to answer me one question ... just one ... But I want you to answer it truthfully and in the name of God your answer will go to the grave with you.'

Ruth turned away from them both, her mouth twitching nervously. She was trapped. Trapped between the chair, the table and her conscience. She had never feared either of her parents, not even as a young child, but she knew what was coming. Even if she fled, and it remained unspoken, she knew that the question would refuse to go away. It would always be there. Better perhaps for it to be aired, where it would echo around the walls before coming to rest. She raised her head and met her father's gaze.

'Did you push him?' He was calm now, in control it seemed. Elizabeth gasped and was about to speak but Hubert silenced her with a point of a finger. 'Well?' he asked again. 'Did you?'

The silence in the room was almost palpable; the air thick and cloying. The question, now asked, hung suspended in the air like a spirit. Their heart beats, quick as mice were the only sound in the room. Ruth seemed to hesitate for a few seconds, frozen to the spot, then, pushing back her chair with considerable force she turned and abruptly left the room.

Elizabeth sobbed. 'How could you Hubert? I know she's impulsive but she would never have ...'

He stopped her before she could finish the sentence. 'Search inside your heart Elizabeth. Remember the way he cried out. Remember the way she fled within seconds of us coming out to see what was going on. Remember the look of guilt on her face. She's never been one to hide her feelings.' He paused, allowing her to absorb his words, his own breath catching in his chest.

'I never wanted it to be this way Elizabeth, believe me ... I have tried and tried to put it out of my mind but have been unable to do so. Too many memories come flooding back; the way she stood behind us as we laid him to rest; the way she avoided speaking about him. No warm words ... nothing. Whenever we spoke of him she would leave the room.' Elizabeth sat, head in hands, sobbing. 'I wanted to believe it was just grief; just her way of handling the loss of her only brother Elizabeth but I know it is not so.' He spoke kindly now, so regretful that he was having to speak such words. 'I think in your heart you know it too my love. We must let her go, for all our sakes we must let her go to the missionary and hope that she can atone for her sins by doing some good for others.'

They held each other then for a long time and cried like they had not cried since the death of their son.

Chapter 36

Marleston England August 1996

The two weeks following my appointment at the solicitors went by in a whirr of activity.

I was glad of the distraction as it meant I had little time to dwell on Ruth's intentions. Summer was at its peak and The Moon and Sixpence was busier than I had ever known it. I had extra shifts to work which meant on most days I would cover both lunch and evening meal. Although the pay was poor, the job had enabled me to really get to know the locals and I was beginning to feel that I truly belonged.

Hope Cottage was coming along well too. Since the plaster board walls had gone up, the renovation had seemed to fly and it was now almost habitable. It did look bare but I could see that with the right paint colours and soft furnishings it could be made cozy.

Mr Ghent's daughter was now back on her feet and he was due home the second week of August, so between working in the pub I was also busy keeping his place up to scratch. Only at night, when I lay in bed alone would my thoughts return to Ruth and the likely outcome of the contest.

I battled with my conscience at the prospect of owning the Vicarage. In all my wildest dreams, I could never have imagined owning such a property. I would have been more than happy with Hope Cottage but I had to admit that the Vicarage was a fabulous house. I could just imagine the grandeur inside. As well as the Vicarage of course there was also the holiday cottage in which I had spent my first week in Marleston. Little could I have even dared to imagine then that I might one day own the place. The whole thing still seemed absolutely ludicrous.

No matter how hard I tried though, I could not stop myself from feeling guilty. After all, it wasn't as if I'd ever even met Elizabeth. Ruth was her daughter and I could not imagine why she would put a stranger before her. I realized that having no children Ruth would have no-one to pass it down to and that, like it or not, I *was* her great niece. Even so I could not help but feel that somehow I did not deserve it. In fact, no matter how hard I tried, I just could not imagine the case going my way; surely such wealth was not in my cards.

I was certain from my encounters with Ruth thus far that she would rather have willed it to a cat's home than have it passed down to me. I had learned enough from Emily's diary to know how much Ruth had hated her. The very fact that she was now prepared to dedicate the time and money to once again contesting her mother's wishes reinforced the fact. After all, in practice it would ultimately make no difference to her as she still remained the rightful occupant until her own death. This only reinforced the power of her hatred towards anyone linked to Emily.

How nice it would have been, I thought, if things were different and instead of hating me she would have welcomed getting to know me as long lost family. Being a peace-maker by nature I would have much preferred this outcome, property inheritance aside. Still, that would never be the case. There would be absolutely no purpose in attempting to win Ruth over. She had to be one of the most hard-hearted people I had ever encountered.

I had saved all that I could from my meager wages over

the past few months. I still could not believe how lucky I had been to have been able to stay at Mr Ghent's rent-free whilst Hope Cottage was being renovated. As I expected, the final bill had come slightly over Steve's estimate but with my savings I just managed to pay my way. By the time Mr Ghent's return was imminent the only jobs that needed finishing were the bathroom installation and the basics in the kitchen and Steve assured me that both would be complete by the end of the week.

Afterward, it would just be a matter of giving the new plaster time to thoroughly dry out before painting then furnishing. Tom and I were looking forward to the decorating. I had always enjoyed it when I had lived back in the North and had already selected my intended colours from the paint charts. I had just enough left in savings to do this as well as purchase a couple of basic pieces of furniture such as a little kitchen table and chairs but the luxury of wardrobes and sofas would have to wait. Tom was lending me two garden recliners for the present and I had bought a cheap rail upon which to hang my clothes.

The night before Mr Ghent arrived home Tom helped me move my few belongings into the spare bedroom at Hope Cottage. Bessie had offered me a spare room at the pub in which to sleep for just a few nights until I had a flushing toilet and running water then I would be able to move in. I was really excited and so glad that I had listened to Tom back in April when he had persuaded me to stay.

The only thing that blighted my current happiness was Ruth. She loomed over me like a threatening thundercloud. Try as I might to persuade myself of the fact that I was now the rightful owner of Hope Cottage, I still could not help but sense her aversion. From what was to be my bedroom window, I could just make out the gables at the front of the Vicarage. I could not help but imagine her sitting inside her own bedroom and concocting her plan to be rid of me. I knew that she would still do her utmost to make life unbearable for me in this village. Perhaps she hoped that by the very act of once again disputing her Mother's wishes I would be forced to sell out of discomfort, what with her being so physically close and holding such a position within the community. Even in my darkest moments though, I was determined that this would not be the case. No ... I had been through enough and would never again allow myself to be ruled by a bully.

Chapter 37

We had just finished painting the last wall in the kitchen when my phone rang. 'Hello, is that Cassie?' the voice on the other end asked.

'It is, who's speaking please?' I knew that it could not have been the solicitor as he would not have called me by my first name.

'It's Phil ... from the college. I was wondering if you were still interested in a few hours lecturing starting in September?'

My heart skipped a beat. 'Oh my goodness! I most certainly am!' I replied without hesitation.

'Well our English department is looking for someone to teach two evening classes and two days. How does that sound? I'm afraid it would only be on a temporary contract but, you know, if things go well and student numbers increase then we might be able to offer something more permanent in the future,' he continued.

'Well I would be absolutely thrilled to take you up on your offer. When would you like me to start? Would it be okay if I came down before the start of term to familiarize myself a bit?' I asked, my voice trembling. I could see from his face that Tom had got the gist of the conversation as he beamed and winked at me from across the room.

Having arranged to visit the college and meet up with Phil again during enrollment week I ended the call.

'What do you think Tom? I can't believe it! Even if it's

just a foot in the door it's still really exciting!' I squealed. 'And I can still do a few shifts at the pub. I wouldn't want to let Bessie down, not after she's been so good to me. I could still do say Friday and Saturday evenings and Sunday lunches couldn't I? It's only a part-time offer see and I'll need every penny I can get my hands on if I'm ever to turn this into a real home. And besides, I enjoy the camaraderie of the pub and it's not like I have any family to look after is it?' My mind was a whirr and my thoughts came gushing out like a torrent.

'It's fabulous news girl!' he answered with a chuckle. 'Things are turning around for you aren't they? Your Mum is looking out for you see, you mark my words!'

I smiled, not wanting to hurt his feelings. Gestures such as these made me wish I could believe the same to be true and yet I could not. In life, Mum had looked out for me every step of the way but I failed to believe that she was still able to do so, even though I wished it so. Still, it was uncanny how things were starting to come together. Perhaps I'd simply had my run of misfortune and was finally turning a corner.

At times like this, I longed to share my news with Mum. At night, when I was alone with my thoughts, I would often speak silently to her, updating her with what was going on and sometimes it even felt as though she were listening. I could imagine her smile and sense her joy, for she was never happier than when *I* was happy and never sadder that when *I* was sad.

Oftentimes, during these past months since losing her, I would be reminded of her suffering, and in particular of her final days but I would also remind myself of the words she had often spoke to me during those dark times, 'Live your life!' she would say. 'It's so precious. Do what makes you happy. Don't worry about what others think. Just look after yourself for me.'

I would stroke her thinning hair then, the baby-fine hair which the chemo had weakened and promise her that I would be fine, that no matter what, I was a part of her and we could never be separated. She would smile then. 'I'm not afraid to die,' she would say. 'I just don't want to leave you.' I would do my best to put on a brave face though her words destroyed me inside. I could not bare to show her how much the thought of losing her hurt because she could do nothing more to help herself and seeing me distressed only made it harder for her.

When I lost her, and was sorting through her possessions, it was her hairbrush that hurt me most. I had bought her a baby brush, soft and pink, in an attempt to stop what was left of her hair from falling out. Sorting through her belongings I had held the brush and pulled the wispy strands from it and it had torn at my heart like nothing else.

Those last few weeks of her life haunted me still but I fought hard to press on with life just as she had wished. She was with me in memory every day yet I still could not believe that she somehow watched me and made my life easier. When the sad memories revisited, I would allow myself some quiet moments with them and then push them away. I would lock them in an invisible box ... until the next time ... for they inevitably found a way to escape again.

She would be proud of me now. I knew that for certain. And she would not have wanted me to give in to Ruth's demands. Throughout her illness she had been a fighter and I was determined to be too.

Chapter 38

The next three weeks passed in a busy blur. It was good to be so engaged as it kept me from dwelling on Ruth and the forthcoming legal issues. It was now early September. Some days would be gloriously warm and bright and others positively autumnal; typical British weather.

The cottage was now finally decorated. I had chosen to make it really cozy with warm hues and inexpensive throws and cushions in natural tones. Even Tom's sun loungers were draped in throws. I loved it. It was the first place I'd ever had that had really felt like home; apart from my childhood home that is. When Simon and I had lived together it had been different. He had owned the property before we had met and so I always felt as if I was on his turf rather than in my own place. But *this* was all mine and I was beginning to feel a sense of peace and belonging which I had never quite experienced before.

On the morning I was due to meet Phil at the college I was up like a lark, glad that I felt more excitement than apprehension. Just as I was leaving the cottage the post arrived. As soon as I saw the brown, official-looking envelope I knew it was unlikely to be good news. Tempted though I was to leave it unopened until I returned I decided instead to have a quick peek. Expecting it to be news of the forthcoming court case I was surprised upon scanning its contents to discover it was actually from the local council.

Within seconds, I had grasped the gist of its contents; my

query for the holiday let on the cottage's land had been rebuked. There was some mention in the validation for the reason being because the cottage was in a conservation area and so on. What surprised me most was my own reaction. Instead of feeling upset I was actually in a way glad. Given that it now looked more likely that I was about to start proper paid employment, I was happy that I no longer needed this source of income as now that I was living here, I could see what a beautiful garden I could eventually have all to myself.

Okay, so I *was* currently penniless but at last I could see a brighter future. I was so glad that I was experiencing this about-turn in thinking. In the past, and especially during my marriage, I had had a tendency to worry. Perhaps Hope Cottage and this village were helping me to once again reunite with the cheery, carefree girl of my youth.

I slung the letter onto the bottom stair of the hallway and hastily left, not wishing to be late for my meeting. Singing along to the radio at the top of my voice, I drove the few miles through glorious countryside towards town without a second thought about what I would have previously considered to be bad news.

Chapter 39

It was the third week of September and I had started my new job the previous week. Luckily, it turned out that enrollment numbers for the creative writing evening classes combined with daytime G.C.S.E. and A level classes were sufficient to afford me to work *three* days a week as well as two evening classes. Luckier still was the fact that none of my hours clashed with peak pub times and so I was still able to work Friday and Saturday evenings as well as cover Sunday lunch for Bessie. It was nice to be so busy. The social side of working at the pub had meant a lot to me during my low times. I had made some good friends and acquaintances in and around the village which I didn't want to lose.

A month on, I had heard no more about Ruth and the impending court case and although I managed in the main to put it out of my mind the thought of what was to come still hung like a storm cloud, threatening to spoil an otherwise blissful day.

From time to time, I had been invited to join some of the college staff for a drink after work at the Smith and Horses in Winchton but so far I had not gone along as they tended to go on Friday evenings when I worked at the pub. Still, they were a friendly bunch and I was already getting to know a few within the English department more closely.

All in all, I truly felt as if my life had turned a corner. Of course, I still had regular cups of tea at Tom's and he occasionally came round to mine though it was presently more comfortable at his, what with my lack of furniture. Still, I was determined to save all I could out of the next three month's wages so that I could complete the basics at Hope Cottage in the upcoming January sales.

Tom's daughter Kate and I had also become closer now that I worked at the college and although we couldn't meet up in the evenings, what with her living several miles away and being busy with the children, we made time for coffee in the refectory once a week where we would catch up.

More than that though, in Kate I had found someone who had experienced the loss of a mother. Her words gave me the confidence to know that the emotional pain would ease with time. She was also very understanding, glad even of my friendship with Tom for as he was getting on in age I provided the security of knowing that there was someone close by whom he could call on should he ever need help.

Strange though that over this past month Ruth had managed to avoid me altogether. As close in proximity as the cottage was to the churchyard and Vicarage, I never once spotted her. Typical, I thought. Now that she has started a war she has gone into hiding. Analyzing this, I realized that it probably meant she wasn't actually as tough as she thought herself, for if she was certain she was in the right, then surely she would not have felt the need to hide away.

I did not want to battle with her; it wasn't me who had initiated the fight. In fact, even when I considered how wealthy I could possibly become in the future, I would have still preferred to have been left alone with my little cottage than to have been involved in this. Life had taught me that so long as one had the basic comforts, happiness was not necessarily to be found in material wealth.

I still wondered though why it was that she had despised

Emily so much and why she should also dislike me without even knowing me. Yes, Emily's diaries had opened my eyes to much of the past and through them I could plainly see that their relationship had been bad, yet I still wondered if there was something more, something which was still to be unveiled to me. Or maybe not. Perhaps, and most likely, I would never get to know the real reason for Ruth's hatred of Emily.

I did not have too much longer to wait though, for the following week, the last week in September, a letter arrived, summoning me to a preliminary court hearing in early October.

Chapter 40

Marleston England 1963

Ruth had not come home when Elizabeth had written to tell her how ill her father was. In the letter, she had explained that he was likely to die within months but even then she had not come to see him.

Not that he had asked for her mind. In the two decades since she had left for Africa Elizabeth could have counted on one hand the number of times Hubert had spoken Ruth's name. In the early days, she had often tried to talk about her. She had even tried to remind him of some little act or words of kindness Ruth had offered as a child but he had always changed the subject. For the first few years or so this had distressed Elizabeth greatly and she had continued to write regularly to Ruth even though any replies were scant and scarce.

Only last night had Elizabeth taken out of her box the few letters she had received from Ruth once again, just to be certain she had not been mistaken, but they had only confirmed what she already knew...that in all this time, Ruth had not *once* asked after her father's health nor in fact had she ever mentioned him.

Many times, especially in the early years, Elizabeth had practically pleaded with her to return, if only for a visit but not once had she taken her up on the offer; nor had she ever invited either of them to Africa. No photo, nothing had she sent which would have enabled Elizabeth to picture her only daughter so far away in her new life.

Hubert would comfort her when she would break down but he could not bring himself to speak kindly of Ruth. He would simply hold Elizabeth's hand before attempting to turn the conversation in another direction.

All through the remaining years of the war Elizabeth had worried and fretted for she knew of Ruth's involvement in the mission and she also knew that war had not escaped Africa. She accused herself of not having done enough to persuade her to stay. As the years had progressed, Ruth's letters had become shorter and more distant than ever.

What had hurt Elizabeth most, and had perhaps made her turn a corner, had been the letter she had received from Ruth in the autumn of 1950. It had simply stated that she was now married to a man named Jonathan who was also part of the missionary. It had provided no detail, no photograph. It had simply stated that she was happy and hoped that Elizabeth would '... allow her to get on with her own life and not bother her again.' It had cut her to the quick and she had secretly cried for days. Although she had shared the news with Hubert she knew that it would only serve to make him angrier and allow him to sever the ties more deeply between them and so she had tried her best to hide her hurt.

Two months had passed now since she had written to Ruth to tell her of Hubert's imminent death and although he hung on, growing weaker by the day, still she had had no reply, no acknowledgment. Still, she had wanted to give her a chance, a chance to put the past behind them and make amends with her own father. She still found it difficult to believe that Ruth could be so hard-hearted as to fail to even acknowledge the news.

And so it was, that just three weeks later, she found herself arranging his funeral alone, without the support of her only remaining child. She had stood at his grave-side that day and for the first time she had felt ashamed of her own flesh and blood. Yes she had many friends within the community and Hubert had been well respected, loved even, for the sheer numbers at the funeral reminded her of that. Yet she felt so alone. The throng of sympathetic onlookers could do nothing to assuage the overwhelming feeling of isolation.

As the first spade of earth hit the coffin she turned away, unable to bear any more and instead stared ahead, towards the place where their precious son lay buried, just a hundred yards or so off in the distance. It was her only solace, for she truly believed without even a shred of doubt that Hubert and Richard would now be reunited.

And so it had been the final letter. Never again had she been tempted to write to Ruth. She finally conceded the fact that Ruth had denied them both, that more than likely she would never again set eyes on her daughter. And it was shortly after that she had changed her will, though it had not been an easy decision. She had searched inside herself for an answer and had imagined having such a conversation with Hubert, the conversation she should have been brave enough to have had with him while he was alive and she had come to her conclusion.

Apart from a nominal sum which both had already willed to charity, Ruth would be kept out of the will and instead all she had would be left to Rebekah. She was sure, having known Hubert so well, that should she have been brave enough to ask his opinion before his death he would have agreed the same. In all likelihood, the only reason he had not raised the subject with her was because he would not have wished to upset her, for he was all too aware that despite all the pain she had caused them, Elizabeth continued to be protective of Ruth.

But he would have been wrong. Ruth could not have hurt her anymore than she had by failing to even acknowledge her own father in his time of need. Over the years, she had gone over and over the conversation that had taken place around the breakfast table on the day Ruth had told them she was leaving. The memory of her face was imprinted on Elizabeth's mind – the look of guilt when Hubert had asked the fateful question. She had tried so hard to eradicate it from her memory but had failed to do so. Even now though, she still did not believe that Ruth had intended to harm Richard that day. She believed, because she simply had to, that if he had fallen because of her then it had been an awful accident, one which not even Ruth could bring herself to discuss. The alternative answer, and the one that she knew Hubert had believed, that somehow Ruth had purposely caused his fall and subsequent death was too unbearable to consider.

And then there was Emily. Her mother had been dead now for some years but sadly Elizabeth had seen that it had happened too late for her. Though still only in her mid-forties, Elizabeth knew that Emily would never live a happy life. Richard had been the only one for her and between losing him and Rebekah and having to look after her mother she had scarcely known a moments happiness. She had had no time to herself during her youth, no-one with whom to share the burden of her role as carer and so had missed out on all the normal stages of growing up. Going out and meeting people, even holding down a job was beyond her as her mother had needed round the clock care for most of Emily's young life.

Elizabeth had witnessed how she had attended Richard's grave almost daily, how she would sit for a few moments in silence, lost in thought before scurrying back down the lane to the cottage.

Emily had remained in touch with her and Hubert over the years but it had become the scantest of friendships. Emily never seemed to have the time to engage in conversation, always having to hurry back to her mother. On one or two occasions, after the death of her grandfather, Elizabeth had tried to visit her at the cottage. She had tried to offer help but Emily had politely but firmly refused it. Elizabeth did not understand why it seemed that Emily almost punished herself in this way. Surely she could have done with some company from time to time. Was it because of the guilt of giving up Rebekah Elizabeth wondered? Though she did not believe for one minute that Emily should feel guilty she could still imagine how deep the scars were imprinted.

As the years had progressed, Elizabeth had also born witness to Emily's steady withdrawal from society. She worried for her. She worried that she may be falling ill in a similar way to her mother. And so it was, that upon her Mother's death, she and Hubert had granted her the deeds to Hope Cottage. As she had stood at her door and handed over the brown envelope containing them a single tear had rolled down Emily's cheek. No smile; and yet there *was* gratitude. Both Elizabeth and Hubert had known that she would not otherwise have been in a position to pay them rent nor would they have wished it so.

She had repaid their kindness over and over for when Hubert had become ill she had turned up one day, unannounced, and had offered to help Elizabeth to nurse him. Throughout the months of his illness, she had taken it in turns to sit at his bedside during the nights and tend to his needs just as his own daughter should have done.

She rarely smiled though and other than the necessary polite conversation regarding his health, could not be drawn into conversation. She was a true nurse; the kindest and most gentle, having had plenty of experience over the years yet Elizabeth sensed a palpable sadness which hung in the air like a dark presence.

If it had not been for Emily's help though, Elizabeth herself might have found it necessary in his latter weeks to have Hubert hospitalized and this would have broken her heart as she sensed that although he felt guilty at their having to do so much for him, he had dearly wished to remain at home.

In all these weeks, not once did Emily inquire after Ruth nor did she state an opinion about her absence. She had stood at Hubert's graveside on the day of his funeral, solemn faced, before immediately returning to her cottage.

Afterward, it was only on rare occasions that she and Elizabeth spoke. If Elizabeth approached Richard's grave whilst Emily was there she would quickly disappear. More often than not by the time Elizabeth reached his grave, she would be gone. This saddened Elizabeth deeply, as she would have loved to have befriended her. After all, they had shared an experience so close, so intimate all those years ago and Elizabeth found it difficult to understand why it was that she chose to be so alone.

At night, she would lie awake wondering if perhaps Emily blamed her. After all it had been she who had arranged Rebekah's swift adoption. She wondered if perhaps she blamed them for not having kept in touch with Rebekah for if they had, perhaps now that her own mother had gone, they might have been able to re-unite. But then if this was so, if Emily did hold a grudge against them, surely she would not have shown the kindness she had when Hubert was ill.

It puzzled Elizabeth greatly and she worried that she would never find out the truth. She worried that perhaps Emily was just becoming ill, that years of depression had rendered her beyond logic. It seemed that the only times during which Emily was capable of engaging with another was when she was in the role of carer.

Chapter 41

Marleston England 1973

Elizabeth had not turned up for evensong and Ruby was concerned. Shortly after Hubert's death, her own husband John had taken over as vicar. Elizabeth had never failed though to attend Sunday evening prayers without an explanation and so Ruby decided to check on her before returning home.

Having secured the church, she walked the short distance to the Vicarage. It was late October and the nights were drawing in. Even though it was just six-thirty it was almost dark as she carefully made her way up the path. The porch was unlit which was odd. This past few weeks, after the service, she and John had returned home with Elizabeth on occasions for a cup of tea and Ruby had noticed that on each occasion, Elizabeth had left the porch light on.

Now, the whole of the downstairs of the Vicarage was in darkness. Ruby could just make out a dim light behind the drawn curtains in one of the front bedrooms. Perhaps she is ill in bed, she thought. Not wishing to disturb her if she was resting, she considered turning back to where John sat waiting in the car. She paused on the path for a moment before deciding instead to continue towards the house. After all, she thought. What if something *is* wrong? We're all a bit long in the tooth now. She knew that Elizabeth was soon to turn eighty and even though she continued to remain fairly fit and well, one could never be too sure at her age.

She climbed the three stone steps which led to the heavy, arched front door of the Vicarage. A solid, old-fashioned brass bell stood waiting and Ruby was just about to ring it when she noticed instead a more modern, electric push bell. She rang it softly, a little guilty at the thought of disturbing her. There was no answer. She tried again, pressing more firmly now and for a few seconds longer. Still no answer. She peered back down the path towards the car, still half tempted to go home. Stepping back down the stone steps, she peered up towards the bedroom light. The curtains remained drawn. The walls of the Vicarage were built of solid stone. It *is* a wonderful house, she thought. It was gothic in style with turrets and stone mullions; a house most could only dream of. 'Elizabeth!' she shouted up towards the window. 'It's Ruby. Are you alright?' She waited for a few moments, half expecting to see the curtains move but the house remained as still and silent as the graveyard in front of it.

Had she not been so friendly with Elizabeth she would have ventured no further but this past year they had become quite close. Even though she herself was almost a decade younger they shared the same interests. Returning to the front door she rang again. The shrill sound of the bell contrasted sharply with the eerie silence which followed it. She decided to try the door. Turning the antique brass handle, she half-opened it, feeling somewhat of an intruder. 'Elizabeth?' she called. 'Are you alright?' She could see that the hallway was in total darkness. She must be inside or surely the door would have been locked, she thought. Pushing the door open to its full extent now she called again. Nothing. She felt along the wall to her right and found a light switch.

A warm glow flooded the hallway. There, at the bottom of the stairs, lay Elizabeth's body. Ruby could see that she was fully dressed, as though ready for church. Her old frame lay twisted at the bottom step. She lay face down. Ruby could detect no movement. In panic, she ran the few steps back to the front door which she had left open. 'John!' she called, as loudly as she could. 'Come quickly!'

Hoping that he would hear, she returned to Elizabeth's side. She was certain she was dead. 'Elizabeth?' Cautiously, she attempted to turn Elizabeth's head. There was no response. Elizabeth's head lay limp in her hands, her face palid and grey. Ruby was on her knees now, her heart racing. Her whole body trembled with shock. She placed two fingers on Elizabeth's neck. There! she was sure she could detect a weak pulse. Oh John, hurry up! she thought, not knowing whether to leave Elizabeth where she lay and phone for an ambulance or wait a few seconds more and hope he had heard her plea.

Her eyes had adjusted to the light in the hallway now and she could see Elizabeth's face more clearly. The left side drooped and she was as white as a ghost yet Ruby was certain she was alive, albeit barely. A voice from the door spoke, 'What's ..?' It was John at last. Breathing heavily from his race to the house, he stooped over both women. 'Is she ..?'

'She's alive! At least, I think she is. Quick ... phone for an ambulance.' Ruby sat on the hall floor, legs straight out in front, cradling Elizabeth's head in her arms. 'It's okay Elizabeth,' she spoke softly in as assuring a tone as she could muster. 'Help is on its way. Hold on dear.' There was no response from Elizabeth.

After what seemed an age but was in actual fact less than ten minutes, the ambulance arrived. The paramedics quickly assessed Elizabeth and told Ruby and John that it appeared as if she had suffered a stroke. Having inquired about next of kin and discovering there were none, they whisked her off to hospital.

Who do we telephone Ruby wondered? She had never really considered how alone Elizabeth must have been until now for she had always seemed quite happy. She had sometimes spoken of her only son and how he had died during the war but she had also mentioned an estranged daughter in Africa though she had never embellished on the story and so Ruby had not wanted to pry further.

Deciding that there was no-one whom she should ring for the moment and locating the keys to the Vicarage in a small, pewter dish beside the front door, they locked the house and followed the ambulance to the hospital. 'I can always attempt to find out the whereabouts of Ruth and write to inform her of her mother's illness later on,' she told John.

Chapter 42

Although Emily rarely spoke to anyone in the village, preferring to keep to herself, she sensed that something was wrong. Most days, as she sat looking out of her front window, she would be aware of Elizabeth's presence in the churchyard. She never let it be known that she watched her as she did not want to engage her in conversation. The memories of the past were just too painful to allow them back out into the open. Nevertheless she still cared for Elizabeth. After all, if it had not been for her she would never have had the opportunity to love. Short lived though it had been, it was the only time in her life that Emily had known true happiness. She locked those precious months spent with Richard and the even shorter precious days spent with Rebekah in a heart-shaped box and only ever opened it when she was alone.

In doing so, from time to time, she was able to re-visit the memories. She could play out her fantasy from the safety of the cottage where she would lay the table for three and bring them their meals. They would laugh and talk before retiring to the sitting room where they would play games together, read, draw and teach Rebekah all sorts of things. If she were to talk to Elizabeth about Richard and Rebekah, then the dialogue would need to be spoken in the past tense and this she could not bear.

But when Elizabeth did not appear at either Richard or Hubert's grave for the second day she knew that something was wrong. As much as she did not want to get involved again she also felt deep down that she owed both her own life, though for this she held little regard, and the life of Rebekah for she had never forgotten that night when both of them had been saved by Elizabeth and Hubert. She knew that Elizabeth was alone now, just like herself, and that being an old lady she was becoming vulnerable. She decided to wait one more day, after all, perhaps she had merely caught a cold.

On the third day she watched more closely and even ventured up the cemetery path towards the church in order to get a better view of the Vicarage. Seeing no sign of Elizabeth from the path, she returned home but remained watching from her little window.

At two thirty she saw a car pull up and a man and a woman approach the house. They seemed to remain inside for some fifteen minutes or so before returning back down the path. Surely if Elizabeth is ill they would not have paid so short a visit she thought. Her palms were clammy and her heart beat as fast as a bird in a trap as she approached them. Apart from the local grocery delivery boy, she had not spoken to anyone for about a year now; yet a sixth sense told her that something was wrong.

Unaware of her somewhat disheveled appearance, she addressed them both. She spoke softly, the sound of her own voice strange to her ears, 'E, excuse me.' She was oblivious to the somewhat surprised reaction her approach had on them both for she did not see what they saw – a middle aged woman with long, greying, uncombed hair and a vacant, sad look in her eyes. They stopped in their tracks but did not speak. She wanted to run, to return to the safety of her cottage, away from these strangers who stared. Her heart beat so loudly now in her chest that she was sure they must hear it. She could not meet their gaze.

She was just about to turn away when the woman spoke,

'Can I help you?' Head down and her back already turned away from them Emily paused. Without turning to face them she asked her question, 'I was just wondering if Elizabeth was alright?' Her voice was timid as a mouse.

'May I ask who you are?' It was the woman's voice again, somewhat haughty though not necessarily unkind. 'I'm a-a neighbour, that's all,' she managed, nodding in the direction of the cottage. 'It's just that I haven't seen her for a few days and I wondered ...'

'Oh I see ... I'm sorry,' the woman replied, this time smiling. 'No actually she isn't ... alright I mean ... she's had a stroke. She's in Winchton Hospital. We've just called round to collect a few of her belongings. Shall I tell her you were asking after her?'

She turned to face them. Her hands shook. She clasped them tightly to disguise the fact. 'Is she *very* ill?' she asked again, unable to hide her concern. She attempted to make eye-contact with the woman in order to try to read the severity of Elizabeth's illness but failed to do so.

'Well things look more promising now. For the first forty-eight hours it was touch and go. She was in a coma. She's out of it now though. Just this morning she awoke and is trying to speak. Who shall I say is asking?' she asked for a second time.

'Emily... just tell her it's Emily. I wish her well.' She turned again then and hurried back towards her cottage without another word.

'Strange one that!' John said, watching her hasty retreat.

She did not even register the gentleman's words as she scurried away.

Emily quickly entered the cottage and stumbled towards the safety of her window to the world. Looking back towards the church, she watched as the strangers drove off. Her mind was in turmoil. What if Elizabeth should die? What if she should never get the chance to tell her how grateful she was? Still, there was nothing to be done about it. The thought of visiting her at the hospital was out of the question. She had not been further than the churchyard in three years. *Agoraphobia* ... she knew that was what people called it ... yet she knew it was greater than that. At times the fear would overwhelm her, threaten to suffocate her. Her throat would constrict and she would shake uncontrollably; then the palpitations would begin accompanied by the tight, aching band which gripped her left arm in a vice.

Many times over the past ten years or so she had thought she was dying but He, this demon who visited, had not taken her. Eventually the feelings would subside and she would simply find herself alone and left to fight over and over again. It had gone on for so long now that she was not even able to remember when it had begun. She only knew that He had grown, become a monster. He was stronger and more ferocious each time He visited. Her fear fuelled Him.

She had recorded her last wishes. An envelope lay in wait on the mantelpiece, addressed to, 'Whomsoever should find my body.' Its contents were brief and unemotional. They merely spoke of what she wanted done with her remains. Even though she was barely fifty years old she knew she would not live for much longer. She knew that this demon would take her one day. He was too powerful to fight but He toyed with her, bringing her back from the edge of death time and time again. Yes, when He had finished playing with her and was ready to move on to another victim He would end it. She wished it would be soon. Sometimes she begged Him to end it but He only laughed in her face ... so she had stopped begging, thinking that if He realized she wanted it to be over He would just enjoy it all the more and make her wait even longer.

So each time He came, she would pretend. She would

simply be still, blank as a new canvas and wait for Him to do his work ... and each time He left she would remain quiet for a few minutes until her heart rate calmed and the invisible iron bands loosened from her arms, before returning to whatever it was she had been doing before His visit. But she could *not* go out into the world; for apart from when she went to the cemetery, He would follow her. He would pounce upon her unexpectedly and embarrass her, make her seem a fool ... so she could *not* go out. No, she had given up on that long ago. At least when He came now, as He frequently did, there was no-one to witness His effect on her. She would suffer His torment in private and wait for Him to abate.

And so she contorted with fear when, just a week later, the same woman she had spoken to in the cemetery turned up at her door and announced that Elizabeth was asking for her.

Chapter 43

A month had passed by and still she tormented herself over whether or not to visit Elizabeth. The woman had kindly offered to take her to the hospital but she couldn't face it. Instead, she asked that should Elizabeth be well enough to come home she should be called upon to visit her at home. She was sure that should this happen she would be able to manage the few extra steps from the cemetery to the Vicarage.

If He followed her there, she would not have far to run home. She even offered to help nurse Elizabeth should she return home. She knew that she had not lost those skills. After all, she had had more experience at nursing then anything else in life. She knew that should this be required, it would be second nature.

It was six weeks after the stroke that Elizabeth was brought home. The woman, who she had learned was named Ruby, had come to tell Emily. She informed her that although paralyzed down one side, Elizabeth could manage to speak a little and although her speech was slurred her overall condition was stable. A private nurse had been arranged to stay at the Vicarage round the clock. This was the only condition upon which she had been allowed home. Ruby had informed Emily that Elizabeth still asked for her. Emily had thanked her and told her to assure Elizabeth that she would visit soon.

Several times over the last three days she had tried to

make it but each time she had had to turn back. The panic had overwhelmed her and she had fled home. Calm and alone again in her cottage she had taken out the gown which she had sewn for Rebekah all those years ago and held it in her lap. It looked tiny in her hands; the delicate lace had begun to yellow. Strange that it was not this baby stage Emily imagined when she thought of the three of them. In her night-time dreams, Rebekah *was* still a tiny baby, and yet in the presence of daylight she had grown to a child of around four or five years of age and had then stopped growing. She was funny and lively, curious and kind and both her and Richard loved her so very much. Perhaps this was why she had put away the gown and had never taken it out again. This gown was the stuff of dreams, sometimes nightmares, when she would hold Rebekah warm in her arms for a few moments before finding her once again wrenched away from her by the Invisible Thing. She would call out to her, reach out for her, feel the cord SNAP ... and then she would be gone again, out of reach, never to return.

So why had she sewn the gown she wondered? She knew from the very first day that she would never see Rebekah again, that she would never get to dress her tiny infant in it...so why? She was sure that had she asked Elizabeth to send it on to her she would have done so. Perhaps the Wilkinsons would even have kindly dressed her in it, for her *birth* mother's sake, even though Rebekah would not have understood the love with which it had been sewn. Those dimly-lit nights which had followed Rebekah's birth seemed pointless now. In the seclusion of her bedroom she had secretly stitched, all the while knowing that the garment would never be worn. She understood the reason why she had now taken the dress out again. It was an attempt to evoke the memory of that night. She hoped that it might give her the strength she needed to make it to Elizabeth.

By the time she rang the bell she felt as though her legs would give way but there was no going back. The kindly looking stranger who invited her in did not dwell on her worn-out dress nor her shoulders, bare despite the wind that howled mercilessly on this early December afternoon. She had merely asked Emily to follow her to Elizabeth's bedroom and had offered her tea.

Once inside, Emily gazed toward where Elizabeth appeared to lay asleep in the bed. She realized that it had been some years since she had last entered this room; for Hubert had been gone a long time. It had not changed. The room just felt sadder, emptier somehow. Tentatively, she approached the bed and sat in the armchair which had been placed beside it. She spoke her name softly, 'Elizabeth?' Elizabeth's eyes flickered open and she gazed towards Emily. Her lights were extinguished, Emily could see that. She remembered that Elizabeth's eyes had always been illuminated by the same warm glow as Richard's but now they just gazed dully towards her. Elizabeth appeared to try to smile but her mouth was lop-sided and instead she dribbled down her chin. The kindly nurse who had shown Emily in appeared as if from nowhere and quickly wiped Elizabeth's face.

It was this one simple gesture which had flicked the switch. Her nursing instincts were immediately triggered. She no longer felt afraid of being out of the comfort of her own environment. She smiled and reached for Elizabeth's hand. 'How are you feeling? I'm sorry that I didn't make it to the hospital, only ...' She stopped. She did not want to lie. She did not want to make up some lame excuse, Elizabeth deserved better than that.

She sat for a while, stroking Elizabeth's hand and talking quietly to her before promising to return the following day. Elizabeth had seemed to understand what Emily had said to her, even though she wasn't able to talk back.

And so it was that Emily had began to visit her daily. She would help out by sitting with her at times, nursing her needs when Elizabeth's own nurse needed to go out or when she needed to attend to other household duties and Emily became a God-send over the weeks. She saved Elizabeth from having to hire a house-maid as well as a nurse.

Chapter 44

Six months had passed since Elizabeth's stroke and it was now approaching the end of April. Elizabeth had made very little progress though she had remained stable and between Emily and the nurse her needs were met.

Emily had been just about to take her leave when Elizabeth had summoned her back with a small movement of the hand. She patted the bed, gesturing for Emily to sit. With her good hand, she retrieved an envelope from beneath her pillow and placed it in Emily's hand. Her index finger hovered above the envelope, urging Emily to open it.

It took Emily some moments before she understood what it was that she was holding. As her eyes scanned the document she noticed that Elizabeth repeatedly pointed towards her, muttering in a slurred voice, 'You ... you.'

In her hands lay the deed to Richard's grave. Plot 204, Marleston Cemetery. Emily's heart pounded. What did Elizabeth mean by this she wondered? Now they would need to play one of their regular guessing games. Emily could see that Elizabeth appeared a little distressed, her eyes pleading with Emily to understand. 'Do you want me to have it?' Emily asked tentatively. Elizabeth nodded and attempted a smile. Then she reached towards the document as if to take it back. Emily handed it to her. Her rheumy eyes scanned the page and then she tapped it. Emily looked again to where Elizabeth pointed. Now she noticed for the first time that the document stated that the plot had been prepared for two. She looked again at Elizabeth. 'You mean you want me to be with him ... when I die?' Elizabeth sighed, relieved that she had understood so easily and nodded. 'Always,' she managed.

'You mean you had planned to give me the opportunity to be reunited with Richard ever since his death?' she smiled.

Again Elizabeth nodded.

Emily had not really cared about what should become of her body upon her death until now. In fact, the envelope which lay on her mantelpiece back at the cottage asked that her remains be cremated and scattered in the river below the cottage. Now, this gift meant that she and Richard could be together again. She bowed down and kissed Elizabeth on the cheek. 'Thank you Elizabeth ... I've never stopped loving him you know.'

Elizabeth nodded, tears in her eyes but she smiled and Emily could sense her relief.

'Yours ... solicitor,' she managed, continuing to clasp Emily's hand.

'You mean it's mine now? You've had it changed with the solicitor?'

'Yes, yes ... Ruth would never ...'

There was no need for her to continue. Emily knew only too well what she meant. She merely nodded to show that she understood.

Gently she took the precious document from Elizabeth and returned it to its envelope. 'I can't thank you enough Elizabeth. It means the world to me. I'll see you tomorrow. You rest now.' She planted another kiss on her cool, white cheek, noticing how paper-thin Elizabeth's skin was and left.

*

It was the twenty third of the month. Elizabeth's nurse had gone to town when Emily heard a commotion downstairs.

A car door had slammed and seconds later so had the front door. At first, she had supposed it to be the doctor for he was due a visit. She could cope with this, as she was now familiar with his presence; after all, it had been he who had delivered Rebekah in this very house, but when she heard unfamiliar footsteps on the stairs she panicked.

Although she was now quite comfortable in this house, she could not bear to socialize with visitors and each time they were due, she would retreat back to her cottage, leaving the nurse to deal with them. This time she had been caught unawares. Before she had time to think, the bedroom door flew open and there stood Ruth. Emily recognized her immediately, even though it had been many years since she had last seen her. Ruth's narrow, pinched expression was ever harder now that she had aged. Her once raven hair was now greying and tightly twisted into a severe bun which sat on top of her head but her steely eyes were instantly recognizable.

She felt herself begin to tremble as Ruth approached the bed, seemingly unaware of who Emily was. She only stared towards her mother who lay asleep. Emily stood to leave and it was then that Ruth recognized her. 'You!' she spat. 'I should have known! You *would* come around at a time like this wouldn't you? Leaching no doubt.'

Panic engulfed her like a wave. She could find no words with which to defend herself. As she headed towards the door, head down, she heard Ruth shout, 'Get out of *my* house!'

As she stumbled towards the top of the stairs she bumped into a man whom she did not recognize. It was only later that evening, when she had calmed down that she understood that he was likely to have been Ruth's husband.

Sadly, this would be the last time that Emily would see Elizabeth. From that day on, Ruth remained firmly ensconced at the Vicarage. Emily had not even had chance to say goodbye. Ruth had made it clear that she was not welcome in the house and Emily would never have found the courage to disobey her. Elizabeth remained too ill to fight her own corner and in fact only lived a few more months.

There were whispers in the village that of course Ruth had only returned to claim her inheritance though such rumours did not reach Emily, since she had no acquaintances amongst the villagers.

She did not even feel able to attend Elizabeth's funeral. Elizabeth's nurse had called round to inform her of Elizabeth's death and to thank her for her help during the time when they had both nursed her. Ruth had of course kept the nurse on during the remainder of Elizabeth's illness. She had told Emily that she had been given little respite over the past few months as Ruth had hardly lifted a finger to help. However, as Emily was not the type to gossip her words of complaint fell upon deaf ears.

On the day of Elizabeth's funeral the rain fell in huge, gulping sobs. Emily watched from the safety of her little front window as they lowered her coffin into the ground. Her gaze never left the coffin so she would not have been able to say how Elizabeth's mourners had coped.

Once the first spade of earth had hit the ground, she ambled into the kitchen without shedding a single tear. She was beyond tears. In fact, she could not remember the last time she had felt them wet her face or sting her eyes. Apart from fear, she was, and had been for many years, almost completely devoid of all emotion. Too blank, too empty now to feel. She simply went through the motions of existing, her stray cats the only company she kept. In fact, the sound of her own frail voice surprised her these days for she would only hear it when she spoke to them and barely recognized it as her own. Of course, *they* did not reply though they showed their gratitude in other ways by curling themselves around her swollen ankles as she sat by her meager fire and rubbing themselves against her as she prepared their food. Since being thrown out of Elizabeth's house, they had now become her only source of interaction with the living.

Chapter 45

Ruth sat stiff as a board as the will was read, her breathing laboured, her piercing eyes cold as steel. For some moments, she could not speak then, her face contorted, she spat the words, 'I will fight it! I will fight with all my strength and I will not give in until the day I die!'

The solicitor had simply returned her steely gaze from the other side of the table. 'The law is the law I'm afraid. These were your mother's wishes and there is little to be done about it.' He had known Elizabeth personally and Hubert too. As a member of the church he was quite aware of Ruth's absence these past decades and so if Ruth was expecting sympathy from him then she would be mistaken.

'Did *you* influence her? If I find out that you did then I'll have you struck off!' she hissed at him.

Struggling to curb his anger, he coolly replied, 'Feel free to look into the records if you wish. You will not find my name on any paperwork connected to your mother. I was not even present when she visited our offices to change the will. You do as you feel you must but you will find nothing to tar my name I can assure you.'

Ruth stood abruptly. 'Come on Jonathan,' she seethed. 'We're leaving. We will ask our own solicitor to contest this ludicrous matter.' She leaned again towards the solicitor who had managed to remain coolly seated behind his desk and added, 'Mark my words, her *bastard* will never get a penny of *my* money. I will prove that my mother was not of sound mind when this ... this piece of rubbish was written!' She swiped her hand across the table, flinging the will from where it lay on the desk to the floor. Dealing him one last vicious stare she stormed from the room.

Chapter 46

Marleston, England October 1996

Once again, Tom was kind enough to accompany me, to offer moral support. I had had to take a morning off work to attend the hearing and had dreaded it all week. If I possibly could have, I would have avoided it altogether. Part of me, the old part who would lie down and play victim would have preferred to have given in and said that Ruth could have her way. I was happy just to have been given the opportunity to begin a new life here in Marleston and as Hope Cottage was becoming more homely by the day I did not desire anything more. However, the other part of me, the new and braver part encouraged me to see it through. After all, why should I just give in ... I had been defeated by a bully in the past and was trying hard never to allow that to happen again.

Even if I had given in to Ruth without a fight, I supposed that the outcome would have remained the same. The law was the law and it was not up to her to render Elizabeth's wishes void. I had learned enough from Emily's diary to believe that Elizabeth and Hubert had been good people and that Elizabeth would not have taken this course of action without much consideration.

I had decided to simply go with the flow and let the outcome be determined by the courts. I had promised myself that after all I had been through over the past year or so, I would not allow what, when it boiled down to it, was simply a matter of money to overshadow my current happiness.

And I *was* happy. Happier than I could remember having been for a long time. Yes, there were dark moments but I was happy now that I had my own home and a life which meant I no longer felt it necessary to please others. No longer did I have to constantly watch my words or consider the possible effect of what I said before I spoke. No longer did I have to seek permission before going out. I had never been able to pre-judge Simon's reaction to my suggestions and I would often set out to please only to have it thrown in my face. The years of being on tenterhooks were over. I could please myself now and yes, all things considered, I *was* happy.

Even so, as I sat waiting, I could not completely swallow my nerves. When the County Court Judge read out my name I felt as though my legs would give way. However, before I knew it, having confirmed I was the legal owner and occupant of Hope Cottage, it was over; court was adjourned to allow the judge time to consider the evidence she needed and we were all dismissed.

I still felt like a criminal though. Unable to meet Ruth face to face I hurried outside and gulped in fresh air before swiftly returning to the car park. Tom and I managed a quick cuppa back at the cottage before I shot off back to college to teach my classes.

Settled again in the safety of home that evening, I reflected on the day. It would not be the end of the matter - today had been just the beginning. I knew that Ruth had failed in her attempt to overturn the will years ago but at the same time I realized that she had not then believed that my Mother would ever be traced. It was little wonder that she had reacted so negatively when she had first learned of my belonging to Emily. She must have quickly put two and two together and realized that Mum would have been

Emily's daughter; the Rebekah who was due to inherit.

Perhaps she hoped now that as Mum was deceased she would have a stronger case, what with the lineage being another step further on. Yet she was not a dull woman; that much was evident from the way she spoke, so why then would she spend so much time and money when she had such little hope of winning? I would have understood her actions more if she had had children of her own as at least then she would have perhaps been justified in feeling that *they* had been innocent victims of Elizabeth's actions. There had to be more to it, it was just a matter of whether or not I would ever discover the real truth.

It was only as I carefully replaced the deeds back in the file that I considered for the first time the name of the cottage. What a contradiction, I thought, that Hope Cottage should be named so aptly on *my* part and yet so *inaptly* on Emily's. I wondered who had named it such. Could it have been Emily's parents? Had they given it it's name after having escaped the tyranny of Emily's grandfather? I quickly realized that this would not have been possible as back then it had been owned by Elizabeth and Hubert. Perhaps then the cottage's name had been the very thing that had motivated them to come and live here.

Or perhaps I was simply thinking too deeply; after all, I guessed that the cottage dated from around the turn of the 19th century and so was possibly older than the Vicarage itself. Perhaps the name pre-dated all of my ancestors and was simply a coincidence.

Chapter 47

I wished I could have seen an image of Emily, just to see if Mum bore any resemblance to her or if indeed I myself did but there was not a single photograph of her amongst the paperwork discovered by Steve. Even if there were no resemblance, it still would have been nice to be able to see if the image of her in my mind matched in the flesh.

Getting up from the kitchen stool, I entered the living room and took out my photo album. It was full of favourite photos collected by both Mum and I over the years. Remembering back to the very first time I had entered the cottage, I removed the photo that I had discovered upstairs in Emily's bedroom and once again examined it closely. Judging by the uniform he wore, I was almost certain it was Richard. No matter how hard I looked though I could see nothing of Mum in him. Perhaps it was because it was a black and white image; maybe if it had been in colour, I would have found some likeness. I put on my reading glasses and peered more closely. Was there something about the eyes? Although he looked sad, there seemed a hint of warmth in them which reminded me of Mum's eyes.

An idea came to me then. Snatching my coat and bag from the hook in the hallway, I jumped in the car and drove off.

The public library was empty except for two elderly men who were silently reading the daily newspapers at a shared table. 'Excuse me,' I approached the desk clerk tentatively, not even sure if I had come to the right place to begin such a search.

She peered down at me over her glasses. 'Yes?' she asked rather curtly.

'I was wondering how I would go about trying to track down old photos of Marleston from around the 1940's. Would there be any old newspapers here which might hold some? I know it's a long-shot but ...'

She cut me off, 'What exactly are you looking for? Photographs of what?' she sighed.

'Well, I've recently discovered that I have long lost relatives in the village. In fact, both my maternal grandmother and grandfather originated from there. His father was the church rector for a long time. I just thought that perhaps there might be photos, you know of annual fetes or some such ... only I've never seen an image of them and I'd love to find one.' I could feel my palms sweating with anxiety.

She continued to examine me sternly, then to my surprise her face suddenly relaxed and she even managed a brief quiver of a smile, 'Oh I see. Well, it'll be like finding a needle in a haystack but I suppose if you have the time.'

'I do, I'm not working today,' I answered, returning her smile to show appreciation and perhaps a little desperation.

'Well I'll show you where they're kept. They're on microfiche. If it's fetes you're after, your best bet is to search through the August months. I know that Marleston always held a large fete in the rectory grounds every August Bank Holiday. In fact, they continue to do so to this day.'

She came out from behind her desk and proceeded to march briskly away, towards the back of the library. Although she didn't suggest I follow her, I did so anyway, feeling like a lap-log behind its master. It came to me then, just as we entered a room at the back. 'What about deaths? Would there be any obituary notices in the newspapers?' I asked.

She turned in my direction and replied rather sarcastically, 'Well of course, but only if the family had listed the death in the obituaries column.'

Thinking on my feet, I mumbled, 'August 1940. Where might I find those?'

She clicked her tongue against the roof of her mouth impatiently and sighed. 'Look, I'll show you how to use this and then you can search for yourself.' After a quick demonstration and the advice that I should probably search the local paper of the time she announced that she needed to get back to her work.

She retreated towards the door, matronly heels clicking on the parquet flooring. Just as she reached for the handle, she turned and glanced back in my direction. 'If you have no luck, try the locals, you know, people in the village. You'd be surprised what they can come up with. Often better than any official records.'

I thanked her. As soon as she was gone, I began scrolling through the date columns on the monitor until I reached 1940. My finger scrolled to the month of August. I had learned from Emily's diary that this had been the month that Richard had died but had no idea of the actual date. Focusing on the obituary pages, it took me just a few minutes to find what I was looking for.

The announcement read, ***'Richard Harrison, beloved son of Hubert and Elizabeth and brother to Ruth. Sadly passed away August 17th.'***

It was followed by a more personal and touching memorial which read, ***'Our hearts are broken by the loss of such a wonderful son but we know he is safe in the arms of Our Lord. Until we meet again, Mum and Dad.'***

The photograph accompanying the piece was a close-up of Richard's face. In it he wore a beret and was dressed in uniform. I therefore guessed that it would have been taken only months prior to his death. I looked more closely. He was smiling at the camera and yet his eyes were solemn. I could now see more plainly the similarity between *his* eyes and Mum's for they both held the same expression. My throat tightened as I stared at his face. Although the rest of his features bore no resemblance to Mum's his eyes almost definitely did. In this image his expression reminded me so much of Mum's during the last few weeks of her life, when she would look at me and try to smile, but the sadness behind her eyes was impossible to hide. The expression in Richard's eyes looked as if he too believed that death was imminent. A little breathless with emotion, I returned to the desk. Informing the clerk that I had found a photograph of my deceased grandfather, I asked somewhat timidly if it would be at all possible to have a copy printed.

She sighed. 'Yes but there will be a five pounds charge and I couldn't do it at the moment, you'd have to call back in a few days time.'

Grateful that I had remembered to bring my bag, I paid her and gave her the precise date of the edition as well as Richard's name. Hastily returning to the microfiche, I proceeded to trawl through more recent editions. I had learned from Mum's paperwork that she had inherited Hope Cottage almost a year before her own death and wondered when exactly Emily had died. Being only too aware that apart from Mum and I, Emily had had no friends or family I still hoped that someone within the community might have placed an obituary for her. No such luck though. Despite trawling back a whole year from the time of Mum's inheritance I found no mention of her. Again it struck me as sad that even her death had not been publicly acknowledged. It was almost as if she had never existed, except that *I* knew she had. To me, her diary and letters were precious evidence of her life.

Another two hours passed by and although I continued to trawl through the newspapers of 1940 I found nothing else except for a mention of the farewell party which Emily had written about in her diary. On this day, the community had gathered at the Vicarage to say goodbye to both Richard and his fellow men before they had left for war. No photographs accompanied this story though. I arranged to pick up the copy of the photograph from the obituary on my way home from college the following Thursday and left.

The clerk's suggestion of asking the locals remained with me though so on the way back I decided to call in on Bessie at the pub to ask her if she knew of anyone who might be able to enlighten me further. 'Oh lass, now why didn't I think of it earlier?' She smiled at me, her round face ruddy from the heat of the oven. 'Your old friend Mr Ghent ... bit of a local historian he is. Now *he* might have something. Why don't you call round and pay him a visit?'

It was music to my ears. Since his return, I had kept in contact with John and had helped out with the animals from time to time. If truth be told, I had missed them and although the past weeks had been very busy I'd still found the time to spend the odd hour with them on Sunday mornings before my shift at the pub. He'd never once mentioned Emily to me though, nor had he ever asked about my inheritance. Perhaps he just didn't want to come across as nosy, I assumed, thinking that if he had been female I would probably have been quizzed by now. Although I would have liked to have visited him there and then I decided I'd leave it until my usual Sunday visit.

And so it was that on the following Sunday, whilst we were both cleaning out the chicken coop, I raised the question. 'I was wondering John,' I paused and looked him in the eye, 'if there was any possibility that you may know of the existence of any photos of my grandmother, Emily. It's just that I have no idea what she looked like and ...well ... I'd love to be able to picture her.'

He stood as straight as his old back would allow and

pondered my question. 'Well Cass, she wasn't much of a mixer you know. Kept out of a lot of what went on the the village, especially in her latter years, but I'll have a look. Got quite a lot of old photos of the village which go far back so you never know.'

'I would be ever so grateful John, for anything I mean. All I've been told is that she was dark-haired, severe looking and...well she'd let herself go it seemed. But I think she'd suffered from mental illness for some time, in fact, for many years.'

He rubbed his chin in thought. 'Aye well, can't say I can add any more to what you already know. Didn't really know her. Don't think anyone did. Wouldn't let anyone in so to speak. Can't help those who don't want to be helped see can we?' He paused, studying my expression closely. 'Still, sad though. Never mind. As long as *you're* alright, that's what matters isn't it?'

'Yes you're right. I just wondered that's all. Were you living round here during the war?'

'Aye, I was, well just outside Marleston. My Da kept the big farm on the hill.' He pointed away from the garden a mile or so into the distance towards a copse of trees. 'Just beyond the tree line it is. I was the youngest of four, two sisters and me older brother Gerald. He still has the farm. His son looks after it now though. I was only thirteen when war broke out. Had to help me Da a lot then 'cos Gerald went off to war. Had a farewell party for him in the Vicarage they did, him and Richard that is. Richard was the vicar's son and a friend of me Da. Sad though. He died during the war yet it wasn't the war that killed him.' He paused, reminiscing. I felt my heart quicken in my chest but said nothing. 'Gerald took it hard, Richard dying. They went off together and were posted together see. Said he was with him when he got injured. Helped get him to safety. But when Richard came home to recuperate he met with a terrible accident which finished him off.' He tutted and shook his head.

I had not taken my eyes off him up to this point. Not wanting to stop his flow I continued even now to nod at him, encouraging him to tell me more. He seemed to understand, for he continued, 'Buried in the churchyard of course. Our Gerald still tends his grave when he can make it down with his arthritis. Always puts a little cross and poppy on for him on Remembrance Sunday in respect for how he fought for his country, even if it wasn't for long.'

Returning to the present, he smiled at me and pitched his fork back into the straw before continuing, 'Anyway, you didn't come to ask about my brother and his friends did you? Get side tracked sometimes I do. Just that it brought back memories that's all. 'Twas a splendid party you know.'

Should I tell him I wondered? It seemed that no-one in the village had ever discovered that Richard and Emily had been in love, or at least how serious their relationship had become, as they had been forced to keep it secret from Emily's grandfather. Would I be betraying their memory if it got out that they'd had a child together? *I* believed there was no shame in it but I also knew that sometimes those of a certain generation still thought otherwise when it came to illegitimacy. And what about Ruth? If it got back to her that I had spread gossip amongst the village how would she take it? None too kindly, I believed. But why should I worry about Ruth? She certainly wasn't concerned about me, except for her desire to be rid of me. I decided to keep it a secret, at least for the time being. I remembered back to my very first day in Marleston, when I had stood at what I now knew to be Richard's grave and had wondered about the poppy cross. Then, I had assumed that it had been placed there on Palm Sunday. Now I knew that it would have lain there since the previous November which pretty much proved that Ruth didn't tend her own brother's grave.

'Do you think you might have any photos of the party?' I asked. 'Only I know Emily attended. She wrote about it in her diary.'

'Aw Cass, I don't think I do but tell you what, next time I go up to the farm, I'll ask Gerald to have a look. I'll be off up there within the week I'm sure.'

'Thanks John. I'd be really grateful for anything,' I said smiling. 'Anyway, better be off now, got to get cleaned up for work. I'm still doing Sunday lunches with Betty at the pub.'

'Okay Cass. If he's got anything, I'll bring them down and show you next Sunday alright? Tell you what, I'll give him a ring later so he has chance to have a look before I call round.'

Chapter 48

The following week was busy as usual but I still found my thoughts returning to the conversation I'd had with John and hoped that he would manage to find a photograph for me. On the Thursday, I picked up the photo of Richard from the library as arranged. Back at the cottage, I put it in a silver frame and placed it on the windowsill facing the churchyard. It seemed apt somehow and gave me a small sense of pleasure. I felt sure that Emily would have approved.

I couldn't wait to go round to John's the following Sunday, though I was half afraid that it would yield nothing. He met me at the back gate and he was smiling. 'Come and have a cuppa before we start,' he said. 'I've managed to get what you wanted. It's not the clearest of images but at least it's a start.'

I followed him inside and sat impatiently while he poured the tea. He passed a brown envelope across the table nodding as he did so. I found my fingers trembling a little as I opened it. Out slid a single photograph, faded around the edges. 'Think they were caught unawares!' he grinned before I'd had the chance to study the image. Looking down, I saw that the photo had been taken inside a marquee, with trestle tables dressed in white. Expecting to see some kind of portrait, my eyes scanned the picture. In the far right corner of the shot, I saw a rather indistinct image of a young man and a young woman standing close together. The man stood almost behind her, his right arm wrapped around her waist. It was not posed. On closer inspection though, I could see how the man smiled at her whilst she in turn looked surprised, anxious even. Her left hand was placed on the arm that held her waist, as if about to remove it. I frowned, trying to get a clearer image of them both. In the background, others were milling about but these two were really the subject of the photo.

John grinned as he spoke, 'Sweet on her he was. There was talk that they'd have married if he had lived and if she had been ... well her own Ma was very sick and she nursed her.' He studied my face, as if to gauge my reaction.

I pointed at the couple. It was difficult to identify Richard as being the same person as the photograph from the paper. This young man appeared happier, healthier, but then I supposed he hadn't been to war at this point. 'Is this them? Emily and Richard?' I asked.

'Aye, the day of the party. The party I told you about last week, the one to see them off so to speak. My brother Gerald took it, only I don't think either of them knew. He dabbled in photography see, always catching folk unawares he was.' He chuckled.

Feeling inside my jacket pocket which I'd slung over the back of the kitchen chair I retrieved my reading glasses. It was only recently that I'd needed them, a sign of age I supposed, but lately I'd found that if I wanted to study anything close then I needed to rely on them more and more. I gazed again at the image. Indeed, Emily looked happy, yet nervous too. Judging by the pose, Richard had caught her unawares and knowing what I did about her grandfather, I knew she would have been terrified of being caught with a man's arm around her. Neither of them directly faced the camera so it was difficult to compare any likeness between either of them with Mum or I. I could see that Emily's long hair was somewhat unruly, just like my own, for strands of it had escaped the pins she had used in an attempt to tie it back. Her stature was fine. She appeared quite tall, unless of course Richard was short though I didn't think so if Ruth's height was anything to go by. *She* struck rather a formidable height for a woman. Emily was svelte. The fingers which held his were long and slender. Her hands reminded me of Mum's and for a moment I could sense her touch. I shivered. It was so strange to be able to put an image to what I had learned about in the diary.

When I looked up again, John was watching me intently from across the table. 'Thank you so much John,' I said thrilled. 'Do you think your brother would mind if I took it to town and had a copy made?'

'No need ... it's yours. He told me to give it to you. Only too pleased to help he was. Also said he'd got more photos up in the attic. Can't promise there's any of Emily of course but he said one day soon, when my nephew's not too busy, he'll send him up there to have a look. Probably got more of Richard 'cos they were friends since childhood but maybe not of Emily.'

He looked so pleased. He could tell from my face how glad I was to finally be able to picture her; though of course he had no idea that what he had shown me was indeed a picture of *both* my grandparents. I once again considered telling him. If his brother had more photographs of Richard then of course I'd *love* to see them. But how could I tell him that without also telling him the truth. I bit the bullet. 'Can I tell you something in confidence John?' I began tentatively.

His expression changed. The smile disappeared and he looked serious. 'Course you can. Never one to break a confidence me.'

And so I gave him the story; at least the bare bones of it. Not once did he interrupt; he just sat quietly, hanging on to every word until I'd finished. 'Well I never!' he exclaimed when I finally stopped speaking. 'What a shame. I mean, if he hadn't been killed it could all have been so different couldn't it? And to think ... he never even knew. What an awful shame!'

'I know. Strange how life turns out sometimes isn't it John?'

'Aye it is Cass. I can see why you wanted to keep quiet 'bout it though. Bit of a devil is that Ruth. You'd have a life of it if she thought you were spreading gossip 'bout her family. Still, no rights really. It's not as if she's such a goody two shoes herself; ran off to Africa for years she did, not long after Richard died and never came back until her own Ma was dying, not even when her own father passed away. Talk of the village she was when she did that. Sticks in my mind.' He tapped his head with one finger as if to indicate the very spot where the memory lay buried. 'He was a good sort her old Da and she couldn't even be bothered to come to his funeral. Nasty piece of work she is. Still, wouldn't encourage you to get on the wrong side of her though.'

'I think it's already too late for that,' I answered with a nervous twitch. I told him about the will and how she was fighting it in court. If Ruth wanted to have secrets then that was up to her but I wasn't the secretive sort so why should I change for her? As far as I could see, neither Mum nor Emily had done any wrong, they had only *been* wronged and I had nothing to be ashamed about.

John was nonplussed. 'I'll not say owt to anyone,' he promised.

'When it's all over John I really won't care but best keep quiet about it for the time being till the court case is over,' I replied. 'Come on, let's get those animals cleaned up. They'll think we've forgotten about them,' I laughed, hearing the cacophony of calls from outside. They were used to being fussed as soon as I arrived and judging by the racket beyond the back door were getting a little impatient.

That night, I lay in bed clutching the photograph. I must have looked at it at least thirty times over the course of the day. I was finally beginning to piece together the missing parts of the puzzle. I wished I could have shown Mum. I felt certain that it would have meant a lot to her to have known where she'd come from. Placing the photo on my bedside cabinet, I turned out the lamp and closed my eyes ...

Chapter 49

She had fallen. I cradled her head in my arms as we sat curled at the bottom of the narrow, steep stairs. Her eyes were closed. I stroked the hair away from her closed eyes and pleaded with her to open them.

I woke with a start, my heart beating fast in my chest. I stared into the darkness of the bedroom. It was just a dream. I tried to comfort myself but it was happening so often lately. In daylight hours I felt that I was coming to term with my loss. Yes, there was never a day when I didn't think about Mum but I knew that I was now beginning to accept that she had gone. I could even call myself 'happy' lately; now that I had found a good job and had started to make friends. Now that I had the cottage and it was all beginning to come together I was even beginning to feel a sense of contentment. So why was it that during the night, when my subconscious took over that the nightmares kept coming? I took a few sips from the glass of water at my bedside and turned over, making myself comfortable again by repositioning the pillow...

A dream within a dream ... In this dream I woke to find myself held in *her* arms. We were in a swimming pool. It was a hot, sunny day. I was aware of the heat from the sun as I awoke. She smiled down at me lovingly, gently. 'Oh ... I fell asleep!' I said as she cradled my head above the water. 'I might have drowned!'

She continued to gaze at me with the reassuring look of

a mother, 'You'll never drown,' she said gently. 'Not while I'm here.' The warm water lapped quietly around both of us. I felt its buoyancy keeping me afloat. I smiled back at her, comforted. She wore a bright turquoise swimsuit. She looked young ... beautiful ... in her prime.

We got out of the pool and dried. 'What do you want to do now?' she asked. The mood was calm, both of us enjoying the laziness of the heat of the day.

'Let's go home, to your house and you can make us lunch,' I said, looking forward to the comfort and familiarity of my childhood home and her cooking. We dressed in silence.

I drove whilst she sat beside me. Soon, we came towards the cemetery. 'Stop here for a moment,' she said, looking at me intently. 'I want to put these in the bin.' She turned around and produced a bunch of dead flowers from the back seat of the car. I stared at her now, a distant niggle of fear returning. Something felt wrong. It dawned on me suddenly that I could not be in my car, sitting beside her. She could not be here for she was dead. Panic coursed through my veins. 'How can you be here?' I asked, aware of the emotion in my voice. I gestured towards the cemetery gates. 'I visit you ... in there,' I watched as her face grew more solemn and her mouth began to quiver. This could not be real for I was certain that she was already lost to me! I continued, pleading for an answer. 'I put flowers on your grave. So how can you be here?' My voice was shrill with anguish.

She began to cry. She stared down at her hands, the warmth of the day instantly extinguished. She spoke then without looking at me, full of regret, as though ashamed. 'I'm sorry,' she sobbed. 'I'm sorry that I was ill, sorry for what I put you through.' She was distraught.

Then *I* felt guilty. Guilty that moments before I had accused her of tricking me, of being here with me when all the time she was really dead. I reached across the front of the car and held her warm in my arms, fiercely protective now. 'Don't say sorry!' I pleaded. 'You couldn't help being ill. You couldn't help what you went through. Don't worry about me. I'll be fine. I promise.' She disappeared then. It was over. I woke up sobbing.

And now I realize that she had visited me that night. It had been her way of apologizing for all the help she'd needed; for all the anguish she must have known I'd been through watching her suffer. But I didn't want her to feel guilty. Who knows what lies around the corner for any of us? We will all be in need at some time.

In the cold light of day, I realized that it must have been the image of Emily that had brought on the dream. Or had it?

In a strange way, the dream helped me heal. Looking back on it, although I still dreamed of her from time to time, each dream that followed grew less traumatic. I had made my peace. I was coming to terms with my loss.

Chapter 50

The phone rang. It was John. 'I've got an invitation for you,' he began. 'Gerald asked if you'd like to come to the farm with me next Saturday to look through the photos. I told him you work the lunch shift at the pub so he suggested around three. What d'you think?' He paused for a second. 'I've told him nothing mind. He just thinks you're interested in the local history. It'll be up to you entirely if you decide to tell him more.'

I was thrilled. I accepted without hesitation and thanked him. Even if Gerald found no more photos of Emily, at the very least I would get to see some of Richard and probably learn more about him too. After all, he and Gerald had been close friends.

Over the coming days, I pondered about how much I should or shouldn't reveal on my visit to the farm. I decided to go with my gut instinct and be true to myself. I would explain who I really was from the start and ask that Gerald keep it to himself for the time being, what with Ruth's looming court case. I didn't want to give her any more ammunition to fire at me than was absolutely necessary. I felt that by confiding in Gerald, we would get off to the most honest start and in this way he would be more likely to open up about Richard.

Saturday dawned bright and sunny and I was bursting with anticipation. The only person I'd told was Tom and he too was excited for me. My shift at the pub over, I raced back to the cottage to quickly shower and change. I'd made a carrot cake earlier that morning as a way of showing my appreciation. Now that it had cooled, I decorated it with cream cheese frosting and carefully placed it in a cake tin before setting off to collect John as arranged. He too seemed more animated than usual and I sensed he also shared some of my excitement.

As soon as we were on our way up the steep hill leading towards the farm I told him my plan – that as soon as the moment was right, I wished to tell Gerald that I was indeed Richard's granddaughter.

'Gerald's not the gossiping type I can assure you lass,' he said, reassuring me that I had made the right decision. 'I think he'll be chuffed to know that part of Richard lives on to be honest. They were very close friends you know, as children, and I know they became even closer when they were conscripted together. Took his death hard he did.'

The farm was wonderful, the farmhouse kitchen in which Gerald sat ready to greet us was warm as toast with an open fire crackling away in the hearth and a tray laid for tea on the table. Initial welcome greetings over, I handed over the cake which was gratefully accepted and the three of us sat down. John broke the ice. 'Cass has something she wishes to tell you Gerald,' he began. 'It'll come as a bit of a shock no doubt.' He glanced from Gerald to me and nodded.

Gerald sat watching, awaiting whatever it was that I was about to divulge but the look on his kindly face read that at his age nothing he heard could surprise him. I inhaled deeply, feeling suddenly nervous. What if he didn't believe me? What if he thought I was just a bit of a gold-digger? I began with a simple statement of fact. 'Richard was my grandfather.' I heard the slight quiver in my voice but managed to look him in the eye. He remained silent, his face blank for a moment so I continued. 'My mum was his and Emily's child.'

I saw him hesitate, trying to assimilate what he had just been told, then he smiled, 'Well I never!' he exclaimed, rubbing the stubble on his chin.

I returned the smile before continuing. 'Can I ask that you keep it to yourself? Just for a while ... only Ruth's taking court action against me at the moment and I don't want to add fuel to the flames.'

He shook his head slowly from left to right, searching my face, presumably for any sign of resemblance before continuing. 'I can see it in the eyes,' he said, seeming not to have heard my request about his keeping silent. 'Well I never! If only he'd known ... he'd have been proud as punch he would.' His voice caught slightly and I thought I saw his pale, grey eyes moisten a little. He continued to search my face. His lips had a bluish tinge and I noticed that he breathed heavily and that his chest rattled as he did so. His eyes were kind. I remained looking in his direction, giving him the opportunity to try and find what he searched for.

It was John who broke the spell. 'Aye Gerald, I knew you'd be pleased. Did you catch what Cass said? Best to keep shtum for the moment, you know as well as the rest of us what Ruth can be like.'

Only now did Gerald take his eyes off me. The smile didn't leave his face. 'Aye I heard. Your secret's safe with me lass. I'll tell no-one. Always been the same she has.'

By this I assumed he meant Ruth. Over the course of the next half an hour or so, I filled him in on more of the details. Not wishing to paint too black a picture of Ruth, I tried to leave her out of the conversation as much as I could.

We had finished our tea and cake. Gerald stood up stiffly and in his slippers shuffled a few steps over to where a dark oak dresser stood. From on top of it he brought down a carrier bag and placed it on the table in front of him. Dipping inside, his fingers trembling, he slid out several photo albums as well as an old cardboard box. 'Now let's see what we can find amongst this lot then,' he smiled. 'I had a bit of a sort before you came.'

I could see now that he had slotted torn shreds of white paper throughout the albums, presumably as a way of marking any pages containing photos of Richard. My heart raced with anticipation. He began by showing me a formal one of Richard and Ruth as children standing with Elizabeth and Hubert. They were all dressed in Sunday best. Elizabeth had her hands placed lightly on Richard's shoulders. From the photo, I guessed that he would have been around the age of eleven. This was the earliest one he had of Richard. It was also wonderful to actually be able to picture both Elizabeth and Hubert. She looked as kind as I had expected. Even though Ruth would only have been about eight or nine at the time, she still managed to wear a rather haughty expression. I could see that she had none of the softness a child of her age would usually have and instead was rather plain and sharp featured.

'I'm afraid I've none of your other grandmother though,' Gerald explained apologetically. 'She was never allowed to mix you see.'

Disappointed though I was, I told him that I understood and that I had not really expected him to find any of Emily. 'I can tell you something though lass,' he continued reassuringly. 'Worshiped her he did. Never told anyone else this in all me life,' he paused now, a grave expression on his face. 'When we were on maneuvers together, he told me that he intended to marry her when the war was over, if he made it home alive. I think I was the only one he ever told. Asked me to keep it to myself else her old man got wind of it. Nasty old beggar *he* was. I never doubted his word though.' He paused, lost in thought.

'Think they'd fallen in love as children when I look back on it. The two of them'd light up when they were together.' He stared beyond, remembering. 'Aye he most certainly thought the world of her, and her him ... Such a shame. To think he never knew ...'

I spoke gently now, trying to appease his obvious sadness. 'His mother and father knew though Gerald, and Ruth... she knew too. It was Elizabeth who helped deliver my Mum, right there in the Vicarage. Emily'd hidden it you see, from her own mother and grandfather. Terrified of him it seems. She'd kept it a secret until the night she gave birth then she'd gone to the Vicarage to ask for help.' I could see the astonishment on his face. He shook his head, tutting quietly. 'She left a diary. That's how I found out. I know how much he meant to her. I think giving up Mum as well as losing him broke her heart. After all, she didn't exactly have much of a life did she?'

'No she certainly didn't lass. Her own father had died and her mother was...well ill with her nerves, a recluse really. Emily's grandfather lived with them. If you ask me *he* was sick in his own way too. A real bully he was.' He stared towards the fire, his eyes following the dancing flames, lost in thought. Only when it spat loudly did he return to the present. 'Poor Emily, she must have been desperate. She'd have had no-one to turn to and things weren't like they are now you know. You couldn't just keep a baby born out of wedlock in those days, 'specially if you didn't have the support of your own family. Aye, she must have been broken-hearted.'

I saw that he was lost in the past. Not wanting to break the spell I remained silent. It wasn't long before he continued. 'Gentle creature she was. I s'ppose you'd call her highly-strung, a bit timid like but that's not surprising given the circumstances. 'Cept when she was with Richard she'd come alive. I suppose she felt cared for, that he was looking after her like.'

'Do you know why Ruth hated her so much? I mean I don't really know what she had against her.'

'Can't say as I do lass. She was always a funny one her; had an inflated sense of her own importance. Wouldn't take much to make her your enemy. I can only guess that it might have been that she considered Emily beneath her you know. After all, they were one of the wealthiest families around. Vicars were important in those days but it was still unusual for a vicar to actually *own* the vicarage. No, they were usually owned by the church.' He paused. 'But he was more than just a vicar. Owned several of the village properties as well. Mind you, the kindest landlords you'd ever be likely to meet I'd say. And Elizabeth, she was a darling; never a bad word to say to anyone. There were many who went to her with their problems.'

It was lovely to hear the kind words spoken about Hubert and Elizabeth.

The afternoon ticked by, the grandfather clock in the hall marking time. Gerald was able to show me several more photos of Richard. Most were of Gerald and Richard together. My favourite was the one of them both horse-riding on the farm. Richard was saddled to a large, brown mare. He looked so healthy and full of life. The last one had been taken on the day of the party. Again it was of both Richard and Gerald. They had both tried to smile at the camera but the expression in their eyes was one of anticipation but also sadness. 'Take them with you lass,' he said as we were about to leave. 'Have copies made of them if you like and I'll have them back in your own good time.'

I thanked him profusely and promised to return them the following week. 'You've brought him to life for me,' I said gratefully.

'And you've brought him *back* to life for me,' he replied,

holding both my hands warmly. 'Just knowing that a part of him lives on means the world. Next time I go down to his grave, I'll tell him how proud he'd have been. He'll hear, I'm sure.'

*

So many questions had been answered and yet with each answer, it seemed that more and more questions remained to be asked, not least of which was why Ruth had hated Emily so and yet instead of dragging her name through the mud, had kept her secret all these years. Was it simply that she did not want to taint her own family name or was there more to it?

Chapter 51

As promised, I had the photos copied and dropped the originals back to the farm a week later. I must have looked at them almost a hundred times over the course of the week. I found myself digging out old photos of both mum and myself and comparing the images. I couldn't help but wonder why I searched so desperately. Was it because I had lost everyone whom I had loved?

Mum had only ever shown me one photograph of my own father. It had been taken whilst they were both still at college. It seemed a relaxed, happy image. It had been taken in a park. He sat bare chested, his long legs in flared jeans stretched out in front of him. Mum knelt behind him, both arms wrapped around his shoulders, her head resting on his neck. The sun was strong and they both squinted towards the camera. Their faces were tanned and both appeared a little disheveled in a typical student kind of way.

She'd told me that they had not been a couple for long though and when she became pregnant with me he had been horrified. Not wishing to trap him, she'd simply let him go and once she had gone home to have me, had never again made contact.

She'd always said that I looked more like her than I did him and I knew this was true. Apart from my paler skin tone, she and I were very similar: the same warm green eyes which I now knew we'd inherited from Richard, the same unruly fair hair. Both of us were tall and even our fingernails were the same shape. Strange, but I'd never really been curious about my own Dad. I'd just accepted that he had been young and carefree, not ready to face the responsibility of bringing up a child and I'd let him go, just as Mum had done. So why I now longed to discover all I could about this long, lost family I did not know. Whether it was coming here, to Marleston, and learning that this was part of both our heritage I could not be sure. All I knew was that I was hungry for more.

Several weeks passed following my visit to the farm and nothing much of importance happened. I continued to tweak little things at the cottage and it felt more like home every day. I'd chosen warm, earthy colours and soft furnishings to decorate the rooms and had given it the feminine touch. It was nice knowing that I only had myself to please. For once, I didn't need to worry about what Simon's choice might have been. Feminine though it was, everyone who visited thought it beautiful. Both Tom and Kate had said how welcoming and cozy I'd made it. It did indeed feel homely in every sense of the word.

*

It was now early November and my life seemed to be jogging along quite smoothly. One afternoon, upon returning home from work, I found an official-looking brown envelope awaiting me. My heart immediately sank. Over the past few weeks, I'd more or less managed to put the court case out of my mind, what with being so busy with the two jobs and helping out at John's, but I instinctively knew that this letter would force me to face it once again. And I was right. It was from my solicitor. Its contents explained that the decision on Ruth's case would be read at the County Court at Winchton on December 3rd and asked that I attend. It also stated that should I require any preliminary advice I should contact the office beforehand before reassuring me that it was unlikely that I would be called to speak as I was not contesting any outcome. My presence was merely requested out of formality and in case the judge should feel the need to ask me any questions.

It seemed that as Ruth had previously lost the battle to contest her mother's will she was unlikely to gain any ground now and that in bringing the matter back to court, she was simply opening up old wounds as well as costing herself a small fortune in fees. Still, it was *her* time and money and if she wanted to spend it on something which gave her hardly any chance of success then that was up to her.

One thing I knew for certain and that was that she could not possibly bring up anything about me personally which could act in her favour as I was an innocent party. I had not even given her the satisfaction of engaging in discussion about the matter and genuinely did not care about inheriting the Vicarage. After all, I was more than happy that Hope Cottage was mine and that I was now more secure. It was a dream come true for me, to finally have a little place to call home, away from the turmoil of the past. In any case, I had no children to pass down any forthcoming wealth to so neither cared whether the Vicarage would eventually become mine or not. If truth be told, the thought of running such a premises scared me somewhat, what with its grandeur and the responsibility of the holiday cottage.

The only thing that stopped me from contacting the solicitor and signing something which would legally hand it all back to Ruth was the thought of Elizabeth and Hubert. From all that I had learned about them over the past months, I still felt certain that there was more to the whole story than met the eye. There must have been something in Ruth's past which had made Elizabeth change her will. It seemed to me that even if they had encouraged Emily to give Mum up for adoption, they had had little choice in the matter and had done so with Emily and Mum's best wishes at heart. They would have been all too aware that in Emily's situation she would have had no chance of raising a child properly. I wondered if they'd considered raising Mum themselves but understood the implications this would have had for them during the 1940's. I was sure that they too had been heart broken at losing their only living connection to Richard and that perhaps they had made the decision to leave the Vicarage to Mum almost as a means of apology.

Still, for several days before the hearing my anxiety levels increased. Once again, Tom had promised to accompany me which I considered rather brave, as this would likely make him an enemy in Ruth's eyes.

'Hey lass, I'm too long in the tooth to be worrying about the likes of her,' he assured me with a smile. 'Wouldn't worry me if she spoke badly of me afterward. In any case, she's hardly the most popular member of the village.'

I thanked him again for his support, 'You're a brick Tom. Honestly you are. I don't know what I'd have done without you. All I know is I most certainly wouldn't be here now.'

'Don't be daft, course you would,' he said, shaking his head.

'No Tom, really I wouldn't. If you hadn't turned up that first day ... you know ... when I'd begun to clear the cottage; if you hadn't helped me and encouraged me to look at all my options I'd have just sold it off for whatever I could have got for it and I wouldn't be in this situation at all.'

I could see that my words pleased him though he still refused to accept praise.

'I wouldn't have found the job at the college, or even the

pub without your help. This place wouldn't be in the state it is now and most of all, I wouldn't have made a new life with wonderful friends if it hadn't been for you.' I looked at him in earnest. 'I know you can't handle me being soft but I just want to take this opportunity to tell you how grateful I am Tom. Your support had been invaluable.'

He flushed with pleasure. 'I know... and I'm glad of your friendship too you know. It can be a lonely old life when you lose the one you love can't it? Come on, let's have a cuppa and stop being so maudlin. You're going to win this you know. She's wasting her time and money bringing it all up again.'

'You know Tom, I have no desire to either win or lose. In fact, I don't feel it's about me. I honestly couldn't care less for the Vicarage. Only I do feel that Elizabeth's wishes deserve to be granted and I think Mum would have been pleased too if she'd known about her father. By what I can gather, he and Emily really did love one another. Perhaps it's time that something good came out of it for the sake of their memory. And in any case, it's all Ruth's until the day she dies and judging by the amount of fight in her, she has a good many years left ahead of her,' I laughed.

'Aye you're right Cass,' he nodded. 'It's about the principle of the thing. Elizabeth and Hubert were good people and so they should have their wishes granted.'

Chapter 52

Although I kept a furtive look out for Ruth over the following weeks, I did not spot her. I was certain now that she was avoiding me. Even though I felt apprehensive in doing so, I would still regularly pay my respects at Richard's grave. After all, I had done nothing wrong and was determined to feel no guilt. Her absence only proved to me her own unease, for surely if she felt she had some genuine recourse against me she would not have felt the need to avoid me so entirely. I was glad that at least the case would be over and done with before Christmas as there were several events planned at the church which I hoped to attend. It wasn't that I was suddenly becoming religious; it was just that the church was a big part of the community in Marleston. It acted as Community Centre and held several charity events throughout the year which most villagers attended.

I often wondered if Ruth looked for me in secret. Did she watch me from a small gap in her heavy brocade curtains? Did my presence at the graveside of her brother, and sometimes of her parents too anger her? I did not pause there out of a wish to antagonize her, it was just that I enjoyed visiting their resting places. I had always felt at peace in cemeteries. There had been a really old one where I'd grown up and Mum and I would often walk through it and study the headstones, wondering about unusual names and the stories of those who rested there.

I suppose some would have considered us morbid, but neither of us ever found the cemetery depressing; it had been merely a place of peace, away from the bustle of the busy town where we had lived.

*

Finally the day of the hearing arrived. I went to work as usual in the morning, though I found it difficult to concentrate on the subject matter I was supposed to be teaching. My lecture didn't finish until one thirty so I had just enough time to race back, pick up Tom who was dressed in his best suit and tie and head back to Winchton. I had not managed to eat since breakfast, having neither the time nor the inclination and so I was grateful when, having parked in the town car park some twenty minutes early, Tom produced a bar of chocolate from his jacket pocket. 'Get this down you Cass. You don't want your sugar level dropping in there now do you? Wouldn't want to come over all faint in front of that lot. Just imagine!' He laughed in an attempt to make light of the situation but I knew he understood only too well how nervous I was.

From where we sat, Ruth was in plain view. Apart from the judge herself, who sat with a severe look on her face, only Ruth, her husband and her solicitor were present. I cast an occasional glance in her direction. However stony-faced she tried to appear I could tell she was nervous. Her pallor was sallow and drawn and her mouth twitched. She clasped her hands tightly in her lap all the while in an attempt to still them I assumed.

Her husband looked afraid. He neither comforted nor ignored her. He merely sat stiffly beside her, occasionally offering the briefest of smiles in her direction. If this doesn't go her way, he'll likely have a hell of a life, I imagined, knowing that she would probably be consumed by the outcome for some time to come. That was just the way she was. She was a bull terrier, once she sunk her teeth into something, or someone, she did not release them easily.

The minutes that followed seemed like a dream. The judge asked us all to stand before reading out her decision, in an official tone, which showed little interest in the subject. Copies of Elizabeth's will were produced by the clerk and soon the whole thing was over. The judge had ruled, as expected, in my favor, though the actual wording appeared to rule in favour of the deceased rather than either Ruth or myself. She simply stated that having considered all that had been presented before her, Elizabeth's last will and testament was sound and therefore, upon Ruth's own demise, Elizabeth's possessions would be passed down to her late granddaughter, Rebekah Wilkinson and therefore to me.

I was numb. Ruth merely nodded sourly in the direction of the judge before rather speedily heading from the court. Her husband had almost to chase her, so hasty was her retreat.

I remained seated a few minutes longer, attempting to catch my breath. Neither Tom nor I had spoken thus far. The judge had risen and left the room almost as abruptly as Ruth and now the only other person who remained in the court was Ruth's solicitor, who busied himself with gathering his paperwork, possibly in an attempt to delay having to face Ruth outside of the court.

Still I failed to take it in. I'd arrived at Marleston just seven months previously with very little to my name and almost as possession-less as an itinerant and yet here I sat, with the knowledge that one day I would likely be one of the wealthiest people in the village. It could not be true! Reality certainly had not sunk in. For the present I experienced no sense of pleasure or even relief that it was all over, just disbelief.

I must have looked pretty ashen too, for the next thing I knew, Tom had taken hold of me by the elbow and was attempting to get me to stand. 'Come on love,' he spoke gently. 'Let's be going. We don't want to end up getting locked in.' He tried to joke to lighten the mood. I found myself being led by him, out of the court room and away from the building towards the car park. I suppose I was grateful that we didn't encounter Ruth on the way. If I had, I certainly would not have been in any state to have spoken to her.

It wasn't until much later that evening when, having made some supper and curling up in front of the fire, reality dawned. It was then that the flood gates opened. I cried for not being able to tell Mum, for the fact that neither Emily nor Richard would ever learn what had become of their union and in a way, I suppose I even cried for Ruth, for in some strange way I pitied her. Right, enough drama, get a grip now Cass, I scolded myself some thirty minutes later. I got up and retreated to the kitchen to re-heat the supper which remained untouched.

Some time later, the phone rang. 'How you doing love?' Tom asked. 'Must have been a bit of a shock today to actually hear it from the horse's mouth I suppose.'

'I've been really upset Tom if I'm honest. I think all the anxiety must have built up. Still, I'm okay now. Just had something to eat and I'm gathering myself together.'

'Good girl. Try not to dwell on things now. Remember that your life will not change for the present. Try to put today behind you and just go forward. Think of the progress you've made these past months and don't let this upset you. You can tackle what lies ahead in the future and by then you'll be much stronger to do so,' he tried to reassure me.

'I know. Thanks Tom. I just find it so hard to take in, that's all. However am I going to face Ruth now? I know she's avoided me these past months but we won't be able to avoid each other indefinitely will we? Our paths are bound to cross at some time aren't they? I'd like to attend the Christmas Fair and I was even thinking about running a stall with my baking but I can't imagine facing her Tom.'

'You do it lass! You've got no reason to hide from her. She's the one who should be embarrassed, not you. Don't you hide away. She'll just have to come to terms with what's happened and accept it like other folk have had to. It's her problem.'

I laughed a little at his straight way of speaking.

'Anyway, you know where I am if you need me ...' He paused for a moment. 'Can I just add ... I'm so pleased for you. You might not be in a position to appreciate it at the moment girl but you will in the future. Just think ... you're secure for life!'

My stomach flipped at the thought of what the inheritance could really mean. 'I know Tom, and thanks again for coming with me today. I suppose it'll all work out in the end. I've come through far worse than this haven't I?'

'Aye indeed. This is a *good* thing, you mark my words. You'll realize in time. Just a bit of a shock that's all. I don't think when you first learned of the possibility from the solicitor all those months ago that you ever really thought it'd come true. But it has and it'll work out for the best, you'll see. Just have to make sure she doesn't try to have you bumped off that's all,' he laughed.

'What a thought! I wouldn't put it past her!' I smiled back, feeling a little cheered. 'Goodnight Tom. See you soon.'

The embers had died down in the hearth. Only a faint, warm glow remained. I put up the guard and went off to bed, exhausted.

Chapter 53

Thankfully Ruth was not in charge of the fair. It was community run and I knew most of the members from the pub. Feeling brave, and not wishing to appear blameworthy in any way, I decided to approach Mabel, the treasurer, when next I saw her at the Moon and Sixpence to ask if I might run a cake stall. I'd always loved baking. Mum had taught me when I was young and we'd spent many a happy afternoon in the kitchen together, both singing away to the radio as we worked. Mabel was only too pleased.

Two weeks had passed since the court case and thus far I had no sense of anyone in the village having got wind of what had happened. The fact was that unless Ruth decided to tell people then they would not know until after her death, as I had already made up my mind that I would keep silent about the matter. After all, it was not until the death of most people that others would ever learn of any inheritance and I certainly didn't want anyone in the village thinking I was a money grabber. In all likelihood, the matter would simply go quiet and no-one would be any the wiser. It would still be uncomfortable though, knowing without doubt that our paths would soon cross. Until now, Ruth had kept herself ensconced in the Vicarage but she would not be able to do so forever.

I had received a letter from my own solicitor at the end of the previous week, asking that I make another appointment to sign some paperwork to finalize the outcome of the court case. College was due to break up at the end of that week and so I rang and arranged an appointment for the day following the end of term so that I would not need to take any more time off work.

It was merely a formality. The solicitor simply told me that he had now been officially informed of the outcome of the case and that a copy of Elizabeth's will would be held at their office. He congratulated me on the outcome and asked how I felt.

'Empty,' I told him truthfully. 'I don't think it's really sunk in. I'm trying to put it out of my mind now and just get on with living my life.'

He appeared a little puzzled. I supposed he'd been expecting me to feel joyful at the outcome but I could not tell a lie. It was only then that it came to me. I looked at him as he frowned across the table. 'Can I ask something?'

'Of course.'

'When someone dies ... I mean, how could I go about finding out what became of their body?' In retrospect, I suppose I'd made little sense, as these current thoughts had nothing really to do with the reason for me being there.

'What do you mean?'

I paused, trying to think more clearly. I didn't really know why the matter had not crossed my mind before. 'Well my grandmother Emily, you know, the partner of Ruth's brother Richard, well when she died, I learned nothing of it until my own mother died shortly after her. Only then did I learn that Mum had inherited Hope Cottage and that it had taken a little time to trace her as they had been estranged all of Mum's life.'

'I see,' he said, still wondering where this was leading.

'Well, I was wondering, how could I go about finding out where she is buried? That is if she's buried at all. I mean I don't know what happened to Emily's body. There was nothing at the cottage which gave me any clue and I didn't get to see her will if indeed there was one ... only Mum's, which passed Hope Cottage down to me. I'd like to know that's all ... if there's a place I could visit, to say thank you.'

'Well if she'd died alone, she'd have had to have written her wishes down somewhere, otherwise the state would have stepped in so to speak. I suppose you could inquire at your own mother's solicitors to see if there was any mention of Emily's last wishes in her will.' He watched me, gauging my reaction. 'If there was nothing written down though, it'd be a matter of chasing it through the local authority in which she died.'

'Thank you. Well at least I know where to start,' I managed a small smile. We shook hands formally and I left.

I knew the name of Mum's solicitor. I would trace their number when I got home and give them a ring.

Chapter 54

Having explained who I was and about Hope Cottage, Mum's solicitors back home in the North promised to look into whatever information they held on record and get back to me. I'd dealt with the same firm after Mum's death and so they seemed vaguely aware of who I was.

Two days later they rang to say that their contacts regarding Mum's inheritance of the cottage had come via a solicitor's firm in nearby Winchton. They were able to inform me that according to the communication received by themselves at the time, the same firm now held the title deeds to the cottage. They were unable to give me any information regarding Emily's will however. I made note of their name and decided that rather than ringing, I would visit their office the following day. Even if they were unable to tell me anything further, I considered I may receive a more accurate account if I visited rather than rung.

What is it about solicitors and Victorian buildings I wondered, having located the address, for the name of their firm was emblazoned above the door to yet another four storey imposing old building. The front door led to a narrow corridor. Steep stairs lay ahead. A half-glazed door on the right read *Reception*. I turned the handle and stepped inside. The clerk eyed me up and down as I entered looking rather bedraggled from the December wind and rain. I stammered a little, not really knowing how to begin. Thank goodness there's no-one else here at the moment, I thought, noting the lack of other clients.

Deciding to begin by pretending I was merely there to confirm that they did indeed hold the title deeds to Hope Cottage, I produced my identification and told the receptionist who I was, explaining that I'd recently inherited it from my own mother. She asked me to take a seat. She left the reception office and went back into the corridor through which I'd entered. I heard her quickly climb the stairs then there was silence. I was alone. I hoped that by the time she returned, no-one else would have come in as I didn't feel that I would be able to question her about Emily's will in the presence of another client.

She returned just a few minutes later. 'Yes,' she said without smiling. 'We do hold the deeds. Are you happy to leave them with us for safe-keeping or did you want to remove them? Only if you did, there would be paperwork to sign and we would need further identification.'

'No, no,' I answered hastily. 'I'm happy that they're here.' It was quite obvious that she expected our conversation to be over at this point. I pulled myself together. 'I wonder if I could ask something else?' She waited, her expression somewhat irritated. 'It's just that Emily Willis was my maternal grandmother as I said and ... well Mum had been adopted as a baby and so was estranged from her. It's only recently that I've found out anything about her and I...well I'd like to get to know a bit more. I was wondering how I might go about finding out if she left any information in her own will regarding her last wishes. I mean I don't know her final resting place or anything and I'd love to find out.'

She sighed, a long, drawn-out sigh. I couldn't be sure whether this was out of impatience that she wasn't actually rid of me yet or out of pondering my question for her face gave nothing away. A few seconds of silence followed.

'If you take a seat again, I'll see if we hold a copy of the will. Even if we do though, I wouldn't be able to pass on any information here and now. You'd need to make an appointment and bring further identification.'

'Thank you. I understand. That's fine,' I answered politely before sitting once again on one of the wooden schoolroom chairs.

This time she did not leave the room but instead tapped away at her computer. Her face gave nothing away. All the while, I was thankful for the fact that still no-one else had walked in. Moments later, she stopped typing and gave a small cough as if to gain my attention. I looked at her. She began to speak. 'It seems that we do hold a copy of the will.' I stood up and approached the desk, smiling obligingly all the while. 'As I said, you'll need to make an appointment if you require further information.'

'Yes please then,' I answered. 'That would be great.'

She brought up the diary on the computer and scanned the screen. 'How about Thursday at two o'clock with Mr Jenkins?'

I knew this was fine as college had finished for the Christmas term so I readily agreed. 'You'll need to bring two forms of identification, preferably passport and driving licence plus a copy of a recent bill with the property address on in your name,' she continued. 'There'll be an initial charge of sixty pounds for a fifteen minute appointment.'

'That's fine,' I answered, realizing that solicitors never did anything for free. 'See you then.'

Two more days to wait. I hoped that I would glean more information about Emily's last wishes from the appointment.

*

'Steven Jenkins,' the solicitor reached forward to shake my hand.

I smiled. 'Cassie Wilkinson,' I answered. 'Pleased to

meet you.'

He gestured for me to sit which I did. 'Now then, I've already been given some basic information by my clerk regarding your request. Have you brought the identification?'

I handed him the envelope containing all of my paperwork as requested. 'Emily Willis was my grandmother. I inherited Hope Cottage after she had passed it down to my mother who also recently died.' When nervous I could not stand silence and so would always fill the space with anything I could think of to say.

'I see.' He examined my I.D., photocopied it at his desk then looked at me. His face was quite friendly, though I could not help but feel as though I were under examination. 'So what exactly would you like to know?'

'Well anything really ... I mean especially what became of her after she died. It would be nice to be able to visit her grave, if there is one that is, to sort of say thank you if you know what I mean.'

'Let's see ...' He reached across his desk and opened a large, brown envelope. I could just make out Emily's name on the front. He slipped out a folded piece of paper and appeared to examine it quite closely, frowning all the while. 'Okay ... This is a copy of the will. I can have a copy made for you should you wish. There will be a small charge but basically it says that she bequeathed the property to her daughter, Rebekah Wilkinson ... your mother I presume?'

'Yes, yes, she was my mother,' I answered eagerly.

He studied the paper again. 'There's not a lot else here but it's all intact and correctly witnessed.' He reached once more into the brown envelope, this time producing another sheet of manilla paper which looked quite aged. I could see that it had been folded and that its folds were worn, as though they had been opened several times over the years.

'This does not form part of the will but was apparently found alongside it when her body was discovered. Would you like me to read it or would you prefer ..?' He held it out across the desk towards me.

My hand shook as I took it from him. 'Yes, thank you,' I managed. Wishing that I'd thought about getting out my reading glasses beforehand, I fumbled for them in my bag. The sheet of paper lay temptingly open but blurred on the desk. I picked it up and read. The hand that had written it had been shaky, the contents barely legible.

I, Emily Willis wish to state that once I depart this world, I would like for my body to be reunited with that of my fiance Richard Harrison in the cemetery at Marleston, the deeds to which are enclosed.

She had signed her name underneath. The signature, though shaky was recognizable as the same as that which had signed the will document.

'Oh my word!' I gasped, putting my hand to my mouth. 'She's been there all the time!' For the past few moments, I had been lost in my own world and unaware of the solicitor's presence. I came back to earth now. I waved the note in front of him. 'Would her wishes have been carried out? Would she have had the right to ..? I mean there was no family to oversee things. She was very lonely you see.' I felt choked. To think that there may have been no-one to ensure her wishes were carried out was awful.

'Yes, yes,' he replied. 'There's a council document here stating that her body was dealt with as she had requested and the burial was paid for from her estate. Apparently there was a little money found in the house in the same envelope which just about covered the cost of her burial. The grave deed she mentions is also here so you can be assured her wishes were carried out.'

He appeared a little embarrassed at having to state the obvious; that this long lost relative of mine had not only died alone but had probably had a funeral devoid of mourners. I found myself feeling a little sorry for his predicament.

'The people in the village ... well I've asked them and all they can tell me is that they didn't know that Emily had been found dead until a week or so later. She was a bit of a recluse you see. Hadn't been well for a long time and well ... she'd lost contact with people. Apparently the police had been called after a refuse collector had noticed that her bin had remained empty for several weeks.' I looked at him, wondering what he must have thought of my ranting.

'Yes of course. It's always sad when these things happen,' he answered, still a little embarrassed. 'Would you like copies made?'

'Yes please,' I answered. He took back the paperwork which I had been holding, ran it through the copier and placed the documents in a fresh envelope. 'Well ... glad to be of assistance.' He reached across to shake my hand again, indicating that the meeting was now over. 'And you know that we hold the cottage deeds? You can pay downstairs before you leave if you wish or we can send you an invoice.'

I packed away my reading glasses and took the envelope containing the copy of the will, the grave deed and the accompanying letter from him. 'Thank you. I'll pay on my way out.'

I felt completely shaken. Yet again, I had learned something new but still felt as if it only opened up further questions. Was it really possible that no-one from the village had attended her funeral? Had there been any kind of service held for her? How on earth had she come to own Richard's grave deed? All of these thoughts whirled around my mind. I couldn't wait to return home and re-examine the letter. I wanted to be alone with my thoughts for a while. It was nice though, knowing that Emily's final resting place lay just outside the cottage. How many times had I visited the plot over the past months? I couldn't begin to count. At least now I gained comfort from the fact that she and Richard had been reunited.

My own beliefs about what happened to us after death were what I suppose one could call *earthly*. I did not believe in any kind of life after death, though I had to admit that strange things did happen after you lost a loved one and that there were times when you almost felt their presence. Instead, I believed in the eternity of nature, that the broken down remains of a loved one would eventually feed the soil and in doing so produce new life, even if it was in the form of grass. Richard's remains, however small, would intermingle with those of Emily. Between them they would be in part responsible for bringing new life. I remembered back to a poem that I had read in my twenties by a Welsh poet named Bob Reeves. He had written about the untimely death of a young friend. The poem personified a person's remains and how they fed the soil, which in turn fertilized the grass and other plants in spring. He wrote about how the lambs would come and feed on the grass and thus the cycle of new life would continue. It had seemed to make so much sense to me, that *this* was the way in which we lived on and it had struck a chord. I had carried his words with me ever since as a sort of philosophy for life after death.

It came to me suddenly ... the grave deed now legally belonged to me. Hastily I retrieved the copy from my bag and re-examined it. It stated that the plot of ground was for two which meant of course that no-one else could be buried within it. Amongst the few, precious possessions which I had brought with me was the casket containing

Mum's ashes. A few weeks before she had died, she had led our conversation towards her final wishes and had said that she preferred cremation. I remembered how I had felt physically sick at having to discuss it with her but she had been adamant. She had also said that she did not really care what I decided to do with her ashes afterward but had hinted that she would like to stay close to me. Had she guessed I wondered? Had she known that I might begin a new life in the cottage she'd inherited? She knew me well enough to understand that I had more of a flight than fight personality so it was possible that she may have guessed I would end up leaving the North and begin a new life for myself here. Perhaps that was what she hinted at when she said she would like me to keep her close. My decision was made. I would contact the local authority and arrange to have Mum's ashes interred in the plot. In doing so, not only would she be reunited with her natural parents but she would also be returning home with me.

In bed though, I tossed and turned over my decision. The more I thought about it the less certain I felt that I would be doing the right thing. What if Mum wouldn't want that? After all, she had never known them. Had she harboured any bitterness about being given up for adoption? In honesty, she had never seemed bitter. She had loved her adoptive parents dearly but they were buried back home, many miles from here. Deep down I felt sure that had she known the circumstances of her birth she would have understood so instead of over-thinking, I needed to follow my instinct which told me it was the right thing to do. Mum would be so close to my new home and at the same time reunited with the two people who would have loved her so much if only they'd had the chance.

Chapter 55

It was the evening before the Christmas fair. I had been busy all day, baking and decorating my cakes and had thoroughly enjoyed myself. Alone, in my little cottage kitchen, radio playing to keep me company, I had whisked and beaten, cooked and cooled and now my table was laden with quite a hearty display.

At around eight o'clock, exhausted but feeling more content than I had for a long time, I sunk into a deep, foamy bath. I had just finished drying myself when the front door bell rang – just one sharp ring. For a few seconds I considered ignoring it but curiosity got the better of me.

Quickly donning my robe, I raced downstairs, hair wrapped in a towel. As I opened the front door, the last person in the world I expected to see stood before me – Ruth! I was so taken aback, I didn't know what to say. I merely stood staring at her, mouth agape whilst she returned my stare with a severe, fixed expression. I tried to speak but failed to do so and so it was she who took the initiative. 'I hear you intend coming to the fair tomorrow,' she said curtly.

She had caught me off-guard. Yes, I had not expected her to welcome me with open arms and, if I was honest, had been dreading seeing her there but I had decided to simply remain at my stall and mingle with the locals whom I now knew quite well. Thinking that she would simply avoid my stall and go about the fair as she would have otherwise done, I thought it unlikely that there would be any need for a scene. Now I was not so sure. Has she really called at this late hour to try and put me off attending I wondered? Thus far, I still had not spoken. Now I simply fiddled at the belted waist of my robe ensuring that it remained secure in the evening chill. How did she always manage to make me feel so vulnerable I thought somewhat crossly, the calm of the day disappearing in an instant. She remained standing at my door, seemingly oblivious to my state of dress.

'Actually Ruth, yes. I'm running a cake stall. I've been busy all day,' I managed uncomfortably.

'May I come in and speak with you?' Her tone was polite for once but firm and unemotional.

'Actually ...' I began but could not really think of a suitable excuse. It was pretty obvious from my appearance that I did not have visitors, nor was I particularly busy. I was a little annoyed though that she had spoiled my evening. I sighed, perhaps a little rudely, 'Well ... I suppose so.'

She stepped inside the little hallway and gazed around. It was likely that long back she would have been familiar with the cottage but I could see that the transformation took her aback. Gesturing towards the living room door I said, 'Please, make yourself comfortable. I'll just pop upstairs and dress.'

Her sturdy heels clip-clopped into the little sitting room which thankfully I had recently afforded to furnish and I noticed her once again cast her gaze. I had prepared the room before my bath, intent on a relaxing evening. A fire glowed warmly in the hearth, scented candles twinkled at various places in the room and Ella Fitzgerald crooned quietly in the background. For most people, the effect would have been instantly calming. She chose the single armchair by the fire, just as I had expected her to, but she sat stiffly. Still she did not smile. I could see the corners of her mouth twitching and this bolstered my confidence a little. After all, this was the first time that she had been on *my* territory. Perhaps the ball was now in my court.

'Shan't be a moment.' I gave a small smile and darted upstairs. Not wishing to spend time untangling my unruly mop of hair, I decided to leave it wrapped in its towel. I quickly pulled on an old pair of jeans and a sweatshirt, all the while my heart beating fast. I paused at the bedroom door to calm my breathing. I wanted at least to *appear* in control. What on earth did she want I wondered, expecting that once I returned downstairs she would most likely try to deter me from attending the fair. There would be no chance of that after my efforts during the day. I was determined. I had not spent almost a hundred pounds and a whole day baking for nothing! No, she would simply have to stay away herself if she did not want to see me tomorrow.

Several deep breaths later, I descended the stairs. 'Sorry about that,' I said as I entered the sitting room. The warm, cozy glow instantly did its magic and calmed me. Considering it rude to keep the music playing, however softly, I crossed the room and switched it off. Wanting to delay the inevitable, and also out of a sense of propriety I asked, 'Cup of tea or coffee perhaps?'

'No thank you,' she replied formally, still without a smile.

I sat at ninety degrees to her on the sofa and tried my best to appear relaxed. Again, I noticed that her mouth twitched in the corners and she looked rather pale. The room was filled with silence, neither of us wishing to speak first and the sudden absence of music seemed to make it more profound. The only sound came from the occasional spitting of the coals in the fire. Inhaling deeply I decided to go first. 'So what did you wish to speak to me about?' I began. Now that the words were out my stomach did a flip. As I readied myself to defend my attendance at the fair, I continued to look in her direction.

A few moments of silence ensued before she spoke. 'As far as I'm concerned, it's over,' she began, turning away from me and instead gazing at the fire as if in a trance.

I had no idea what she was getting at and so didn't know how I should respond to her statement so I decided to wait for her to enlighten me further.

Still avoiding my gaze she continued. 'You might as well know the truth for I have no fight left in me.'

I wondered then for the first time if perhaps her unexpected visit had less to do with the fair and more to do with Emily and the past. For the present, she offered no more and just continued to stare at the flames in the hearth, her eyes watering from lack of blinking as well as the heat.

When she did not enlighten me further I tried again. 'What do you mean Ruth? I must admit, this is rather unexpected.' I tried to make my voice sound as controlled as I could and was very glad that she was on my premises and not her own. Her whole demeanor seemed suddenly small. Yes, she was a tall lady and with her severe hairstyle and pointed features she gave the impression of a formidable character. Was it simply because she was sitting down that I perceived her as small now or was it that she seemed to have had the wind knocked out of her sails I wondered.

Again, a few seconds of silence, then taking her eyes away from the dance of the fire and looking at me for the first time since I had entered the sitting room she spoke. 'I have not come to ask forgiveness. No, there is only One who has the power to forgive.' She paused for a few seconds but when I remained silent she continued. 'I am an old woman. An old woman with so many regrets, so many wrongs that cannot be undone but I cannot fight any longer. I wish to tell you of the past. I neither want nor expect to receive your forgiveness, nor am I looking for sympathy.' Her eyes still bore dark and fierce yet she suddenly sighed, hard and long and with this sigh appeared to deflate even further.

She seemed to be waiting for me to react. 'Okay Ruth. So what is it that you wish to talk about? Have you come to tell me why you hated Emily so much?'

She held my gaze. 'Yes, in a way I have ... but there's more, much more. When you hear what I have to say, you may even feel it necessary to contact the police and if that is what you wish, then you should go ahead and do so for I am beyond judgment now. I merely wish to rid myself of the secrets that have poisoned me throughout my life. I wish to speak of them, to give them air; perhaps then I may finally achieve some sense of peace.'

My curiosity was alight. She looked so frail, so old and worn that I almost pitied her. 'Listen Ruth, whatever it is you have done, it is not for me to judge and yes, I will listen if that is what you want but let me fetch us a drink first.' I stood, feeling the need to escape for a moment.

She groaned impatiently and flapped her hand, gesturing for me to sit again. 'No ...' her voice broke. 'If I stop now, I might change my mind. Please ... just listen.'

The old Ruth was desperate to gain back control. I sat back down as bidden, leaning forward slightly to show that she had my full attention.

Chapter 56

'I killed him,' she began. I held my breath, wondering whom she could possibly mean. She had turned her attention back to the fire now. She appeared almost oblivious to my presence. It was as if I was not there, but rather she spoke to the flames. I said nothing, but felt my heart beat quicken.

Then she gave a small, mocking laugh. 'Of course I did not *mean* to kill him but still ... I am guilty, as guilty as if I'd taken a gun to him.' She paused for some moments but I dared not interrupt. 'That night, the night he returned home from war. He was injured you see, his leg ... but more than that ... I sensed his weakness. From the moment I saw him slumped in the armchair, I knew it had beaten him and I felt triumphant. *His* weakness fed *my* strength. Finally, *I* had the upper hand!'

I was afraid to break the spell. It felt like a dream, or as if I were watching a soliloquy in the theatre. Surely what I was hearing could not be true. This was not how real life panned out. Blood rang in my ears, a high-pitched whine and my face burned red.

She continued and I, her sole audience member, listened. 'He went off to bed and shortly afterwards so did I. I remained in my room and waited. I wanted the opportunity to have it out with him you see. By acquainting himself with her ...' She glanced up now and I saw that her eyes addressed the farewell party photograph of Emily and

Richard on the mantelpiece. 'He brought shame to our family. How could he fall in love with one so low?'

My instinct was to stop her and defend Emily. 'Now hold on!'

She simply waved her hand at me and shushed me and I found myself once again obeying her school-ma'am demeanor. 'You can say what you have to say when I have finished,' she snapped impatiently.

Yes, the old Ruth was still there; yet there was also a desperation in her that I had not witnessed before. I realized that I was her pawn, merely a chosen spectator and so I remained quiet. I would let her speak her mind and then I would have my say; I would defend the grandmother I had never known but whom I was certain had been so wronged by this woman.

And so she continued, but her story now seemed to veer in another direction. She sighed heavily. 'I worshiped her when I was a child.' She glanced up, smirking at the absurdity of such an idea. I understood that she meant Emily. 'She was beautiful. She was serene. She had a natural grace that I *so* longed to have. Even when she was dressed in rags ... the way she carried herself ... she was almost other-worldly, a heavenly creature. And she was happy! We would play in the woods, the three of us and she would laugh and smile. She was always good; always did the right thing. She never stayed out later than instructed, never got dirty, even during play ... and *he* adored her.' She paused again, lost in the past. 'I think he loved her even in childhood you know.' I stirred in my seat, enthralled yet at the same time horrified by what I was hearing.

She spoke calmly, steadily, as if she had all the time in the world. 'And then her father died ... and that was when she changed. Up until then I would watch her, even when she did not know I was watching. I would emulate her stance, the way she walked, the way she threw back her head when she laughed but I could never *be* her. Even as a child I knew my short-comings. I was plain and stern; my features would glare back miserably at me whenever I looked in the mirror. I was her polar opposite. She was soft, I was hard. She was caring, I was intolerant of others ... yet deep down all I wanted was to be like her.' She gave a slight shiver, even though the room was very warm then inhaled deeply and continued. 'When her father died, and the old man came to live with them she changed, almost over night. Only rarely now did she join us to play. I noticed how she lost weight, how she appeared frailer, more timid, and do you know? I was glad! I rejoiced in the fact that her years of innocence were over, glad that she suffered, glad that she was burdened by him. Her candle had been snuffed. And then it became obvious that her own mother was ill too and I clapped my hands in joy!'

The room felt cloying somehow, heavy, as if it were becoming filled with the weight of her words. Here she sat, unburdening herself and all the while the room took on her negativity and grew laden. I wondered if it remembered ... this little room that had become such a place of contentment to me; perhaps it remembered all that had gone before. Perhaps it stirred now, with the knowledge of all that she spoke about for it suddenly occurred to me that this very room would have witnessed much of the misery about which she spoke. The thought frightened me for I did not want it tainted. I had enough ghosts in my past but I had banished them to the North. I did not want my little abode tarnished by her. I was almost tempted then to ask her to leave. Why should I allow her to eradicate her own guilt and in doing so taint my life in this way?

But I remained silent. There was a part of me that was still hungry for the truth and I knew that the more I learned of the past, the more I understood of Emily and this house, the more I would be able to put her to rest. So I waited, and I listened ...

'I'd hoped that he would stop loving her, that he would see how she had changed, how her light had been extinguished, how instead of blossoming she wilted. I hoped he would see it and that he would stop loving her. But he didn't. He *still* loved her. In fact, if anything, what she was going through only seemed to make him love her even more!' She gave a small laugh. 'Always the hero was Richard. The kind of boy who would nurse a sick animal back to health. And that was what she had become - a sick, wild animal. I knew that he intended to marry her and I could not bear the thought of it. Yes, I was proud, in the worse sense of the word. I was vain and I didn't want our family name tainted by one so poor, so uncultured. But I was jealous too.'

Her anger was a storm now. The more she spoke, the more she seemed to grow in stature. It was as if the memories fuelled her strength. Then she stopped, a puzzled look on her face. When she next spoke she again took up the first part of her story.

'And so on that night, I waited. I did not undress and get into bed for I knew that sooner or later he would need the bathroom. After all, he had gone to bed at eight o clock. I waited to confront him. I would tell him what I thought of her and her family and ask him how he dared to bring shame on our family.' With the last few words her voice had risen to almost a screech. She inhaled deeply and calmed herself a little. Now she looked sad. 'I loved him though. I had always loved him. He was my older brother, my soldier. He should have been my protector, but instead of protecting *me* he only noticed *her*.'

She seemed thoroughly entranced by the flames of the fire. Her eyes danced in tune to their wild rhythm. Her next breath was almost a sob. 'And finally he came. It was well past midnight and the house was silent. I heard him stir in his room. I sensed him struggle to get to his feet. I listened silently, like a lion stalking its prey, as he hobbled to the bathroom and back again and then, before he could reach his room I stepped out onto the landing.'

Still I dared not interrupt. She was lost in the past. To have interrupted her now seemed dangerous, as when awakening a sleep-walker. 'We both stood at the top of the stairs. I could see that he was shaken by my sudden appearance; disappointed at having to speak with me, his own sister. It had been an age since I had felt that he had loved me, in fact, I had sensed his distaste for me for some time. I had become a bad smell under his nose. I hated him... and yet I loved him.' She paused again but didn't look towards me. 'We argued. It was as simple as that. We argued and I took advantage of his weakness. He was injured. The longer he stood the more he found it difficult to balance on his crutch and so I saw my chance and I took it ...'

I think then I understood what it was she had done, before she actually spoke the words. I almost did not want to hear it and yet I felt I had no choice in the matter. She had chosen me as her priestess and I had no choice other than to sit and hear her confession. I had so far seen no sign of penitence though.

'I pushed him...and he fell.' She paused and glanced towards me for the first time. 'I have asked myself over and over again if I intended to kill him and the truth is this ... I simply wished for it to be over, that I should never need to hate him, and love him; to despise her and yet have her in my life. I wanted it to be over ... so yes, perhaps in a way I did want him dead. I managed to convince myself that I had only done what the war had intended for I knew from the day he'd left that he would not make it through the war alive.'

She stared me in the eye still with no hint of remorse or guilt. Her piercing gaze still dared me to interrupt. I could see that she was not yet finished and so, desperate though I was to speak, I allowed her the privilege.

'And so I considered it over. Finally I felt a sense of relief.'

She watched me now, as if attempting to glean my reaction. I tried to give nothing away. I wanted to hear it all first, every last condemning word.

'I thought that perhaps we would be able to get on with our lives. I cared nothing for Emily or what would become of her. Yes, she had lost Richard and with him any hope of making a life for herself but I did not care. In fact I was glad.' She laughed again, sneeringly, her face contorting even further.

'But there was worse to come. I had no idea that their relationship had come to *that*. Imagine my horror when months later I returned one morning to discover that even in killing him I had not managed to rid our family of hers. She had borne his child ... and in our very own home! I felt defiled by the thought of what had happened. Mother tried to make the situation sound like a gift. *A gift!*' She laughed almost hysterically at this. 'I glanced at the baby, but only for a second, just to be sure. Though I denied it there was no mistake. I *knew* she was his, that he had come back to mock me even from the grave ... and it was then that I knew for certain that it was I who must leave.'

I longed now to interrupt. She was talking about my own Mother. I was desperate to spring to her defense. I opened my mouth to speak but before I could she cut me off again.

'What was more, I knew without doubt that Father blamed me for his death, long before he said so, and of course he was right. Mother grieved as any doting mother would and she tried to protect me. Of course she knew that I had been with him when he had fallen but she did not, *would* not allow herself to believe that I had in any way contributed to his fall ... but *I* knew that *Father* knew. He knew and he despised me, his own daughter. I could bear it no longer and so I made some contacts and went abroad, away from this place.' Her hand flicked as if beating off a pesky fly. 'I could no longer bear to see the accusation every time I looked in his eyes ... and so I left.'

She re-adjusted her posture and in doing so, seemed once again to deflate. 'And so time passed, and when Mother wrote to tell me how ill Father was I ignored her pleas and remained resolute. I did not want to see the hatred in his eyes as he lay dying, for that is what I would have seen. How had he not understood that I had only been trying to protect them? Protect him and my family from certain bad genes! No, he would never have understood, and so I chose not to come home. Let him go to his precious son and let Richard confirm that it had indeed been I who had ended his life. I no longer cared.'

I was still struggling to comprehend all that I had just heard. Regardless of the fact that Ruth had been consumed by jealousy, I could think of no justifiable reason for her having gone to the lengths that she had. It was obvious that she was sick, sick of mind, for no reasonable human being could have done such a thing and yet be so remorseless. By the way she had told her story, I had the impression that although she knew she had done wrong, somehow, she had been able to justify her actions to herself; somehow, in the depravity that was her mind, she still felt that it was *she* who had been wronged. It was quite unbelievable. A cauldron of anger bubbled inside me.

Still she was not finished. 'And what was more, I learned after I did return that Father had convinced Mother of my guilt for why else would she have cut me out of the will? Why else would she have named your mother as beneficiary? Oh, so she made a token gesture of allowing me to remain in my home until my death but still! No, what Mother did to me was inexcusable. It was obvious that he had poisoned her mind against her own flesh and blood.'

I could no longer sustain my silence. I almost spat the words. 'Really Ruth! Can you not see how much you hurt them? What you did robbed your parents of their only son and also their future daughter-in-law and grandchild!' She frowned in my direction but I did not stop. I had heard her out and now it was my turn, 'And you have the nerve to speak of your mother's own flesh and blood! Well can you not see that we too are her flesh and blood?' My voice was almost a shriek. I could not remember a time when I had felt so angry, so disgusted, not even when Simon had told me he was leaving nor when I discovered that he was to become a father. Then, I had felt hugely sad, vulnerable, cheated even, but I had never known such anger.

Still her face bore no sign of acknowledgment of the depths of her wrong doing. Her features quivered a little but there were no tears or shame in her expression. It seemed as though she was now allowing me to have my say for she nodded towards me, almost encouragingly and so, voice trembling I continued. 'I find it simply hard to believe! You murder your own brother and yet you behave as if it is *you* who deserve pity, as if it is *you* who have been wronged!' I laughed with disbelief. 'Do you know Ruth? I pitied you at the beginning of your story. I will be honest with you; I've been afraid of you Ruth. I even felt guilty about what happened, as if I were in some way responsible for cheating you out of your inheritance! I do not want your money Ruth. I have not preyed on your property. All I wanted when I came here was to begin a new life for myself. Let me tell you, I too have known sorrow, but of course you would not care about that! Not once have you ever acknowledged me as a real person, someone with feelings, someone who, like you has known loss. No! All you cared about was ridding yourself of any link with the past.' I paused, breathless. As I spoke, the truth seemed to dawn on me. In speaking my thoughts out loud I was becoming enlightened as to her motivations.

I laughed then, a small, cynical laugh. 'I think I see it Ruth. I think I finally understand the reasons why you detest me so much. It is not *me* you hate but yourself. My being here only serves to remind you of the past, of your evil deeds and thoughts and you cannot bear it!' I continued to hold her gaze now, all fear of her extinguished.

'In me you see the past and it haunts you,' I continued. 'Every day, when you look out of your window you see this cottage and you see me coming and going. Perhaps you even see Richard in me, for I have already been told that I have his eyes. Do you Ruth?' I wanted to hurt her now. Never before had I behaved in such a manner but it was empowering. 'Do my eyes reflect his, perhaps the moment when you pushed him? Did you see his fear reflected in my eyes over the past months when you looked at me? Well, let me tell you ... I will never again fear you Ruth. You can crawl back into your hole. I have not yet decided whether or not I will take it any further.' I stood now, abruptly. 'I want you to leave.'

She had paled. I think if I am truthful I was still a bit surprised that she had not fought back. She stood and I marched ahead of her to the front door. As soon as she was outside I closed the door and stood with my back against it, breathing hard.

I did not recognize myself. I peered into the hall mirror and did not recognize what I saw. My featured were pinched, my complexion pale. I did not like what I saw. Continuing to stare at my image, I watched as the tension in my face slowly began to ease; until my expression took on its familiar softness and then I nodded, satisfied.

Returning to the living room, I slumped down heavily

in the chair which she had so recently vacated. After all, it was *my* favourite chair and I would not allow her to taint it. My heart-beat gradually slowed and my hands became more steady. Had I over-reacted I wondered? Perhaps all the anguish of the past had simply bubbled over. I could not be sure; all I knew was that I had not been myself. I shuddered. I was not comfortable with that part of me and yet at the same time I had to acknowledge that I felt somehow purged.

Minutes passed. I got up and went to the kitchen. Shaking my still-damp hair free of the towel, I put on the kettle. I would need time to consider what had just happened and what, if anything I would do about it, for already it was as though a dream.

Chapter 57

Although I had intended to have an early night, it was past one in the morning when I finally made my way to bed. I had tried to reinstate a serene atmosphere by putting on soft music, re-lighting the candles and making a hot drink but nothing had worked. My mind was exhausted and yet at the same time alert.

Glancing at the clock by my bedside, I realized that I had already tossed and turned for over an hour. It was past two-thirty in the morning and still sleep evaded me. I wondered how I was ever going to function at the fair in the morning. I would need to be in the church by eight thirty at the latest to set up my stall. I knew one thing though, I was no longer afraid of Ruth. Perhaps what had happened was for the good. At least now I knew the truth and could finally begin to understand what Emily had suffered.

A thought came to me then. Had she guessed? Had Emily herself ever been suspicious of Richard's fall? All things considered I thought it unlikely and was glad of this.

Eventually, I must have drifted off to sleep for the next thing I was aware of were the church bells ringing. I was jolted from slumber, and experienced the shock of what I had been told the previous night anew. It reminded me of when Mum had died; how every morning for several weeks I would experience the shock of her loss as my first waking thought over and over again, as if the nightmare were on repeat. It had taken me some time to get through this stage of grief.

Over breakfast, I calmed myself. Determined not to repeat the self-destructive behaviour which had consumed me after losing Mum and following my divorce, I decided to do my utmost to press on with the day ahead.

I flicked on the radio and was pleased that a favourite tune was playing. I sang along. At least the day had dawned bright and sunny. Over the dishes, I decided to allow myself to dedicate a few minutes of thought to the previous evening and then I must put it to rest. I realized that this would take some doing but for the sake of my own health I understood that putting things behind me was the only way to move on.

*

The fair was a success. I was so busy and the church was so crowded that I had little time to think about Ruth. In fact, it wasn't until I was packing away at the end of the day that I spotted her. The hall was almost empty now, though the throng of people who had been present throughout the day still managed to keep the draughty old building warm.

She stood a little way off, appearing to fuss over an untidily stacked pile of prayer cushions. I could see that she merely play-acted the task and in reality seemed to be waiting. I wondered if she was waiting to speak with me again and hoped that she was not. I was not yet ready for another battle.

Doing my best not to face in her direction, I quickly finished packing and lifted the now-empty crate to leave. Holding it aloft in both arms, I did my best to avoid her as I began my procession along the aisle of the church. I sensed her presence though. All the while, I felt her eyes on me. I was certain that she was following me. I could feel the warmth of her body, could hear her breathing close by. I hurried as quickly as I could, the bravery of the night before vanished. On reaching the main door I was grateful that the previous person had left it ajar, for it meant that at least I did not have to delay my exit by putting down the crate and re-opening it.

Not once did I glance back. The further away I got and the closer to home, the more distance there seemed between us. Finally I reached my front door. Now I had to put down the crate in order to retrieve my keys. I noticed that I was still a little shaken. Inside now and safe! Plodding to my little kitchen, I realized that I had neither eaten nor drunk a single thing all day since breakfast.

I could not stomach food. Stirring some hot milk over the stove, I stared out of the front window into the pitch darkness. I must have imagined that she had followed me for there was no sign of anyone in the churchyard. I realized that the feeling of strength that I had experienced the previous night when I had thrown her out was not truly empowering; it was simply a reaction of anger. Still, I would stick to the promise I had made myself. Once I had satiated my thirst, I would retreat to my living room, get a fire going and allow myself to make my decision.

Chapter 58

It was done. It had been an easy decision and had not taken long to reach. Now I must put it out of my mind and go forward with my life. After all Ruth had said, I was beyond doubt that she was correct in her assumptions. Both Hubert and Elizabeth must have known the terrible thing that she had done.

I concluded therefore that it was not for me to judge. *They* had chosen not to take up the matter with the law and I understood their reasons. After all, appalling though Ruth's behaviour was, she was still their child. I knew that when a child does wrong, even as an adult, parents often feel responsible; as if they are in some way to blame. They believe that the wrong doing committed must be a result of something that they themselves did or failed to do.

I did not believe that Ruth would be judged by a God upon her death; nor would it be my place to pass judgment. I could only hope that one day, she would herself truly acknowledge her own wrong doing and that in itself would be punishment enough.

The sense of relief over having made my decision was immense. Now I knew I must put it to rest and not allow myself to mull it over any further. I had also decided to keep it secret. I would tell no-one, not even Tom, for really it was not my story to tell; I had been a listener, not a participant in the story.

On the other hand, I no longer felt any sense of guilt about the future, about the prospect of one day inheriting the Vicarage. I would deal with that if and when it happened. For the time being, I would just get on with my own life, in the best way I could and continue to deepen the friendships I had made since my arrival.

*

Although it was late December, the night had been mild and by morning I was desperate for some air. Hurriedly dressing in my favourite old jeans and sweater, I made my way across the little lane towards the grave. This morning though, the December wind blew hard. It had cleared away the clouds of the previous night and the air was pure and crisp. Little white fronds of frost clung to the earth.

Reaching the raised mound I looked down, expecting to see the holly wreath that I had placed there the previous week in readiness for Christmas, and indeed there it lay. Peering closer, I now saw that a small, white envelope had been attached to the wreath. It was addressed to me. I tore it open. Inside was a note...

'Returning that which is rightfully yours and was wrongfully taken. Should you wish to have the stone reinstated you will find it at the Monumental Mason's in Midhurst High Street. I took it because I could not bear to see their names side by side. It has taken me a long time to realize I was wrong.'

I stood up straight in order to catch my breath, my heart racing. Finally I understood the mystery over which I had pondered since the first day I had arrived at Marleston. But there was something else too, another white card attached to a single red rose had been flimsily secured to the grass by a tent peg. It had managed to turn round in the wind and so I could not see the writing. Heart racing,

I carefully squatted and turned the card to face me.

Brother…it is too late to ask for forgiveness, too late to turn back time.
Perhaps I loved you too much; perhaps that is just an excuse.
It is too late to tell you I'm sorry.
But I know in my heart that I am.

I did not want to dwell on how it was that Ruth had managed to have the headstone removed without being in possession of the grave deed. I could only assume that because she was the only remaining member of Richard's family and what with her connections to the church and cemetery it had not been questioned. But what a gift! Now, I would be able to have it inscribed with all three names.

I turned away from the mound and wrapped the scarf more tightly about my neck. A stray tear ran down my cheek. The wind was fierce. I swept it away with a gloved hand.

Printed in Great Britain
by Amazon